I NEVER PROMISED YOU
A ROSE GARDEN

I NEVER
PROMISED YOU
A ROSE GARDEN

HANNAH GREEN

UNABRIDGED

PAN BOOKS LTD : LONDON

First published 1964 by Victor Gollancz Ltd.
This edition published 1967 by Pan Books Ltd.,
33 Tothill Street, London, S.W.1.

Printed in Great Britain by
Cox & Wyman Ltd., London, Reading and Fakenham

TO MY MOTHERS

1

THEY RODE THROUGH the lush farm country in the middle of autumn, through quaint old towns whose streets showed the brilliant colours of turning trees. They said little. Of the three, the father was most visibly strained. Now and then he would place bits of talk into the long silences, random and inopportune things with which he himself seemed to have no patience. Once he demanded of the girl whose face he had caught in the rear-view mirror: 'You know, don't you, that I was a fool when I married – a damn young fool who didn't know about bringing up children – about being a father?' His defence was half attack, but the girl responded to neither. The mother suggested that they stop for coffee. This was really like a pleasure trip, she said, in the fall of the year with their lovely young daughter and such beautiful country to see.

They found a roadside diner and turned in. The girl got out quickly and walked towards the rest rooms behind the building. As she walked the heads of the two parents turned quickly to look after her. Then the father said, 'It's all right.'

'Should we wait here or go in?' the mother asked aloud, but to herself. She was the more analytical of the two, planning effects in advance – how to act and what to say – and her husband let himself be guided by her because it was easy and she was usually right. Now, feeling confused and lonely, he let her talk on – planning and figuring – because it was her way of taking comfort. It was easier for him to be silent.

'If we stay in the car,' she was saying, 'we can be with her if she needs us. Maybe if she comes out and doesn't see us . . . But then it should look as if we trust her. She must feel that we trust her . . .'

They decided to go into the diner, being very careful and

obviously usual about their movements. When they had seated themselves in a booth by the windows, they could see her coming back around the corner of the building and moving towards them; they tried to look at her as if she were a stranger, someone else's daughter to whom they had only now been introduced, a Deborah not their own. They studied the graceless adolescent body and found it good, the face intelligent and alive, but the expression somehow too young for sixteen.

They were used to a certain bitter precocity in their child, but they could not see it now in the familiar face that they were trying to convince themselves they could estrange. The father kept thinking: How could strangers be right? She's ours . . . all her life. They don't know her. It's a mistake – a mistake!

The mother was watching herself watching her daughter. 'On my surface . . . there must be no sign showing, no seam – a perfect surface.' And she smiled.

In the evening they stopped at a small city and ate at its best restaurant, in a spirit of rebellion and adventure because they were not dressed for it. After dinner, they went to a movie. Deborah seemed delighted with the evening. They joked through dinner and the movie, and afterwards, heading out farther into the country darkness, they talked about other trips, congratulating one another on their recollection of the little funny details of past vacations. When they stopped at a motel to sleep, Deborah was given a room to herself, another special privilege for which no one knew, not even the parents who loved her, how great was the need.

When they were sitting together in their room, Jacob and Esther Blau looked at each other from behind their faces, and wondered why the poses did not fall away, now that they were alone, so that they might breathe out, relax, and find some peace with each other. In the next room, a thin wall away, they could hear their daughter undressing for bed. They did not admit to each other even with their eyes, that all night they would be guarding against a sound other than her breathing in sleep —a sound that might mean . . . danger. Only once, before they lay down for their dark watch, did Jacob break from behind his face and whisper hard in his wife's ear, 'Why are we sending her away?'

'The doctors say she has to go,' Esther whispered back, lying rigid and looking towards the silent wall.

'The doctors.' Jacob had never wanted to put them all through the experience, even from the beginning.

'It's a good place,' she said, a little louder because she wanted to make it so.

'They call it a mental hospital, but it's a place, Es, a place where they put people away. How can it be a good place for a girl – almost a child?'

'Oh, God, Jacob,' she said, 'how much did it take out of us to make the decision? If we can't trust the doctors, who can we ask or trust? Dr Lister says that it's the only help she can get now. We have to try it!' Stubbornly she turned her head again, towards the wall.

He was silent, conceding to her once more; she was so much quicker with words than he. They said good night; each pretended to sleep, and lay, breathing deeply to delude the other, eyes aching through the darkness, watching.

On the other side of the wall Deborah stretched to sleep. The Kingdom of Yr had a kind of neutral place which was called the Fourth Level. It was achieved only by accident and could not be reached by formula or an act of will. At the Fourth Level there was no emotion to endure, no past or future to grind against. There was no memory or possession of any self, nothing except dead facts which came unbidden when she needed them and which had no feeling attached to them.

Now, in bed, achieving the Fourth Level, a future was of no concern to her. The people in the next room were supposedly her parents. Very well. But that was part of a shadowy world that was dissolving and now she was being flung unencumbered into a new one in which she had not the slightest concern. In moving from the old world, she was moving also from the intricacies of Yr's Kingdom, from the

9

Collect of Others, the Censor and the Yri gods. She rolled over and slept a deep, dreamless, and restful sleep.

In the morning the family started on its trip again. It occurred to Deborah, as the car pulled away from the motel and out into the sunny day, that the trip might last forever and that the calm and marvellous freedom she felt might be a new gift from the usually too demanding gods and offices of Yr.

After a few hours of riding through more brown and golden country and sun-dappled town streets, the mother said, 'Where is the turn-off, Jacob?'

In Yr a voice shrieked out of the deep Pit: *Innocent! Innocent!*

From freedom, Deborah Blau smashed headlong into the collision of the two worlds. As always before it was a weirdly silent shattering. In the world where she was most alive, the sun split in the sky, the earth erupted, her body was torn to pieces, her teeth and bones crazed and broken to fragments. In the other place, where the ghosts and shadows lived, a car turned into a side drive and down a road to where an old red-brick building stood. It was Victorian, a little run-down, and surrounded by trees. Very good façade for a madhouse. When the car stopped in front of it, she was still stunned with the collision, and it was hard to get out of the car and walk properly up the steps and into the building where the doctors would be. There were bars on all the windows. Deborah smiled slightly. It was fitting. Good.

When Jacob Blau saw the bars, he paled. In the face of this, it was no longer possible to say to himself 'rest home' or 'convalescent care'. The truth was as bare and cold for him as the iron. Esther tried to reach him with her mind: We should have expected them. Why should we be so surprised?

They waited, Esther Blau trying still to be gay now and then. Except for the barred windows the room was like an ordinary waiting room and she joked about the age of the magazines there. From a distance down the hall they heard the grate of a large key in a lock and again Jacob stiffened, moaning softly, 'Not for her – our little Debby. . . .' He did not see the sudden, ruthless look in his daughter's face.

The doctor walked down the hall, and steeled himself a little before entering the room. He was a squared-off, blunt-bodied man and now he dived into the room where their anguish seemed to hang palpably. It was an old building, a frightening place to come to, he knew. He would try to get the girl away soon and the parents comforted enough to leave her, feeling that they had done the right thing.

Sometimes in this room, at the last minute, the parents, husbands, wives, turned with loathing from the truth of the awful, frightening sickness. Sometimes they took their strange-eyed ones away again. It was fear, or bad judgement well meant enough, or – his eyes appraised the two parents again – that straying grain of jealousy and anger that would not let the long line of misery be severed a generation beyond their own. He tried to be compassionate but not foolish, and soon he was able to send for a nurse to take the girl to the wards. She looked like a shock victim. As she left, he felt the wrench of her going in the two parents.

He promised them that they could say good-bye to her before they left, and surrendered them to the secretary with her pad of information to be gotten. When he saw them again, leaving after their good-bye, they, too, looked like people in shock, and he thought briefly: wound-shock – the cutting-away of a daughter.

Jacob Blau was not a man who studied himself, or who looked back over his life to weigh and measure its shape. At times, he suspected his wife of being voracious, picking over her passions again and again with endless words and words. But part of this feeling was envy. He, too, loved his daughters, though he had never told them so; he, too, had wished confidences, but was never able to open his own heart; and, because of this, they had also been kept from venturing their secrets. His oldest daughter had just parted from him, almost eagerly, in that grim place of locks and bars, turning away from his kiss, stepping back. She had not seemed to want comfort from him, almost shrinking from touch. He was a man of tempers and now he needed a rage that was cleansing, simple, and direct. But the anger here was so laced with pity, fear, and love that he did not know how he could free himself of it. It lay writhing and stinking inside him, and he began to feel the old, slow waking ache of his ulcer.

2

THEY TOOK DEBORAH to a small, plain room, guarding her there until the showers were empty. She was watched there also, by a woman who sat placidly in the steam and looked her up and down as she dried herself. Deborah did what she was told dutifully, but she kept her left arm slightly turned inward, so as to hide from sight the two small, healing puncture wounds on the wrist. Serving the new routine, she went back to the room and answered some questions about herself put to her by a sardonic doctor who seemed to be displeased. It was obvious that he did not hear the roaring behind her.

Into the vacuum of the Midworld where she stood between Yr and Now, the Collect was beginning to come to life. Soon they would be shouting curses and taunts at her, deafening her for both worlds. She was fighting against their coming the way a child, expecting punishment, anticipates it by striking out wildly. She began to tell the doctor the truth about some of the questions he was asking. Let them call her lazy and a liar now. The roar mounted a little and she could hear some of the words in it. The room offered no distraction. To escape engulfment there was only the Here, with its ice-cold doctor and his notebook, or Yr with its golden meadows and gods. But Yr also held its regions of horror and lostness, and she no longer knew to which kingdom in Yr there was passage. Doctors were supposed to help in this.

She looked at the one who sat fading amid the clamour and said, 'I told you the truth about these things you asked. Now are you going to help me?'

'That depends on you,' he said acidly, shut his notebook, and left. *A specialist,* laughed Anterrabae, the Falling God.

Let me go with you, she begged him, down and down beside him because he was eternally falling.

So it shall be, he said. His hair, which was fire, curled a little in the wind of the fall.

That day and the next she spent on Yr's plains, simple long sweeps of land where the eye was soothed by the depth of space.

For this great mercy, Deborah was deeply grateful to the Powers. There had been too much blindness, cold, and pain in Yr these past hard months. Now, as by the laws of the world, her image walked around and answered and asked and acted; she, no longer Deborah, but a person bearing the appropriate name for a dweller on Yr's plains, sang and danced and recited the ritual songs to a caressing wind that blew on the long grasses.

For Jacob and Esther Blau the way home was no shorter than the way to the hospital had been. Although Deborah was not with them, their freedom to say what they really wanted to say was even more circumscribed than before.

Esther felt that she knew Deborah better than her husband did. To her, it had not been the childish attempt at suicide that had begun this round of doctors and decisions. She sat in the car beside her husband wanting to tell him that she was grateful for the silly and theatrical wrist-cutting. At last a dragging suspicion of something subtly and terribly wrong had had outlet in a fact. The half-cup of blood on the bathroom floor had given all their nebulous feelings and vague fears weight, and she had gone to the doctor the next day. Now she wanted to show Jacob the many things he did not know, but she knew she could not do it without hurting him. She looked over at him driving with his eyes hard on the road and his face set. 'We'll be able to visit her in a month or two,' she said.

Then they began to construct the story that they would tell their acquaintances and those relatives who were not close or whose prejudices did not allow for mental hospitals in the family. For them, the hospital was to be a school, and for Suzy, who had heard the word 'sick' too many times in the past month and had been puzzled too often and deeply before that, there was to be something about anaemia or weakness and a special convalescent school. Papa and Mama would be told that everything was fine ... a sort of rest home. They already knew about the psychiatrist and his recommendation, but the look of the place would have to change in the telling, and the high, hard scream that they had heard from one of the barred windows as they left, and that had made them shiver and grit their teeth, would have to be expunged. The scream had made Esther wonder if they had not really been wrong after all; the scream would have to be kept locked in her heart as Deborah in That Place.

Doctor Fried got up from her chair and went to the window. It faced away from the hospital buildings and over a small garden beyond which lay the grounds where the patients walked. She looked at the report in her hand. Against the weight of three typewritten pages were balanced the lectures she would not be able to give, the writing she would have to neglect, and the counselling of doctors that she would have to refuse if she took this case. She liked working with patients. Their very illness made them examine sanity as few 'sane' people could. Kept from loving, sharing, and simple communication, they often hungered for it with a purity of passion that she saw as beautiful.

Sometimes, she thought ruefully, the world is so much sicker than the inmates of its institutions. She remembered Tilda, in the hospital in Germany, at a time when Hitler was on the other side of its walls and not even she could say which side was sane. Tilda's murderous hate, bound down on beds, tube-fed, and drugged into submission, could still fade long enough to let the light in now and then. She remembered Tilda looking up at her, smiling in a travesty of genteel politeness from the canvas-bound bed, and saying,

'Oh, do come in, dear Doctor. You are just in time for the patient's soothing tea and the end of the world.'

Tilda and Hitler were both gone and now there was more and more to tell the younger doctors who were coming out of the schools with too little experience of life. Is it fair to take private patients when any real improvement may take years, and when thousands and tens of thousands are clamouring, writing, phoning, and begging for help? She laughed, catching in herself the vanity she had once called the doctor's greatest enemy next to his patient's illness. If one by one was good enough for God, it would have to do for her.

She sat down with the folder, opened it, and read it through:

BLAU, DEBORAH F. 16 yrs. Prev. Hosp: None
INITIAL DIAG: SCHIZOPHRENIA.

1. *Testing:* Tests show high (140–150) intelligence, but patterns disturbed by illness. Many questions misinterpreted and overpersonalized. Entire subjective reaction to interview and testing. Personality tests show typically schizophrenic pattern with compulsive and masochistic component.

2. *Interview (Initial):* On admission patient appeared well oriented and logical in her thinking, but as the interview went on, bits of the logic began to fall away and at anything which could be construed as correction or criticism, she showed extreme anxiety. She did everything she could to impress examiner with her wit, using it as a formidable defence. On three occasions she laughed inappropriately: once when she claimed that the hospitalization had been brought about by a suicide attempt, twice with reference to questions about the date of the month. As the interview proceeded her attitude changed and she began to speak loudly, giving random happenings in her life which she thought to be the cause of her illness. She mentioned an operation at the age of five, the effects of which were traumatic, a cruel baby-sitter, etc. The incidents were unrelated, and no pattern appeared in them. Suddenly, in the middle of recounting an incident, the patient started forward and said accusingly, 'I told you the truth about these things – now are you going to help me?' It was considered advisable to terminate the interview.

3. *Family History:* Born Chicago, Ill. October, 1932. Breast-fed 8 mos. One sibling, Susan, born 1937. Father, Jacob Blau, an accountant whose family had emigrated from Poland 1913. Birth normal. At age 5 patient had two operations for removal of tumour in urethra. Difficult financial situation made family move in with grandparents in suburb of Chicago. Situation improved, but father became ill with ulcer and hypertension. In 1942 war caused move to city. Patient made poor adjustment and was taunted by schoolmates. Puberty normal physically, but at age 16 patient attempted suicide. There is a long history hypochondria, but outside of tumour the physical health has been good.

She turned the page and glanced at the various statistical measurements of personality factors and test scores. Sixteen was younger than any patient she had ever had. Leaving aside consideration of the person herself, it might be good to find out if someone with so little life experience could benefit from therapy and be easier or harder to work with.

In the end it was the girl's age that decided her, and made the report weigh more heavily than the commitment of doctors' meetings to be attended and articles to be written.

'*Aber wenn wir* . . . If we succeed . . .' she murmured, forcing herself away from her native tongue, 'the good years yet to live . . .'

Again she looked at the facts and the number. A report like this had once made her remark to the hospital psychologist, 'We must someday make a test to show us where the *health* is as well as the illness.'

The psychologist had answered that with hypnotism and the ametyls and pentothals such information could be obtained more easily.

'I do not think so,' Dr Fried had answered. 'The *hidden* strength is too deep a secret. But in the end . . . in the end it is our only ally.'

3

FOR A TIME – HOW long by Earth's reckoning Deborah did not know – it was peaceful. The world made few demands so that it seemed once more as if it had been the world's pressures that had caused so much of the agony in Yr. Sometimes she was able to see 'reality' from Yr as if the partition between them were only gauze. On such occasions her name became Januce, because she felt like two-faced Janus – with a face on each world. It had been her letting slip this name which had caused the first trouble in school. She had been living by the Secret Calendar (Yr did not measure time as the world did) and had returned to the Heavy Calendar in the middle of the day, and having then that wonderful and omniscient feeling of changing, she had headed a class paper: NOW JANUCE. The teacher had said, 'Deborah, what is this mark on your paper? What is this word, Januce?'

And, as the teacher stood by her desk, some nightmare terror coming to life had risen in the day-sane schoolroom. Deborah had looked about and found that she could not see except in outlines, grey against grey, and with no depth, but flatly, like a picture. The mark on the paper was the emblem of coming from Yr's time to Earth's, but, being caught while still in transition, she had to answer for both of them. Such an answer would have been the unveiling of a horror – a horror from which she would have awakened rationally; and so she had lied and dissembled, with her heart choking her. Such a danger must no more be allowed aloud, and so that night the whole Great Collect had come crowding into the Midworld: gods and demons from Yr and shades from Earth, and they had set up over their kingdoms a Censor to stand between Deborah's speech and actions and to guard the secret of Yr's existence.

Over the years the power of the Censor had grown greater and greater, and it was he who had lately thrust himself into both worlds, so that sometimes no speech and no action escaped him. One whisper of a secret name, one sign written, one slip of light could break into the hidden place and destroy her and both the worlds for ever.

On Earth the life of the hospital moved on. Deborah worked in the craft shop, grateful that the world also offered its hiding places. She learned to do basketwork, accepting the instruction in her acerbic and impatient way. She knew that none of the workers liked her. People never had. On the ward a large girl had asked her to play tennis and the shock had sounded down to the last level of Yr. She saw the pencil-doctor a few more times and learned that he was 'ward administrator' and the one who gave permission for 'privileges' – steps in similitude to the normal world – to get up and go out on the ward, to go to dinner, on the grounds, then out of the hospital itself to the movie or store. Each was a privilege and had a certain connotation of approval that seemed to be expressed in distances. To Deborah he gave permission to walk unrestricted on the grounds, but not outside. Deborah said to the large girl, whose name was Carla, 'Well, I'm a hundred square yards sane.' If there were such things as man-hours, and light-years, surely there was foot-sanity.

Carla said, 'Don't worry. You'll get more privileges soon. If you work hard with your doctor, they ease up a little. I just wonder how long I'll have to stay here. It's been three months already.' They both thought of the women at the far end of the ward. All of them had been in the hospital for over two years.

'Does anyone ever leave?' Deborah asked. 'I mean be well and leave?'

'I don't know,' said Carla.

They asked a nurse.

'I don't know,' she said, 'I haven't been here that long.'

There was a groan from Lactamaeon, the black god, and a derisive laugh from the Collect, which were the massed images of all of the teachers and relatives and schoolmates standing eternally in secret judgement and giving their endless curses.

Forever, crazy girl! Forever, lazy girl!

Later, one of the little student nurses came to where Deborah was lying, looking at the ceiling.

'It's time to get up now,' she said in the wavering and frightened voice of her inexperience. There was a new group of these students working out their psychiatric training in this place. Deborah sighed and got up dutifully, thinking: She is astounded at the haze of craziness with which I fill a room.

'Come on now,' the student said. 'The doctor is going to see you. She's one of the heads here and a very famous doctor, too, so we must hurry, Miss Blau.'

'If she's that good, I'll wear my shoes,' Deborah replied, watching the young woman's expression widen with surprise and her face fight with its look of disapproval. She must have been told not to show anything so strong as anger or fear or amusement.

'You really should be grateful,' the student said. 'You're very lucky to get to see her at all.'

'Known and loved by madmen the world over,' Deborah said. 'Let's go.'

The nurse unlocked the ward door and then the stairway door, and they went down to the lower floor, which was open, and out of the back of the building. The nurse pointed to a green-shuttered white house – a small-town, oak-lined-streets type of white house – standing incongruously just inside the hospital grounds. They went to the front door and rang. After a while a tiny, grey-haired, plump little woman answered the door. 'We're from Admissions. Here she is,' the nurse said.

'Can you come back for her in an hour?' the little woman said to the student.

'I'm supposed to wait.'

'Very well.'

As Deborah stepped through the door, the Censor began to thrum his warnings: *Where is the doctor? Is she watching from behind a door somewhere?* The little housekeeper motioned towards a room.

'Where is the doctor?' Deborah said, trying to stop the rapid juxtaposition of walls and doors.

'I am the doctor,' the woman said. 'I thought you knew. I am Dr Fried.'

Anterrabae laughed, falling and falling in his darkness. *What a disguise!* And the Censor growled, *Take care ... take care.*

They went into a sunny room and the Housekeeper-Famous-Doctor turned, saying, 'Sit down. Make yourself comfortable.' There came a great exhaustion and when the doctor said, 'Is there anything you want to tell me?' a great gust of anger, so that Deborah stood up quickly and said to her and to Yr and to the Collect and to the Censor, 'All right – you'll ask me questions and I'll answer them – you'll clear up my "symptoms" and send me home ... *and what will I have then?*'

The doctor said quietly, 'If you did not really want to give them up, you wouldn't tell me.' A rope of fear pulled its noose about Deborah. 'Come, sit down. You will not have to give up anything until you are ready, and then there will be something to take its place.'

Deborah sat down, while the Censor said in Yri: *Listen, Bird-one; there are too many little tables in here. The tables have no defence against your clumsiness.*

'Do you know why you are here?' the doctor said.

'Clumsiness. Clumsiness is first and then we have a list: lazy, wayward, headstrong, self-centred, fat, ugly, mean, tactless, and cruel. Also a liar. That category includes sub-heads: (a) False blindness, imaginary pains causing real doubling-up, untrue lapses of hearing, lying leg injuries, fake dizziness, and unproved and malicious malingerings; (b) Being a bad sport. Did I leave out unfriendliness? ... Also unfriendliness.'

In the silence where the dust motes fell through the sun shaft, Deborah thought that she had perhaps spoken her true feelings for the first time. If these things were so, so be it, and she would leave this office at least having stated her tiredness and disgust at the whole dark and anguish-running world.

The doctor said simply, 'Well, that seems to be quite a list. Some of these, I think, are not so, but we have a job cut out for us.'

'To make me friendly and sweet and agreeable and happy in the lies I tell?'

'To help you to get well.'

'To shut up the complaints.'

'To end them, where they are the products of an upheaval in your feelings.'

The rope tightened. Fear was flowing wildly in Deborah's head, turning her vision grey. 'You're saying what they all say – phony complaints about non-existent sicknesses.'

'It seems to me that I said that you are very sick indeed.'

'Like the rest of them here?' It was as near as she dared go, already much too near the black places of terror.

'Do you mean to ask me if I think you belong here, if yours is what is called a mental illness? Then the answer is yes. I think you are sick in this way, but with your very hard work here and with a doctor's working hard with you, I think you can get better.'

As bald as that. Yet with the terror connected with the hedged-about, circled-around word 'crazy', the unspoken word that Deborah was thinking about now, there was a light coming from the doctor's spoken words, a kind of light that shone back on many rooms of the past. The home and the school and all of the doctors' offices ringing with the joyful accusation: There Is Nothing The Matter With You. Deborah had known for years and years that there was more than a little the matter – something deeply and gravely the matter, more even than the times of blindness, intense pain, lameness, terror, and the inability to remember anything at all might indicate. They had always said, 'There is nothing the matter with you, if you would only . . .' Here at last was a vindication of all the angers in those offices.

The doctor said, 'What are you thinking about? I see your face relax a little.'

'I am thinking about the difference between a misdemeanour and a felony.'

'How so?'

'The prisoner pleads guilty to the charge of not having acute something-itis and accepts the verdict of guilty of being nuts in the first degree.'

'Perhaps in the second degree,' the doctor said, smiling a little. 'Not entirely voluntary nor entirely with forethought.'

Deborah suddenly recalled the picture of her parents standing very single and yet together on the other side of the shatter-proof locked door. Not aforethought, this thing, but more than a little with malice.

Deborah became aware of the nurse moving about in the other room as if to let them know that the time was up.

The doctor said, 'If it's all right with you, we will make another appointment and begin our talks, because I believe that you and I, if we work like the devil together, can beat this thing. First, I want to tell you again that I will not pull away symptoms or sickness from you against your will.'

Deborah shied away from the commitment, but she allowed her face a very guarded 'yes', and the doctor saw it. They walked from the office with Deborah striving assiduously to act as if she were somewhere else, elaborately unconcerned with this present place and person.

'Tomorrow at the same time,' the doctor told the nurse and the patient.

'She can't understand you,' Deborah said. 'Charon spoke in Greek.'

Dr Fried laughed a little and then her face turned grave. 'Someday I hope to help you see this world as other than a Stygian hell.'

They turned and left, and Charon, in white cap and striped uniform, guided the removed spirit towards the locked ward. Dr Fried watched them walking back to the large building and thought: Somewhere in that precocity and bitterness and somewhere in the illness, whose limits she could not yet define, lay a hidden strength. It was there and working; it had sounded in the glimmer of relief when the fact of the sickness was made plain, and most of all in the 'suicide attempt', the cry of a mute for help, and the statement, bold and dramatic as adolescents and the still-fighting sick must always make it, that the game was over and the disguising ended. The fact of this mental illness was in the open now, but the disease itself had roots still as deeply hidden as the white core of a volcano whose slopes are camouflaged in wooded green. Somewhere, even under the volcano itself, was the buried seed of will and strength. Dr Fried sighed and went back to her work.

'This time ... this time can I only call it forth!' she sighed, lapsing into the grammar of her native tongue.

4

SUZY BLAU took the story of the convalescent school quite well, and when Esther told her own parents she tried to shade the hospital into a rest home. But they were undeceived and furious.

'There's nothing the matter with her brains! That girl has a good wit,' Pop said. (It was his highest compliment.) 'It's just that the brains in this family skipped a generation and fell on her. She is me, my own flesh. The hell with all of you!' He walked out of the room.

In the following days Esther pleaded for their support in her decision, but only when Claude, her elder brother, and Natalie, her sister – the favourites of the family – admitted to Mom and Pop that there could be a need, did the old man relent a little, for Deborah was his favourite grandchild.

At home Jacob was silent but not at peace with what he and Esther had done. They went to see Dr Lister twice, and Jacob listened, trying to be comforted by the belief that they had done the right thing. Confronted with direct questions, he had to agree, and all the facts were trying to make him say 'yes', but he had only to submit to his feelings for the smallest moment and his whole world rang with misgivings. When he and Esther quarrelled, the crucial thing remained unspoken, leaving an atmosphere of wordless rancour and accusation.

At the end of the first month a letter arrived from the hospital relating Deborah's activities in very general terms. She had made 'a good adjustment' to the routine and staff, had begun therapy, and was able to walk about the grounds.

From this noncommittal letter Esther extracted every particle of hope, going over and over the words, magnifying each positive sign, turning the remarks this way and that for the facets of brightest reflection.

She also struggled to sway the feelings of Jacob and Pop, practising her arguments with her image in the mirror. Pop knew in himself somewhere, she believed, that the decision was not wrong, that his anger at Deborah's hospitalization was only an expression of his injured pride. Esther saw that her dominating, quick, restless, and brilliant immigrant father now showed certain signs of mellowing; only his language was as brusque as ever. Sometimes it even seemed to her that with Deborah's illness coming to a head, the whole thrust and purpose of their lives was forced under scrutiny. One night she asked Jacob abruptly, 'How did we share in the thing? What awful wrongs did we do?'

'Do I know?' he answered. 'If I knew would I have done them? It seemed like a good life – a very good life she had. Now they say it wasn't. We gave love and we gave comfort. She was never threatened with cold or hunger . . .'

And Esther remembered then that Jacob, too, had had an immigrant past; had been cold, wet, hungry, and foreign. How he must have sworn to keep those wolves from his children! Her hand went up to his arm, protectively, but at the gesture he turned a bit.

'Is there more, Esther? Is there more?'

She could not answer, but the next day she wrote a letter to the hospital asking when they might visit and see the doctor.

Jacob was glad for the letter and waited, going over the mail every day for the answer, but Pop only snorted, 'What are they going to do – tell you it's a mistake? The world is full of jackasses. Why should that place be immune?'

'Nonsense!' Jacob said, more angrily than he had ever spoken to his father-in-law. 'Doctors have ethics to live up to. If they find out it's a mistake, they'll let us take her home right away.'

Esther realized that he was still waiting for the diagnosis to be reversed, the miracle to happen, the locked doors to

swing wide, the film of the last year of living to be ru
backwards, and everyone to be able to laugh at the ludicrou.
way life worked – backwards, backwards until it was all un-
lived and erased. She pitied Jacob suddenly, but she could
not let him go on thinking that she wanted to visit the hospital for that reason. 'I wanted to tell the doctors – to ask
them – well, our lives have changed . . . and there are things
that Deborah may not even know that made us do what we
did. There are reasons for so much of it that all our good
will could not change.'

'We lived simple lives. We lived good lives. We lived in
dignity.' He said it believing it utterly, and Esther saw that
some of what she had said reflected on him and on her relationship with him, both before she was married and after,
when she should have changed allegiances and hadn't. She
couldn't bear to hurt him now. It was pointless anyway; so
much of the struggle was past. For everyone but Deborah it
was a dead issue, and who could know what it was to her?

And sometimes, in the first months, there were periods of
calmness, even of happiness. Suzy, alone in the house, began to come into her own, and Jacob realized, even as he
denied it, that before Deborah had gone he had been tip-
toeing, deferring, frightened of something nameless for a
long time.

One day a group of Suzy's school friends trooped in, laughing and joking, and Esther asked them all to dinner on the
spur of the moment. Suzy shone, and when they had gone,
Jacob said good-naturedly, 'Those stupid kids. Were we
ever that stupid? The little one with that cap!' He laughed,
and catching himself in the real enjoyment, said, 'My god –
I laughed so much tonight. When before did I have so much
fun!' And then: 'Has it really been *that* long? Years?'

'Yes,' she said, 'it has been that long.'

'Then maybe it's true that she was . . . unhappy,' he said,
thinking of Deborah.

'Sick,' Esther said.

'Unhappy!' Jacob shouted and left the room. He came
back a few minutes later. 'Just unhappy!' he said.

'Your parents write that they wish to make a visit,' Dr Fried said. She sat on the other side of the heavy twelfth-century iron portcullis that Deborah occasionally found separating them. The portcullis had been raised this time, invisible, but when the doctor had mentioned parents and a visit Deborah heard the sudden heavy rasp, and down it clanged between them.

'What is it?' the doctor said, not hearing the clang of lowering, but perceiving its effect.

'I can't really see you and I can't really hear you,' Deborah said. 'You are behind the gate.'

'Your medieval gate again. You know, those things have doors on them. Why don't you open a door?'

'The door is locked, too.'

The doctor looked at her ashtray. 'Well, those gatemakers of yours must not be too smart or they would never build their barriers with side doors and then not be able to open them.'

Deborah was annoyed when the doctor took her private facts and moved them and used them to her own ends. The bars were thickening against the doctor. The soft, accented voice was closing and closing to silence behind the metal wall. The last words were: 'Do you want them to come?'

'I want Mother,' Deborah said, 'but not him. I don't want him to visit me.'

Her words surprised her. She knew that she meant them, that they were somehow important, but she didn't know why. For many years words had come out of her mouth for which her mind could not remember giving the order. Sometimes only a feeling would sweep over her. The feeling would be given voice, but the logic behind it, by which the world might have been convinced, remained mute, and so she lost faith in her own desires. It made her defend them all the more blindly. Part of her present feeling, she knew, was delight in her power to reward and punish. Her father's love for her was her weapon against him, but she had a knowledge, however hard to express, that his pity and love were dangerous to her now. She knew that this hospital was good for her. She knew also that she could not defend her knowledge, that she could not express why this was really where she belonged. Considering her own muteness and the eloquence of the locks and bars, Jacob might be overcome by the horror and sadness she had seen in him when they had first brought her there. He might decide to end this 'imprisonment'. The women on Disturbed were always howling and shrieking. One of them might tip the balance the wrong way. Deborah knew all this, but she could not utter it. Also, there was her sense of power.

She saw the doctor's mouth moving, and imagined that it was spewing questions and accusations. She began to fall, going with Anterrabae through his fire-fragmented darkness into Yr. This time the fall was far. There was utter darkness for a long time and then a greyness, seen only in bands across the eye. The place was familiar; it was the Pit. In this place gods and Collect moaned and shouted, but even they were unintelligible. Human sounds came, too, but they came without meaning. The world intruded, but it was a shattered world and unrecognizable.

Once in the past, while in the Pit, she had been scalded, because although she had seen the stove and boiling water, its purpose and form had had no meaning. Meaning itself became irrelevant. And, of course, there was no fear in the Pit because fear had no meaning either. Sometimes she even forgot the English language.

The horror of the Pit lay in the emergence from it, with the return of her will, her caring, and her feeling of the need for meaning before the return of meaning itself. There had been one day (also in school) when she had risen from the Pit while a teacher pointed to a word in her book, saying, 'What is it . . . this word?' She had tried desperately to make intelligibility of white ground and black lines and curves. Nothing. It had taken every bit of strength to remember sufficient English to say, 'what?' The teacher had been angry. Was she trying to be a smart aleck? 'What is the word?' Nothing. She had been unable to extract a single bit of reality from the lines and spots on the white ground. Someone tittered in the background and the teacher, apparently fearing compromise of her authority, left the mute

Deborah and disappeared into the greyness. Present became nothing; world, nothing.

Again in Dr Fried's office, the terror of emergence had not yet begun. Deborah was still deep in the Pit and it was yet unimportant whether there was language or meaning or even light.

Esther Blau tore open the letter eagerly and, as she read, was first puzzled and then angry. 'It says that she wants me to come, but she has told the doctor that she wants me alone this time.' She was trying to make it easier for Jacob by not using the words that were in the letter: '. . . will not see Mr Blau.'

Jacob said, 'Well, we'll drive down and see her for a while, and then you two can have a nice visit if you want.'

She edged the fact a little closer. 'Well, Jacob, they think that both of us would be too much just now. I can drive down myself or take the train.'

'Don't be silly,' he said. 'It's nonsense. I will go.'

'It isn't nonsense,' she said. 'Please, Jacob—'

He took the letter from the table and read it, and the anger that came first was more for his wife, who had had to try to cover up for him and spare him, than for the words themselves. 'Who does she think she is?'

'She's sick, Jacob – I told you – Dr Lister told you.'

'All right!' he said. 'All right.'

The hurt had now come to overwhelm the anger. 'You can't go alone. I'll drive you down and stay in the background. If she changes her mind, she can see me.'

'Of course.' It was giving in again, Esther knew. She would be pulled from both sides all the way, but she had to let Jacob do this for her. Maybe he could see the doctor there and be reassured. She got up and took the letter from him, hoping that the trip would dull the pain of the unequivocal words of denial.

When she went into their bedroom to put the letter away, she heard Suzy talking with a friend on the phone. She was saying, 'But I don't know . . . it's not just something you can plan for. . . I told you. My sister Debbie is very sick. No.

28

... They get these reports every month. No ... it's not that. It's that if the next one is bad, they won't feel like having anything here. ... Sure. Well, I'll let you know if it's all right.'

A sudden, helpless anger leaped into Esther's head, and her eyes burned with it for a moment. Deborah! Deborah – what has she done to us all?

5

Dr Fried saw Esther Blau in the doctor's bright, cluttered office. It was important to Dr Fried to know whether Deborah's mother would be an ally in this treatment or an adversary. Many parents said – even thought – that they wanted help for their children, only to show, subtly or directly, that their children were part of a secret scheme for their own ruin. A child's independence is too big a risk for the shaky balance of some parents. On Esther's impeccable surface Dr Fried saw intelligence, sophistication, and straightforwardness. There was also an intensity that made her smile a little hard. How those two blunt wills must have struggled over the years!

They sat down in the comfortable chairs, the doctor breathing a little heavily and feeling somewhat dowdy as she faced Esther's formidable jewellery. She examined her again. The woman was sane: she accepted the heavy penalties of reality and enjoyed its gifts also. Her daughter did not. Where was the difference to be found?

The mother was looking about the room. 'Is this – is this where Deborah comes?'

'Yes.'

Relief showed on the carefully composed surface. 'It's pleasant. No – bars.' She got the word out, straining so hard for relaxed matter-of-factness that the doctor almost winced.

'Right now it hardly matters. I don't know if she trusts me enough to see the room as it really is.'

'Can she get well? I love her so very much!'

If it is so, Dr Fried thought, the love will meet a strong test in what they are all about to undergo. She said, 'If she is going to get well, we are all going to have to be patient and to work like anything.' The colloquialism sounded strange in her accent. 'She will need a tremendous amount of energy to give to this, to fight her own impulses for safety ... and so you may find her tired and not keeping herself groomed as she should. Is there something that worries you particularly about her now?'

Esther tried to frame her thoughts. It was too soon to think about Deborah's progress really; the worry was something else. 'You see – all these days ... all these days we've been thinking and thinking how and why this could have happened. She was so much loved! They tell me that these illnesses are caused by a person's past and childhood. So all these days we've been thinking about the past. I've looked, and Jacob has looked, and the whole family has thought and wondered, and after all of it we just can't see any reason for it. It's without a cause, you see, and that's what is so frightening.'

She had spoken louder than she wished, trying to convince the chairs and the tables and the doctor and the whole institution with its bars and screaming people whose reasons for being there must be different ... must be.

'Causes are too big to see all at once, or even as they really are, but we can tell our own truths and have our own causes. Tell me what you know about Deborah and yourself in *your* own way and as you knew it.'

'I suppose I should start with my own father.'

Pop had come from Latvia. He had a clubfoot. Somehow these two things represented him more fully than his name or occupation. He had come to America a young man, poor and foreign and lame, and he had borne down on his new life as if it were an enemy. In anger he had educated himself; in anger he had gone into business, failed, succeeded, and made a fortune. With his fortune and his anger he had bought a great home in an old neighbourhood of the inbred and anciently rich. His neighbours had every manner he admired, and in turn they despised his religion, his accent, and his style. They made the lives of his wife and children miserable, but he cursed them all, the neighbours and wife and children, in the crude, blunt words of his abhorrent past. The true conquest, he saw, would not be for him, but for his seed, educated and accentless and gently conditioned. The Latvian and Yiddish curses that they had learned at his knee he tried to temper with tutoring in genteel French.

'In 1878,' Esther said, 'the daughters of noblemen took harp lessons. I know because I had to take harp lessons, even though playing the instrument had gone out of fashion, even though I hated it and had no talent for it. It was one of the flags to capture, you see, and he had to try to win it, even through me. Sometimes when I played, Pop would pace the floor and mutter to his nobleman, "Look, damn you – it's me, the little cripple!"'

Pop's 'American' children had grown up knowing that all their worth and gentility and culture and success was only a surface. For a glimpse of their true value they had only to look into their neighbours' eyes or to hear Pop's remarks if the soup was cold or the suitor came late. As for the suitors, they were to be flags also; the proud banners of great families; the emblems of conquests in alliance, as it had been among the great in the old country. But wilful Esther had chosen beneath her family's hopes. The boy was smart enough, well-spoken, and presentable; still he had put himself through accountancy school and his family was 'a bunch of poor greenhorns', beneath Esther, beneath the dream in every way. They had argued and fought and at last, on the strength of Jacob's prospects for the future, Pop had given in. Natalie had married well enough for the family to afford a gamble. Soon both of the young wives were pregnant. Pop began to think of himself as the founder of a dynasty.

And Esther's daughter was blonde! a singular, thrilling, impossible, fair-skinned blonde. She was Esther's redemption from secret isolation, and for Pop she was the final retort to a long-dead village nobleman and his fair-skinned daughters. This one would go in gold.

Esther recalled then the time of the depression and the cast of fear that had surrounded everything. It was fear and – Esther groped for the word that would evoke those years – unreality. Jacob had entered his working life at the very nadir of opportunity. The accounts that he had sworn to take in order to deserve Esther as a wife – the boring and routine, the scraps that others threw away – were simply not there. For every column of figures there were a hundred minds waiting, as hungry and well educated as his. Yet they lived in one of the best new sections of town. The daughters of the dynasty had to live well and Pop paid all their bills. When Deborah was born it was into the handmade lace – the heirloom of some great European house felled by the revolution. Capturing an old flag was better than weaving a new one, and the princely carriage caps that Deborah wore for her outings had once been fitted to the head of a prince. Though the peasant's mud-village past was already a generation removed, there was still in that peasant a peasant's dream: not simply to be free, but to be free to be titled. The New World was required to do more than obliterate the bitterness of the Old. Like the atheist saying to God, 'You don't exist and I hate You!' Pop kept sounding his loud shouts of denial into the deaf ear of the past. When Jacob was earning fifteen and then twenty dollars a week, Deborah had twelve hand-embroidered silk dresses and a German nurse.

Jacob could not pay for her food. After a while they moved back into the family home, surrounded by a new generation of neighbourhood scorn. Even as a prisoner of her own past, Esther saw that Jacob was unhappy, that he was taking charity from a man who despised him, but her own fear made her subtly and consistently side with her father against her husband. It seemed then as if having Deborah had made her allegiance right. Jacob was consort of the dynasty, but Deborah – golden, gift-showered Deborah – always smiling and contented, was a central pin on which the dream could turn.

And then they found that their golden toy was flawed. In the perfumed and carefully tended little girl a tumour was growing. The first symptom was an embarrassing incontinence, and how righteously wrathful and rigid governess was! But the 'laziness' could not be cured by shaming or whipping or threats.

'We didn't know!' Esther burst out, and the doctor looked at her and saw how passionate and intense she was under the careful, smooth façade. 'In those days the schedules and the governesses and the rules were god! It was the "scientific" approach then, with everything sterile and such a horror of germs and variation.'

'And the nursery like a hospital! I remember,' said the doctor laughing, and trying to comfort Esther with her laughter because it was too late for anything but remorse for the mistaken slaps and the overzealous reading of misguided experts.

At last there were examinations and a diagnosis and trips from doctor to doctor in search of proof. Deborah would have nothing but the best of course. The specialist who finally did the operation was the top man in the Midwest, and far too busy to explain anything to the little girl or stay with her after the miracles of modern surgery were over and the ancient and barbaric pain took their place. Two operations, and after the first, a merciless pain.

Esther had forced herself to stay cheerful and strong, to go to Debby's room always with a smile. She was pregnant again and worried because of the earlier stillbirth of twin sons, but to the hospital staff, the family, and Deborah, her surface never varied, and she took pride in the strength she showed. At last they learned that the operations had been successful. They were jubilant and grateful, and at Deborah's homecoming the whole house was festive and decorated, and all the relatives were present for a party. Two days later Jacob got the Sulzburger account. Esther found old names coming to mind from nowhere.

At the time the Sulzburger account had seemed to be the most important thing in their lives. It was a series of very lucrative smaller accounts and they had gone a little crazy with it. At last Jacob could be free, more than a consort in his own house. He bought a new one in a quiet and modest neighbourhood not too far from the city. It was small, with a little garden and trees and lots of children close by with lots of different last names. Deborah was cautious at first, but before long she began to open, to go out and make friends. Esther had friends, too, and flowers that she could take care of herself, and sunlight, and open windows, and no need for servants, and the beginnings of her own decisions. One year – one beautiful year. Then one evening Jacob came home and told her that the Sulzburger account was a vast chain of fraud. He had been three full months discovering how and where the money was going. He said to Esther on the evening before he went to resign it, 'A fraud that's as diverse and clever as this one is has a kind of beauty in it. It's going to cost us – everything. You know that, don't you? . . . But I can't help admiring that mind. . . .'

They had to give up the house and a month later they were back in the family home once again. There was very little money, but Esther's parents decided to give the house to them; there was too much room without the whole family and the parents had rented an apartment in Chicago. But the big house *had* to stay in the family, of course. And so the hated place became the Blau house.

Deborah went to the best schools in the winter and the best camps in the summer. Friendships came hard to her, but they do to many people, Esther thought. The family had not known until years later that the first summer camp (three silent years of it), was cruelly anti-Semitic. Deborah had never told them. What Esther and Jacob saw were the laughing teams of girls at play and singing over toasted marshmallows the old camp songs about Marching on to Victory.

'Was there nothing to show you that she was ill or suffering – just reticence?' Dr Fried asked.

'Well, yes. . . I mentioned school – it was small and friendly and they all thought well of her. She was always very bright, but one day the psychologist called us and showed us a test that all the children had been given. Deborah's answers seemed to show him that she was "disturbed." '

'How old was she then?'

'Ten,' Esther said slowly. 'I looked at my miracle, trying to see her mind, if it were true. I saw that she didn't play with other children. She was always at home, hiding herself away. She ate a lot and got fat. It had all been so gradual that I had never really seen it until then. And – and she never slept.'

'A person must sleep. You mean she slept little?'

'I knew that she must sleep, but I never *saw* her asleep. Whenever we came into her room at night, she would be wide awake, saying that she heard us coming up the stairs. The steps were heavily carpeted. We used to joke about our light sleeper, but it was no joke. The school recommended that we take her to a child psychiatrist, and we did, but she only seemed to get more and more disturbed and angry, and after the third session she said, "Am I not what you wanted? Do you have to correct my brain, too?" She had that way of speaking even at ten, a kind of bitterness that was too old for her. We stopped the visits because we never wanted her to feel that way. Somehow, even without realizing it, we got into the habit of listening, even in our sleep, for—'

'For what?'

'I don't know. . . .' And she shook her head to ward off a forbidden word.

When the Second World War began it was no longer possible to maintain a fifteen-room house. Esther struggled on while they tried to get rid of it, feeling overwhelmed by its huge, musty rooms and the awful compulsion to 'keep things up' in the critical eyes of Mom and Pop and the rest of the family. At last they found a buyer, dropped the weight of the past gratefully, and moved into an apartment in the city. It seemed a good thing, especially for Deborah; her little oddities, her fears, and her loneliness would seem less strange in the anonymity of a large city. She was still not really happy, but her teachers thought highly of her in the new school and the studies went well without any great effort on her part. She took music lessons and did all the ordinary things that young girls do.

Esther tried to think of something that would make

Deborah's present condition believable. Well . . . she was intense. Esther remembered speaking to her about it now and then, telling her not to take things so very seriously, but it was part of both of them, and not something to be stopped just by a decision or request. In the city Deborah discovered art. The opening of her interest was like a torrent; she spent every spare moment drawing and sketching. In those first years, when she was eleven and twelve, she must have done thousands of pictures, not to mention the little sketches and bits of drawing on scrap paper at school.

They had taken some of the drawings to art teachers and critics and were told that the girl was, indeed, talented and should be encouraged. It was a bright and easy answer to Esther's grey, vague suspicions, and she tried to pull it up over her eyes. To the whole family it suddenly seemed to explain all the sickness and sensitivity, the sleeplessness, the intensity, and the sudden looks of misery, covered quickly by a blank hardness of the face or the bitter wit's backthrust. Of course . . . she was special, a rare and gifted spirit. Allowances were made for her complaints of illness, for her vagueness. It was adolescence; the adolescence of an exceptional girl. Esther kept saying it and saying it, but she never could quite believe it. There was always this or that nagging sign that seemed to taunt her perceptions. One evening Deborah had gone to the doctor for another one of her mysterious pains. She had come home strangely blank and fearful. The next day Deborah had left early on some errand and not come home until late. At about four in the morning, Esther had awakened for some unknown and instinctive reason and she had gone to Deborah's room with a certainty that now, in the telling, brought her a strange feeling of guilt. The room was empty. When she had looked in the bathroom, she had found Deborah sitting quietly on the floor, watching the blood from her wrist flow into a basin.

'I asked her why she didn't just let it go into the sink,' the doctor said, 'and she answered interestingly, I thought. She said that she had not wanted to let it get too far away. You see, she knew, in her own way, that she was not attempting suicide, but making the call for help, the call of a mute and confused person. You live in an apartment house; you have from your windows a death much quicker and surer at every hand and yet this – and she knew you to be light sleepers because she was.'

'But did she decide to do this? Could she have planned it?'

'Not consciously, of course, but her mind chose the best way. She is, after all, here. Her call for help was successful. Let us go back a way now, to the camps and the school. Was there always trouble between Deborah and the campers and schoolmates? Did she work her own troubles out or did she call on you for help?'

'I tried to help, certainly. I remember quite a few times when she needed me and I was there. There was the time when she had just started school and was having trouble with a little clique there. I took them all out for a big day at the zoo and that broke the ice. In the summer camp sometimes people didn't understand her. I was always friendly with the counsellors and that would ease the way a little. She had great trouble with one of the teachers at the public school in the city. I had the teacher in to tea and just talking a bit, explaining Deborah's fears of people and how sometimes they were misinterpreted, I helped her to understand Deborah. They were friends through the rest of school, and at the end the teacher told me that having known Deborah had been a real privilege, that she was such a fine girl.'

'How did Deborah take this help?'

'Well, she was relieved, of course. These troubles loom so large at that age and I was glad to be a real mother to her, helping in things like that. My own mother never could.'

'Looking back at those times – what was the feeling of them? How did you feel during them?'

'Happy, as I said. The people Deborah had trouble with were relieved and I was happy to be helping her. I worked hard to overcome my own shyness, to make it fun always to be where I was. We sang and told jokes. I had to learn how to bring people out of themselves. I was proud of her and often told her so. I told her often how much I loved her. She never felt unprotected or alone.'

'I see,' the doctor said.

It seemed to Esther that the doctor did not see. Somehow the wrong picture was there before them, and Esther said, 'I fought for Deborah all her life. Maybe it was the tumour that started it all. It was not us – not the love that Jacob and I had for each other or for our children. It was in spite of all our love and care, this awful thing.'

'You knew for a long time, didn't you, that things were not right with your daughter? It was not only the psychologist at the school. When did it seem to you that the trouble started?'

'Well, there was that summer at camp – no – it was before that. How does one sense just when the atmosphere changes? Suddenly it just seems to be, that's all.'

'What about the camp?'

'Oh, it was the third year she had been going. She was nine then. We had come up to see her towards the end of the season and she seemed unhappy. I told her how I had gotten over bad spots of growing up by going in for sports. It's a good way to get recognition and friends when you are young. When we left, she seemed all right, but somehow, after that year ... something ... went out of her. ... It was as if she had her head down from then on waiting for the blows.'

'Waiting for the blows ...' the doctor said musingly. 'And then there came a time, later – a time when she began to arrange for blows to fall.'

Esther turned towards the doctor, her eyes full of recognition. 'Is that what the sickness is?'

'Maybe it is a symptom. I once had a patient who used to practise the most horrible tortures on himself, and when I asked him why he did such things, he said, "Why, before the world does them." I asked him then, "Why not wait and see what the world will do," and he said, "Don't you see? It always comes at last, but this way at least I am master of my own destruction."'

'That patient .. did he get well?'

'Yes, he got well. Then the Nazis came and they put him into Dachau and he died there. I tell you this because I am

38

trying to tell you, Mrs Blau, that you can never make the world over to protect the ones you love so much. But you do not have to defend your having tried.'

'I had to try to make things better,' Esther said, and then she sat back, thinking. 'Somehow, as I see it now, there were mistakes – great mistakes – but they are more towards Jacob than Deborah.' She paused, looking at the doctor incredulously. 'How could I have done such things to him? All these long years .. since that overpriced apartment, the years of Pop's charity, the years and years I let him come second, even today – if "Pop thinks so" or "Pop wants it". Why – when he was my husband and his wishes were so simple and modest?' She looked again. 'It's not enough, then, just to love. My love for Jacob didn't stop me from hurting him and lowering him in his own eyes as well as my father's. And our love for Deborah didn't stop us from . . well, from causing . . . this . . . sickness.'

Dr Fried looked at Esther and listened to the words of love and pain coming from the carefully composed mother of a girl sick to death with deception. The love was real enough and the pain also, so that she said very gently, 'Let us, Deborah and I, study for the causes. Do not agonize and blame yourself or your husband or anyone else. She will need your support, not your self-recrimination.'

Brought back to the present, Esther realized that she would now have to face the Deborah of the present. 'How – how can I know the right thing to say while I am talking to her? You know, don't you, that she won't let Jacob see her, and she had such a strange, sleepwalker's look when I last saw her?'

'There is only one thing that is really dangerous, especially now, because she is so sensitive to it.'

'And what is that, Doctor?'

'Why, lying, of course.'

They rose because the time was over. Too short, Esther thought, to say a fraction of what needed to be said. Dr Fried saw her to the door with a last small gesture of comfort. She was thinking that the patient's versions would be radically different from the ones her mother ascribed to both

39

of them. The helpful parent, the grateful child. But if it were not so, the child would not be a patient. The quality of and the difference between these versions of reality would help to give depth to each of their interpretations of it.

Leaving the doctor's office, it seemed to Esther that she had not put her case correctly. Perhaps her attempt to help had been, after all, interference. The hospital had given her permission to take Deborah out by herself. The two of them would go to a movie and dinner in town, and they would talk. 'I swear to you,' Esther said to the Deborah in her mind, 'I swear to you that I will not use you. I will not ask you what we did or didn't do.'

She went to the small hotel room to tell Jacob that Deborah still refused to see him. The doctor had said that they must not force her, that perhaps what she had done was not so much a slighting of Jacob as an attempt, poor and misdirected, to make her own decisions. Esther had thought that this was only placating, but she had said nothing. Poor Jacob – and I am in the middle again – the deliverer of the blow.

And after a while Jacob stopped insising, but Esther saw him in the back of the theatre, watching Deborah instead of the film. And as they came out she saw him standing in the shadows alone, watching her, and on the corner as they went into the restaurant, he was standing in the cold path of early winter.

6

'TELL ME ABOUT your life before this hospital,' the doctor said.

'My mother told you all about it,' Deborah answered bitterly from the high, cold regions of her kingdom.

'Your mother told me what she gave, not what you took; what she saw, not what you saw. She told me what she knew of that tumour of yours.'

'She doesn't know much about it,' Deborah said.

'Then tell me what you know.'

She had been five, old enough to be ashamed when the doctors shook their heads about the wrongness inside her, in the feminine, secret part. They had gone in with their probes and needles as if the entire reality of her body were concentrated in the secret evil inside that forbidden place. On the evening that her father made the plans for her to appear at the hospital the next day, she had felt the hard anger of the wilful when they are dealt with and moved about like objects. That night she had had a dream – a nightmare – about being broken into like a looted room, torn apart, scrubbed clean with scouring powder, and re-assembled, dead but now acceptable. After it had come another about a broken flowerpot whose blossom seemed to be her own ruined strength. After the dreams she had lapsed into a mute, stunned silence. But the nightmares had not taken into account the awful pain.

'Now just be quiet. This won't hurt a bit,' they had said, and then had come the searing stroke of the instrument. 'See, we are going to put your doll to sleep,' and the mask had moved down, forcing the sick-sweet chemical of sleep.

'What is this place?' she had asked.

'Dreamland,' had come the answer, and then the hardest, longest burning of that secret place she could imagine.

She had asked one of them once, an intern who had seemed to be discomfited at her suffering, 'Why do you all tell such terrible lies?' He had said, 'Oh, so you will not be frightened.' On another afternoon, tied to that table yet again, they had said, 'We are going to fix you fine now.' In the language of the game-playing liars she had understood that they were going to murder her. Again the transparent lie about the doll.

What terrible scorn they had had to give that lie so often! Was it to have been worse than murder? What could they have had in their demented minds, those killers with their false 'fine'? And afterward, through the brutal ache: 'How is your doll?'

As she told it, she looked at Dr Fried, wondering if the

41

dead past could ever wake anything but boredom in the un-caring world, but the doctor's face was heavy with anger and her voice full of indignation for the five-year-old who stood before them both. 'Those damn fools! When will they learn not to lie to children! Pah!' And she began to jab out her cigarette with hard impatience.

'Then you're not going to be indifferent ...' Deborah said, walking very gingerly on the new ground.

'You're damn right I'm not!' the doctor answered.

'Then I will tell you what no one knows,' Deborah said. 'They never said they were sorry; not one of them. Not for going in so callously, not that they made me take all that pain and be ashamed of feeling it, not that they lied so long and so stupidly that their lies were like a laughing at me. They never asked my pardon for these things and I never gave it to them.'

'How so?'

'I never lost that tumour. It's still there, still eating on the inside of me. Only it is invisible.'

'That punishes you, not them.'

'*Upuru* punishes us both.'

'*Upu* – what?'

Yr had opened suddenly, in horror that one of its guarded secrets had slipped into the earthworld, the sunny office with the booby-trap furniture. The language of Yr was a deep secret, kept always more rigidly away from people as it crept towards greater control of the inner voice. *Upuru* was Yr's word for the whole memory and emotion of that last hospital day – that day after which all things had seemed to grey to dimness.

'What did you say?' the doctor was asking, but Deborah had fled, terrified into Yr, so that it closed over her head like water and left no mark of where she had entered. The surface was smooth and she was gone.

Looking at her, drawn away from words or reasons or comforts, Dr Fried thought: The sick are all so afraid of their own uncontrollable power! Somehow they cannot believe that they are only people, holding only a human-sized anger!

A few days later, Deborah returned to the Midworld looking out on Earth. She was sitting with Carla and some others on the corridor of the ward.

'Do you have town privileges?' Carla asked her.

'No, but they let me go out when my mother was here.'

'Was it a good visit?'

'I guess so. She couldn't help trying to get me to figure out what made me sick. We were no sooner sitting down when it came out in a big rush. I knew she had to ask it, but I couldn't tell her – even if I knew.'

'Sometimes I hate the people who made me sick,' Carla said. 'They say that you stop hating them after you've had enough therapy, but I wouldn't know about that. Besides, my enemy is beyond hating or forgiving.'

'Who is it?' Deborah asked, wondering if it could only have been one.

'My mother,' Carla answered matter-of-factly. 'She shot me and my brother and herself. They died; I lived. My father married again, and I went crazy.'

They were hard words, and stark, with no euphemisms such as one always heard outside. Starkness and crudity were two important privileges of the hospital, and everyone used them to the fullest. To those who had never dared to think of themselves, except in secret, as eccentric and strange, freedom was freedom to be crazy, bats, nuts, loony, and, more seriously, mad, insane, demented, out of one's mind. And there was a hierarchy of privilege to enjoy these freedoms. The screaming, staring ones on Ward D were called 'sick' by others and 'crazy' by themselves. Only they were allowed to refer to themselves by the ultimate words, like 'insane' and 'mad', without contradiction. The quieter wards, A and B, were lower on the upside-down scale of things and were permitted only lighter forms: nuts, cuckoo, and cracked. It was the patients' own unspoken rule, and one learned without benefit of being told. B-ward patients who called themselves crazy were putting on airs. Knowing this, Deborah now understood the scorn of the rigid, dull-eyed Kathryn when a nurse had said, 'Come on now, you are getting upset,' and the woman had laughed, 'I'm not upset; I'm cuckoo!'

Deborah had been two months in the hospital. Other patients had come and some had gone up to 'D' among the 'insane', and some to other hospitals.

'We're getting to be veterans,' Carla said, 'old hands at the funny-farm.' And perhaps it was true. Except for 'D', Deborah was no longer frightened of the place. She did what she was told and, apart from that wielder of horrors, Dr Fried, in her innocent-looking white house, there was no mark of excessive caution put on anything by the Censor.

'How long is the time until we know if we're going to make it or not?' Deborah asked.

'You kids are just in the honeymoon phase,' said a girl sitting near them. 'That takes about three months. I know, too. I've been in six hospitals. I've been analyzed, paralyzed, shocked, jolted, revolted, given metrazol, amatyl, and whatever else they make. All I need now is a brain operation and I'll have had the whole works. Nothing does any good, not this crap or anything else.' She got up in the very doomed, dramatic way she had and left them, and Lactamaeon, second in command of Yr, whispered, *If one is to be doomed, one must be beautiful, or the drama is only a comedy. And therefore, Unbeautiful . . .*

Kill me, my lord, in the form of an eagle, Deborah said to him in the language of Yr. 'How long has she been here?' she asked Carla in the language of Earth.

'More than a year, I think,' Carla said.

'Is this . . . forever?'

'I don't know,' Carla answered.

The winter hung around them. It was December, and outside the windows the tree limbs were black and stark. A group in the dayroom was decorating a tree for Christmas. Five staff and two patients – God, they tried so hard to make the madhouse look like home. It was all lies; their laughter hung very false among the ornaments (no sharp edges and no glass), and Deborah thought that at least they had the decency to be embarrassed. At the doctor's house the dragging forth of her history, and the retreats, camouflaging, and hiding went on. Except for her contact with Carla and Marion on the ward, she was drawing away from the world even the under-voice that answered questions and stood in place of herself when she wished to be in Yr. 'I can't describe the feeling,' she said, thinking of the Yr metaphors which she had used to tell herself and the Yri ones what she wished. In recent years thoughts often came, and happenings also, for which there seemed no sharer on the hard earth, and so the plains, pits, and peaks of Yr began to echo a growing vocabulary to frame its strange agonies and grandeurs.

'There must be some words,' the doctor said. 'Try to find them, and let us share them together.'

'It's a metaphor – you wouldn't understand it.'

'Perhaps you could explain it then.'

'There is a word – it means Locked Eyes, but it implies more.'

'What more?'

'It's the word for sarcophagus.' It meant that at certain times her vision reached only as far as the cover of her sarcophagus; that to herself, as to the dead, the world was the size of her own coffin.

'With the Locked Eyes – can you see me?'

'Like a picture only, a picture of something that is real.'

The exchange was making her terribly frightened. Because of it the walls began to thrum a little, vibrating like a great, blood-pumping heart. Anterrabae was reciting an incantation in Yri, but she couldn't understand his words.

'I hope you are happy with your prying,' she said to the fading doctor in her chair.

'I am not trying to frighten you,' the doctor said, not seeing the walls writhe, 'but there is still much to do. I wanted to ask you, since we had spoken about the tumour operations, how the world went grey suddenly after that, what the rest was like, the rest of those early years.'

It was difficult speaking to a half-present shape in the greyness outside of Yr, but there was an aching sense of loss and misery about the past and if this doctor could give a form to it, the memory might be easier to endure. Deborah began to pick through the happenings, and wherever she looked there was failure and confusion. Even at the hospital where the tumour had been so successfully removed those years ago, she had somehow not been equal to the game they were playing. Its rules had been lies and tricks and she had seen through them but had not known how to respond to the play – to fall in with it and believe. The convalescence had also been hypocritical, since the illness itself had not passed.

When her sister Suzy had been born, Deborah's senses had told her that the intruder was a red-faced, puckered bundle of squall and stink, but the relatives had all come crowding into the nursery, crowding her out in their wonderment at the beauty and delicacy of the newborn child. They had been shocked and angered at the truth she felt so naturally: that she thought the thing ugly, did not love it, and could not conceive of it as ever being beautiful or a companion.

'But she is your sister,' they had said.

'That was not my doing. I wasn't even in on the consultation.'

With that remark the family's discomfort about her had begun. A clever and precocious comment for a five-year-old, they had said, but cold, almost cruel. An honesty, they had said, but one which rose from anger and selfishness and not from love. As the years went by the aunts and uncles had stood off from Deborah, proud but not loving; and Suzy had come behind with a careless, bright sweetness, all woman-child, and had been loved without reservation.

Like a dybbuk or the voice of a possession, the curse proclaimed itself from Deborah's body and her mouth. It never left her. Because of the operation she was late starting school and stood apart from the first friendships and groups that the little schoolmates had formed in her absence. A kind and sorrowing mother, recognizing the fatal taint, took hold and played hostess to the girls of the most popular group. Deborah had been too heartsick to dissuade her. Perhaps through a lovely mother, taint or no, Deborah would be tolerated. And it was somewhat so. But in the neighbourhood the codes of long-established wealth still prevailed and the little-girl 'dirty Jew', who already accepted that she was dirty, made a good target for the bullies of the block. One of them lived next door. When he met her, he would curse her with the deep-rooted, hierarchical curse he loved: 'Jew, Jew, dirty Jew; my grandmother hated your grandmother, my mother hates your mother *and I hate you!*' Three generations. It had a ring to it; even she could feel that. And in the summer there was camp.

They said it was nonsectarian, and it might have been so for the niceties which differentiated various sorts of middleclass Protestants, but she was the only Jew. They scrawled the hate-words on walls and in the privy (that place where the evil girl with the tumour had screamed once at the release of burning urine).

The instincts of these hating children were shared, for Deborah heard sometimes that a man named Hitler was in Germany and was killing Jews with the same kind of evil joy. One spring day before she left for camp she had seen her father put his head on the kitchen table and cry terribly, wrenching men's tears about the 'checks-and-the-poles'. In the camp a riding instructor mentioned acidly that Hitler was doing one good thing at least, and that was getting rid of the 'garbage people'. She wondered idly if they all had tumours.

Deborah's world revolved around an inborn curse and a special, bitter-sweet belief in God and the Czechs and the Poles; it was full of mysteries and lies and changes. The understanding of the mysteries was tears; the reality behind the lies was death; and the changes were a secret combat in which the Jews, or Deborah, always lost.

It was at the camp that Yr had first come to her, but she did not tell the doctor of it, or of the Gods or the Collect with their great realms. From her absorption in the telling of events she looked out again and saw the doctor's expressive face indignant for her. She wanted to thank this Earth person who was capable of being moved to anger. 'I did not know that they endowed Earth-ones with insides,' she said musingly, and then she was very tired.

Yr was massed against her when she got back to the ward. Sitting on a hard chair, she listened to the cries and screams of the Collect and the roaring of the lower levels of Yr's realms. (*Listen, Bird-one; listen, Wild-horse-one; you are not of them!* The Yri words sounded an eternity of withdrawal. *Behold me!* Anterrabae fell and said, *You are playing with the Pit forever. You are walking around your destruction and poking a little finger at it here and there. You will break the seal. You will end.* And in the background: *You are not of us*, from the cruel-jawed Collect.

Anterrabae said, *You were never one of them, not ever. You are wholly different.*

There was a long, profound comfort in what he said. Quietly and happily, Deborah set out to prove the distance across the yawning gap of difference. She had the top of a tin can, which she had found on one of her walks and picked up, both knowing and not knowing what she expected of it. The edges were rippled and sharp. She dragged the metal down the inside of her upper arm, watching the blood start slowly from the six or seven tracks that followed the metal down below the elbow. There was no pain, only the unpleasant sensation of the resistance of her flesh. The tin top was drawn down again, carefully and fastidiously following the original tracks. She worked hard, scraping deeper, ten times or so up and back until the inside of the arm was a gory swath. Then she fell asleep.

'Where's Blau? I don't see her name here.'

'Oh, they moved her up to Disturbed. Cates went in the room this morning to wake her up and saw a real mess – blood on the sheets and on her face and an arm all cut up with a tin can. Ugh! A tetanus shot and right up in the elevator.'

'It's funny ... I never figured that kid was really sick. Every time I saw her I thought: There goes the rich girl. She walked as if we were too low to look at. It was all beneath her; and the sarcastic way she said things – not what she said, really, but the coldness. A spoiled little rich kid, that's all.'

'Who knows what's inside them? The doctors say that all of them are sick enough to be in here and that the therapy is damn hard in those sessions.'

'That snooty little bitch never did anything hard in all her life.'

7

SHE WAS terrified of the Disturbed Ward, from which all pretensions to comfort and normalcy had been removed. Women were sitting bolt upright in bare chairs, and sitting and lying on the floor – moaning and mute and raging – and the ward's nurses and attendants had big, hard, muscular bodies. It was somehow terrifying and somehow comforting in a way that was more than the comfort of the finality of being there. Looking out of a window barred and screened like a fencer's mask, she waited to find out why there seemed to be some subtle good about this frightening place.

A woman had come up behind her. 'You're scared, aren't you?'

'Yes.'

'I'm Lee.'

'An attendant or something?'

'Hell no, I'm a psychotic like you. .... Yes, you are; we all are.'

The woman was small, dark-haired, and troubled, but she had looked out of herself far enough to see another's fear, and, being a patient, had all the direct and immediate access that no staff member could attain. She has courage, Deborah thought. I might have belted her one, for all she knew. And Deborah suddenly knew what was good about D ward: no more lying gentility or need to live according

49

to the incomprehensible rules of Earth. When the blindness came, or the hard knots of pain from the nonexistent tumour, or the Pit, no one would say, 'What will people think!' 'Be ladylike,' or 'Don't make a fuss!'

In the bed next to hers was the secret first wife of Edward VIII, abdicated King of England, who had been spirited to this place (it was a House of Prostitution) by the Ex-King VIII's enemies. When the nurse locked Deborah's possessions in the small built-in cupboard, the woman – who was sitting on her bed discussing her strategy with the invisible form of the Prime Minister – rose and came to Deborah, her face full of pity. 'You're so young to be in this evil house, my dear. Why, you must still be a virgin. I've been raped every night since I came.' She went back to her discussion.

'Where will I meet you alone here?' Deborah cried to Lactamaeon and his others.

There are always ways, Yr echoed. *We will not crowd or overcrowd the guests of this unsecret unwife of the abdicated King of England!* Yr rang with laughter, but the Pit was very close.

'Escorted?' the doctor asked Deborah, looking quizzically at the attendant standing beside her.

'She's upstairs now, on D ward,' the attendant answered evenly, and then posted herself outside the normal-looking, booby-trapped, civilized office.

'Well, what happened?' The doctor saw the lostness and the fear and its mask of truculence on Deborah's face. Deborah sat down, hunching over the vulnerable abdomen and the lower area, where waited the easily awakened tumour.

'It was something I had to do, that's all. I scratched my arm a little – that's all.'

The doctor looked at her intently, waiting for a sign of how honestly she might be ready to search. 'Show me,' she said. 'Show me the arm.'

Deborah undid the sleeve, burning with shame.

'Wow!' the doctor said in her funny, accented colloquial English. 'That's going to make a hell of a scar!'

'All my dancing partners will wince when they see it.'

'It is not impossible that you will dance someday, and

that you will live in the world again. You know, don't you, that you are in big trouble? It's time to tell me fully what brought you to doing that business there.'

She was not frightened, Deborah saw, or horrified, or ridiculing, or making any of the hundred wrong expressions that people had always shown in the face of her trouble. She was only completely serious. Deborah began to tell her about Yr.

At one time – strange to think of it now – the gods of Yr had been companions – secret, princely sharers of her loneliness. In camp, where she had been hated; in school, where strangeness set her apart more and more as the years went on; Yr had grown wider and wider for her as the solitude deepened. Its gods were laughing, golden personages whom she would wander away to meet, like guardian spirits. But something changed, and Yr was transformed from a source of beauty and guardianship to one of fear and pain. Slowly Deborah was forced to assuage and placate, to spin from queenship of a bright and comforting Yr to prison in its darker places. She was royalty among gods on the days of the high calendar, debased and wretched on the low. Now she was also forced to endure the dizzying changes between worlds, to bear the world's hatred voiced in the chanting curses of the Collect, to be subject and slave to the Censor, who had been given the task of keeping the world of Yr from blowing its secret seeds to ground on Earth, where they would spring up wide open to flowering lunacy for all the world to see and recoil from in horror. The Censor had assumed the role of tyrant over both worlds. Once her guardian, the Censor had turned against her. In her mind, the proof of Yr's reality had become its very cruelty, for it was like the world, whose promises were all lies and whose advantages and privileges were, in the end, evil and agony. A sweetness turned into a need, the need into a force, the force into total tyranny.

'And it has a language of its own?' the doctor asked, remembering the alluring words and the withdrawal that came after them.

'Yes,' Deborah said. 'It is a secret language, and there is a

Latinated cover-language that I use sometimes – but that's only a screen really, a fake.'

'You can't use the real one all the time?'

Deborah laughed because it was an absurd question. 'It would be like powering a firefly with lightning bolts.'

'Yet you sound quite competent in English.'

'English is for the world – for getting disappointed by and getting hated in. Yri is for saying what is to be said.'

'You do your drawing with which language – I mean when you think of it, is it in English or Eerie.'

'Yri.'

'I beg your pardon,' the doctor said. 'I am perhaps a little jealous since you use your language to communicate with yourself and not with us of the world.'

'I do my art in both languages,' Deborah said, but she did not miss the threat of the doctor, and the claim she was putting on the communication.

'Our time is over,' the doctor said gently. 'You have done well to tell me about the secret world. I want you to go back and tell those gods and Collect and Censor that I will not be cowed by them and that neither of us is going to stop working because of their power.'

The first secret had been given, but the day was still there when Deborah and the attendant went back through it to the hospital. No lightning or growl from Yr. The last ward door was locked behind her, and they were beginning to serve lunch. There had been a change of head nurses on the ward and the new one was giving metal spoons instead of wooden ones. There were two missing in the count. As the search grew more earnest, Doris, a new girl, began to laugh. 'Keep calm everybody! Keep calm!' For Deborah, those were the last clear Earth-words for a while; there was a pleat in time.

Ward D's administrator was saying, 'What are you feeling like?' Deborah couldn't speak without great difficulty, so she drew with her hands – a surging. She had trouble seeing.

'You look pretty frightened,' he said.

The surge began to make noise also. After a while the voice came through again. 'Do you know what a cold-sheet pack is? I'm going to have one set up for you. It's kind of uncomfortable at first, but when you're in it a while, it may calm you down. It doesn't hurt – don't worry.'

Watch out for those words . . . they are the same words. What comes after those words is deceit, and. . . The stroke from the tumour made her writhe on the floor. A bursting vein of terror released itself and then there was the darkness, even beyond the power of Yr.

The consciousness that came after a time was blunt. She became aware that she was lying on a bed with an icy wet sheet stretched under her bare body. Another was thrown over her and it was also pulled tight. Then she found herself being rolled back and forth between the sheets while others were wound about her body. Then came restraints, tightening, forcing her breath out, and pushing her deep into the bed. She did not stay for the completion of whatever was being done. . . .

Sometime later Deborah came free of the Pit with perceptions as clear as morning. She was still wrapped and bound tightly in the pack, but her own heat had warmed the sheets until they seemed the temperature of her own exertions. All the anguish and fighting only served to heat the cocoon; the heat, to wear her out. She moved her head a little, tiring from the effort. It was all she could move.

After a while someone came in. 'How are you feeling?'

'Yes . . .' Her voice sounded surprised. 'How long have I been here?'

'About three and a half hours. Four hours is standard and if you're okay we'll let you up in half an hour.' He left. Her joints were beginning to ache from the pressure of the restraints, but reality was still there. She was amazed that she had been able to come from the deepest place without the anguish of rising.

After what seemed like a long time, they came to let her up. As they were freeing her, she studied the construction of the cocoon. There was an ice pack under her neck and a hot-water bottle at her feet. Sheets were spread over and under the complex of wrappings which made up the mummy case. Over the sheets were three canvas strips, wide and long, which were pulled tightly across her body at the chest, stomach, and knees, and tied to the bed on the other side. A fourth strip was knotted around her feet and pulled down to be tied around bars at the foot of the bed. The wrappings were large sheets that fitted around the body; three of them interlapped like white wet leaves, and one, on the inside, held the arms to the sides.

Deborah was weak when she got up, and had difficulty walking, but her world-self had risen. When she was dressed, she went back to her bed to lie down. The unsecret unwife of the abdicated King of England was full of solicitude. 'You poor little whore,' she said, 'I saw what they did to you for not sleeping with that doctor! They tied you so that you couldn't move and then he went in and violated you.'

'What a prize!' Deborah answered acidly.

'Don't lie to me! I am the unsecret unwife of the abdicated King of England!' the Wife shouted. Her phantoms flowed to her, and she began to chat with them in a parody of all of gentility's gossip and rattling teacups. Politeness made her introduce Deborah, from whom the streaky marks of sheet creases were just beginning to fade: 'And this is the little tart I was telling you about.'

8

'DISTURBED ... what does disturbed *mean*?' Esther Blau said, looking at the report again. She was hoping that the word would change or that some other word would appear to modify it so that it could be transmuted into the pleasant fact she wanted. In its briefly impersonal way, the monthly report counselled patience, but the facts it contained were unambiguous, and the signature at the bottom was that of another doctor, the administrator of the Dis-

turbed Ward. Esther wrote immediately to the hospital and
shortly received a reply saying that a visit would not be
wise.

With a fear verging on panic, Esther wrote to Dr Fried.
Perhaps she might go down again, not to see Deborah, since
the hospital thought it unwise, but to confer with Deborah's doctors about this change. The answer was the attempt of an honest person to reassure. It, too, counselled
patience. Of course, if she and her husband felt it necessary
to come, they would be given appointments, but this seeming setback was in itself no reason for anxiety.

Esther remembered the screams from that high, double-
barred place, and she shivered. Reading the letter over again
and again, she located the subtle strain of its meaning, like a
hidden message. She must not let her fear, or Jacob's, inter-
fere with what was happening to their daughter. She must
wait and endure. Quietly, she put the letter and the report
away with the others. She did not look at it again.

'I wonder if there is a pattern . . .' Dr Fried said. 'You
give up a secret to our view and then you get so scared that
you run for cover into your panic or into your secret world.
To Yr or there.'

'Stop making my puns,' Deborah said, and they laughed a
little.

'Well then, tell me what the rhythm is, of these upsets of
yours.' She was looking at her patient intently, interested in
that world which had been a refuge once, had suddenly gone
grey, and was now a tyranny whose rulers Deborah had to
spend long days of her life propitiating.

'One day . . .' Deborah started. 'One day I was walking
home from school and Lactamaeon came to me and said,
Three Changes and Their Mirrors, and then Death. He
spoke Yri and in Yri the word that means death also means
sleep, insanity, and the Pit. I didn't know which he meant.
The first change, I knew, was riding home from the hospital
after the tumour kas supposed to be out. Its mirror was the
broken flower that I saw years later. The second change
was being shamed in the camp, and its mirror was an episode

55

with a car when I was about fourteen. The third was moving to the city, and its mirror, foretold, was what made the prophecy come true. Whether it was cutting my wrist or coming here I don't know, but it was the death that Lactamaeon spoke of.'

'Two of the changes happened before the god, or whatever, announced them, didn't they?'

'But the third didn't and the mirrors didn't.' And she began to tell of the weaving together of prologue and destiny that was the fabric of her secret world.

When the tumour was removed, everyone had been jubilant. They had driven her home from the hospital through a light rain and they had been laughing. Deborah had stood up in the back of the car and looked out at the grey skies and the wet streets where people were pulling their coats close. Reality was not inside this car with her singing mother and cheerful father, but towards the murky sky finishing with its rain, exhausted and dark. It occurred to her that this darkness was now, and was forever going to be, the colour of her life. Years later, after other realities had been argued for between her soul and the world, Lactamaeon reminded her of that day of knowledge.

Even before she had gone to that hospital there had been a dream: a white room – the hospital room as she imagined it – and an open window through which she saw a brilliant blue sky where a swiftly changing white cloud rode. In the window a flowerpot stood and a red geranium was growing in it. 'You see—' the dream voice said, 'there are flowers in a hospital and strength, too. You will live and be strong.' But suddenly in the dream the air went dark and the sky through the window blackened, and a stone thrown from somewhere smashed the pot and broke the plant. There was the sound of screaming and the foreknowledge of something horrible. Many years later a bitter-voiced art student – another Deborah entirely – passed by a broken flowerpot that had fallen into the street. The dirt had spilled out and a red flower hung tangled in its own roots and stem. Lactamaeon, beside her, whispered, *See – see. The change has come and the mirror of the change is here. It is completed.*

Two more changes and two more mirrors of those changes and then *Imorh* (that word like death or sleep or insanity; a word made like a sigh of hopelessness).

The second change came when she was nine and it came with her shaming. It was the first day of her third year at the camp, and still fighting against what she felt was the injustice of having been born as herself, she reported the two girls who had ridiculed her and refused to let her walk with them. The camp director gave her a hard look. 'Who actually said those words to you: "We don't walk with stinking Jews—" Was it Claire or Joan?'

Because it was the first day, Deborah was confused over names and faces in the swarm of girls. 'It was Claire,' Deborah answered. Only when Claire was called and hotly denied saying the words did Deborah realize that Claire had only listened and nodded agreement and that the speaker had been Joan.

'Claire denies this. What do you say now?'

'Nothing.' The train of ruin was keeping its track. She stopped struggling and said no more. That night there was one of the comradely campfires that campers remember years later with wistful sadness at the innocence of their youth. The director gave an impassioned speech about 'a liar in our midst who uses her religion to get pity and involve innocent girls in trouble – one among us who would stoop to any evil, any dishonour.' He would not mention names, he said, but they all knew who it was.

Some days later when she managed to get away for a while by herself, she heard a voice from somewhere saying in a sweet, dark sound, *You are not of them. You are of us.* She looked for the voice but it was part of the mosaic of leaves and sunlight. *Fight their lies no longer. You are not of them.* After a while, hoping to hear the voice, becoming sadder with the loss of it, she found it again in the night of stars, inaudible to the others walking with her, the same rich voice saying like a poem, *You can be our bird, free in wind. You can be our wild horse who shakes his head and is not ashamed.*

The shaming was the second change, but the rising of

57

the gods, the first intimations of what would become Yr, made the shaming secondary. The hatred of the people in the world was, rather than a wound, suddenly a proof of the truth of Yr and it was reflected in its mirror, suddenly, when Anterrabae called her from a crowd in a car and she had to make them stop and let her go. In the camp the world had held her hour after hour, but henceforth she could no longer be kept, for she belonged *otherly*, as Yr said.

The third change was the move to the city. Mother had thought it would be such a happy change. They could have their own place at last, even if it were an apartment, and Deborah would find friends of her own age. She had laughed as they left the old house, for she knew they were taking the ruin with them. In the city the fatal taint would stand out with even more clarity and the issues themselves would be clearer. At last, the old hate and loneliness could no longer be attributed to their being Jewish. But the hate of the old place had grown familiar. In the city the new scorn and the new loneliness cut their channels deep in the parts of her feeling that had not yet been toughened.

This time the mirror came as another embarrassment: a gym teacher singling her out for some scornful comment on her clumsiness. She had fallen headlong into the Pit. She spent three days of waking nightmare, invisible to her own soul and inaudible to her own ears.

Then, one evening shortly before her sixteenth birthday, she was returning from a doctor's office, heavy with the non-existent pain of her nonexistent tumour. Anterrabae and Lactamaeon were with her and so were the Censor and the Collect. Amid the noise of their conflicting demands and curses, she suddenly realized that she had lost another day somehow. In an inexplicable way time pleated up again, and it was another time and she was being chased by a policeman. When he caught up to her, he asked her what was wrong; she had been running in great terror from something. She assured him that nothing was the matter, even ducking into a building to get away. When she came out again, she was walking to the slow, deep rhythm of a drum-beat. *It has come. The Imorh at last is here.* There came a

long, calm sounding of the rhythm and a great peace because there was no more need to struggle or resist.

The three changes and the three mirrors, all as Lactamaeon had said.

'But I could not be sure. I am good at getting deceived,
you know. It's even one of my names in Yr, The Always Deceived.'

'Since two of your three changes happened before the
gods were even presences to you, I wonder if they did not
seem wise by hindsight. I wonder if they do not deceive you
only to conform to your own picture of the world.' The
doctor leaned forward in the chair, feeling Deborah's exhaustion at revealing the things which seemed to Deborah
to most truly motivate her. A secret language concealing a
still more secret one; a world veiling a hidden world; and
symptoms guarding still deeper symptoms to which it was not
yet time to go, and those in turn concealing a still, still deeper
burning wish to live. She wanted to tell the stunned-looking
girl in front of her that this sickness, which everyone shied
from and was frightened of, was also an adjustment; these
hidden worlds – all of them – and tongues and codes and
propitiations were for her the means to stay alive in a world
of anarchy and terror.

'You know ... the thing that is so wrong about being
mentally ill is the terrible price you have to pay for your
survival.'

'At least being nuts is being somewhere.'

'Exactly so, but it is still in a group, with other people.'

'No! No!'

'At a terrible price, you belong.'

'Not to anyone *here*! Not to you or the world! Anterrabae
told me that a long time ago. I belong to Yr!' But Deborah
knew that the doctor was, perhaps, in a small way right. She
had opened her mind to the words the way an eye used to
darkness, veiled with its lashes, opens cautiously to the
light, and, finding it even a little blinding, closes itself too
late. The light had come, and come invincibly, even after
the eye had renounced it. It was too late to unsee. She was,
after all, at home on D ward, more than she had ever been

59

anywhere, and for the first time as a recognizable and defined thing – one of the nuts. She would have a banner under which to stand.

After the session Dr Fried went to her kitchen and began to brew some coffee. Mirrors and changes! Aren't all human eyes distorting mirrors? Here again, as a hundred times before, she was standing between one person's truth and another's, marvelling at how different they were even when there was love and the share experiences of many years. After the tumour business and the anti-Semitism of the camp there must have begun the malignant and pernicious loneliness that is the ground of mental illness; all of the love that Esther gave had been reinterpreted by Deborah. If the daughter was damned surely, she must feel that her mother knew it and was offering pity instead of love and feeling martyrdom instead of pride.

When the coffee began to perk, she looked at it, suddenly feeling a little old and baffled. The mother was formidable. 'Charming . . needing very much to be charming and a great success at everything . . .' she murmured to the empty cup in front of her. 'She is competitive, I think. . . She dominates, but there is honest love too. . . Ach!' And she leaped up with a word in the true and familiar language of her own childhood and youth because the coffee had boiled over and was spilling from under the lid.

Deborah walked back to the ward, yearning for somewhere she could go to be completely alone. In this place aloneness was an ambiguous state, for though the hospital was full, the floors were full, and the wards were full, all the occupants were separated. In all the hospitals she had heard about there were atomized armies of persons who had severed their claims to membership in all the world's other groups and orders. Some of the patients on her ward had been stopped motionless. Some, like the prostituted Wife of the Assassinated Ex-President, had set up their own kingdoms and never even seemed to approach, as Deborah did, the edges of terrestrial reality.

Many of the patients had the preternatural ability to tell,

60

almost at a glance it seemed, where another person's weaknesses lay and how great and compelling those weaknesses were. But coupled with this power, as if the forces of self-ruin were afraid of it, was the utter inability to use the knowledge consciously. They had all been taught to be 'civilized'. never to laugh at cripples or stone the deformed or stare at old men in the road. They obeyed these commandments, but when it came to unseen lamenesses, they perceived secrets with accustomed eyes, and they heard the hidden pleas of the so-called sane with well-attuned ears, and they were merciless. But their cruelty was beyond their own grasp or control.

Deborah saw one attendant attacked by the patients night after night. The attackers were always the sickest ones on the ward – out of contact, far from 'reality'. Yet they always chose to go against the same man. On the day after a fight that had been more violent than usual there was an inquiry. The battle had become a free-for-all; patients and staff were bruised and bleeding and the ward administrator had to ask everyone questions. Deborah had watched the fight from the floor, hoping that an attendant would trip over her foot, so that she might play a little parody of St Augustine and say later, 'Well, the foot was there, but I didn't make him use it. Free will, after all – free will.'

The ward administrator spoke to everyone about the fight. The patients were proud of their lack of involvement; even the mutest and most wild-eyed managed a fine disdain and they purposely thwarted all of the questions.

'How did it start?' the doctor asked Deborah, alone and very important for her moment in the empty dayroom.

'Well ... Hobbs came down the hall and then there was the fight. It was a good fight, too; not too loud and not too soft. Lucy Martenson's fist intruded into Mr Hobbs' thought processes, and his foot found some of Lee Miller. I had a foot out, too, but nobody used it.'

'Now, Deborah,' he said earnestly – and she could see the hope in his eyes, something to do with his own success as a doctor if he could get the answer when another might fail – 'I want you to tell me ... Why is it always Hobbs and why

61

never McPherson or Kendon? Is Hobbs rough on the patients without our knowing about it?'

Oh, that hope! – not for her, but for her answer; not for the patients, but for a moment in his private dream when he would say matter-of-factly, 'Oh, yes, I handled it.'

Deborah knew why it was Hobbs and not McPherson, but she could no more say it than she could be sympathetic to that raw, ambitious hope she saw in the doctor's face. Hobbs *was* a little brutal sometimes, but it was more than that. He was frightened of the craziness he saw around him because it was an extension of something inside himself. He wanted people to be crazier and more bizarre than they really were so that he could see the line which separated him, his inclinations and random thoughts, and his half-wishes, from the full-bloomed, exploded madness of the patients. McPherson, on the other hand, was a strong man, even a happy one. He wanted the patients to be like him, and the closer they got to being like him the better he felt. He kept calling to the similarity between them, never demanding, but subtly, secretly calling, and when a scrap of it came forth, he welcomed it. The patients had merely continued to give each man what he really wanted. There was no injustice done, and Deborah had realized earlier in the day that Hobbs' broken wrist was only keeping him a while longer from winding up on some mental ward as a patient.

She did wish to say this, so she said, 'There is no injustice being done.' It seemed to the doctor a cryptic statement – with a patient in bed, another with a broken rib, Hobbs's wrist, another with a broken finger, and two nurses having black eyes and bruised faces. He rose to go. He had not helped her to say any more than she wished to say, and she saw that he was angry and disgusted with her for having helped to frustrate his daydream. Then the door opened quickly, and he turned. It was Helene, another patient, carrying her lunch tray into the dayroom. Apparently they had given out lunch while Deborah was in with the doctor.

For a moment Deborah thought that Helene simply wanted to eat in the dayroom, where it was sunny, but seeing her face – no, it was not for the sun. The doctor looked up sharply and said, 'Go back to your place, Helene.' With a single, graceful step back and a pivot of the arm, smooth on its fluid bearings, Helene sent the tray crashing down on Deborah's head. Deborah had seen the beautiful ballet-like motion and she was yearning after the beauty of it when the world suddenly exploded in an avalanche of warm, wet food – stew, shreds of things, and the glancing edge of the tray. She turned towards the ward doctor and saw him cowering against the wall, saying in a voice very different from his professional drawl: 'Don't hit me, Helene – don't hit me! I know how hard you can hit!' Right behind his cry the attendants came rushing in to overwhelm the ballet with their heavy arms and hard, frightened faces. There seemed to Deborah to be quite a few of them for one small woman, even though she was like a thresher and they, wheat. She murmured beneath the mess dripping from her face and hair, 'Good-bye, Helene, go in sixes.'

'What did you say?' the doctor asked, straightening his clothes and struggling to do the same with his expression.

'I said, "*Relevez, soufflé,* dragged away." '

She heard the bed being moved for the cold pack. The doctor left hurriedly to cope with some screaming that had started in one of the back rooms. Deborah stood alone in the mess wondering if she were bleeding.

Because of the excitement, it was half an hour before she could get an attendant to unlock the bathroom so that she could clean up a little. Here, as elsewhere, the attackers were favoured above the attacked. They were not so far from the world after all. Deborah thought a curse against the whole business. They might have quelled Helene roughly, but they were caring about her; they were concerned. When she had freed herself of Helene's lunch, she went to her bed, where her own cold food was waiting, having been half eaten by a patient who slept near the window.

'Eat, dear,' said the Wife of the Abdicated, sitting on her bed, 'they'll get it out of you later.'

'No . . . ,' said Deborah, looking at the stew, 'I've done this already.' The Wife of the Assassinated looked at her sharply, 'My dear, you'll never get a man, looking like that!'

She turned from Deborah to attend her conference, and, suddenly, Deborah knew why Helene had come in and tried to hurt her. About an hour earlier, before the doctor had called her, Helene had come to Deborah and, speaking quite clearly, had shown her some pictures which had come in a letter. Helene was kept in a seclusion room, for she was universally feared for her angers and violence, which could break bones when she wished. The door had been open to-day, though, and no one had noticed her going to see Deborah or had heard them sharing the small confidences of the pictures. She had gone on for a while telling Deborah who this one was and that, and had come to a picture and said, 'She was with me in college.' A nice girl, standing in the real world, that nightmare no man's land. Helene had taken the picture back from her and lain down on Deborah's bed, saying, 'Go away – I'm tired.' Because she was Helene, Deborah had left the room and gone into the hall and soon the attendant had found Helene and told her to go back to her room. Deborah understood now that Helene had attacked her because she had to discredit her as a witness to the shame and misery that the picture evoked. The mirror had to be dirtied so that it would no longer reflect the sudden secret vulnerability beneath the surface of hard fists and eyes and obscenity.

'Philosopher!' Deborah muttered to herself and picked a piece of food from behind her ear.

9

'WE HAVE THE changes and we have the secret world,' Dr Fried said, 'but what was going on in your life in the meantime?'

'It's hard to get close to; it all looks like hate – the world and camp and school. . . .'

'Was the school also anti-Semitic?'

'Oh, no, it was truer there. The hate was all for myself,

the good, hard in-spite-of-lessons-on-manners dislike. But every time mere dislike turned to active anger or hate, I never knew why. People would come to me and say, ". . . after what you did, . . ." or ". . . after what you said, . . . even I won't defend you any more . . ." I never knew what it was that I had done or said. The maids in our house left one after another, until it was like a continuous procession, and I kept having to "apologize", but I never knew for what or why. Once I greeted my best friend and she turned from me. When I asked why, she said, "After what you did?" She never spoke to me again, and I never found out what had happened.'

'Are you sure that you are not hiding some truth here – something you needed to do that angered these friends?'

'I've tried and tried to imagine, to think, to remember. I have no idea at all. None.'

'How did you feel about this happening?'

'After a while it was just a greyness and the surprise of the inevitable.'

'Surprise of the inevitable?'

'Where there is no law but this awful destruction, coming and always coming closer – the *Imorh* – the shadow of it is always inevitable. Yet – and why I don't know – I keep suffering from its oncoming and from being hit and hit over and over from directions which I don't expect.'

'Perhaps it is only that you are looking to be shocked and frightened in this world.'

'You mean arranging deceits?' Deborah felt the ground beginning to go dangerous.

'But you had to make the deceits yourself, did you not? Or understand nothing.'

A picture came to Deborah from the years when she was only waiting for the end. She had been removed from the anti-Semitic camp, but the colour of life had been set and only the despair could deepen. She was always off by herself sketching, they had said, but she never let anyone see the pictures. She had begun to carry that sketchbook around everywhere, clutching it like a kind of shield, and once, among a laughing, idle group of boys and girls, a picture had dropped out of the book without her knowing it. One of the boys had picked up the paper. 'Hey – what's this? Who dropped it?'

It was an intricate picture with many figures. One by one the members of the group disclaimed it: no, not mine, not mine, no, no ... down the line, and finally he looked again at Deborah.

'Is this yours?'

'No.'

'Oh, come on – admit it.'

'No.'

As Deborah looked at the boy more closely, she saw that he was trying to help her – that if she would admit the work and take her 'punishment' in the laughter of the others, he would defend her. He wanted to be a benefactor, but she did not know at what cost to her.

'Is it yours?'

'It is not mine.'

'You see—' she told the doctor bitterly, 'they made me repudiate my art.'

'But don't *you* see that the boy was begging you not to repudiate it, and none of the others laughed, really. You were only afraid that they might laugh. You alone made yourself lie.'

She looked at the doctor, angry and fearful. 'How many times does one tell the truth and die for it!'

She got up angrily, went to the doctor's desk, and took a sheet of paper and began to draw an answer to the seeming accusations of all of them: the doctor, who seemed to be blaming her; the Collect and its endless disapproval; the words of so many. She drew furiously for a while and when she was finished, she handed the picture to the doctor.

'I see clearly the anger, but there are symbols here which you should explain. Crowns ... sceptres ... birds ...'

'Those are nightingales. So lovely. See, the girl has all the advantages, all that money can buy, only the birds use her hair for nests and to polish those crowns, and they burnish the sceptre with her bones. She has the finest of crowns

66

and the heaviest of sceptres and everyone says, "Lucky girl, with all that!" '

Dr Fried saw her patient turning and running, turning and running in her fear. Soon there would be no place to go and she would have to meet herself as she planned her own destruction. She looked at Deborah. At least the battle was being fought in earnest now. The old apathy was gone. She began to feel in herself a rising hope and with it an excitement that was like no other; the echo coming out of so deep a place still bore the sound of this girl's potential health. She withheld the excitement from her face so that Deborah would not see it and damn herself forever by defiantly trying to prove that this Yr of hers was a fact.

'Crown and nightingales!' Deborah was saying caustically. 'Keep the thing and you can show it to the learned doctors you lecture to. Tell them that you don't have to be sane to understand linear perspective.'

'It does depend on the kind of perspective,' the doctor said. 'But I think I'll keep this for myself – to remind me that the creative strength is good enough and deep enough to bring itself to flower and to grow in spite of this sickness.'

Deborah was sitting on the floor of the ward, idly waiting for a meeting with Anterrabae, when she saw Carla coming towards her down the hall. 'Hey, Deb . . .'

'Carla? I didn't know you were up here.'

Carla looked very tired. 'Deb – I had enough of hate all boxed in. I decided to come up here where I can yell and yell until I get hoarse.' They looked at each other and smiled, knowing that 'D' was not the 'worst' ward at all, only the most honest. The other wards had 'status' to keep up and a semblance of form to maintain.

The people on the edge of Hell were most afraid of the devil; for those already in hell the devil was only another and no one in particular. So Wards A and B whispered their little symptoms and took their sedatives and were terrified of loud noises or overt agony or towering despair. Women's Disturbed rocked like a boat sometimes, but its inmates felt free of the subtle, treacherous currents of secret madness.

Sometimes the patients talked to one another about their lives before, or shared information from the grapevine. Such was the instinct of the idle and displaced for some union with the world, however they wished to deny it. Now their world was peopled with psychotics and bounded by walls and wards.

'Where were you before?'

'Crown State.'

'Jessie was there. I knew her in Concord.'

'What ward in Concord?'

'Five and Eighteen.'

'I had a friend on Seven. She said it was a real bughouse.'

'Hell, it was! Hesketh was head of the place. He was nuttier than the patients.'

'Hesketh ...' Helene, passing by them, started from her trancelike procession down the hall. 'Short and kind of thin? Blue eyes – a slurring of his r's. Did he turn his head up like this?'

'Yeh, that's him.'

'The bastard! I got beaten up by him at Mount Saint Mary's.' And she continued on, moving away from them and back into her trance. Lee Miller rubbed her ear reflectively. 'Mount Saint Mary's ... I remember ... Doris was there; Doris Rivera.'

'Who the hell is she?'

'Oh, kid, she was before your time, a veteran of every treatment I ever heard of and she was as crazy as a bedbug. She was up here for three years.'

'Where did they send her then?'

'Nowhere. She's living outside now and working.'

They were incredulous. Did someone really know? Could someone really name the name of a success – one for whom this place had been means and not end? They deluged Lee with questions until she said, 'Listen, I knew Doris when she was up here on "D", but I don't know her formula for success and I haven't seen her since she left! All I know is that she's out and has a job. Now, damn it, leave me alone!'

The patients turned and began to scatter to the dayroom, the bathroom, the far end of the hall, and their beds. The evening went into night. The Wife of the Assassinated made one of her monthly breaks for freedom – a headlong, blind dash to the closing ward door as the dinner trays left.

Deborah stood listening to the endless recitals of her wrongs in the chant of the Collect, and into the middle of their noise Anterrabae cried, *See if you can ever got out and live. See if you can ever go out and work and be a person!* The threat made her dizzy with fear. The outside world and its beings were as foreign to her as if she had never eaten at the same tables with them or been caught in the up-current of their death-dealing and unfathomable lives. All the simple-looking actions that she could not counterfeit, she saw again, flatly, like a series of still pictures. Young girls saying hello, walking together, going unafraid to school; the pretty girls, courting and marrying. She remembered Helene and the anguish which had made her wish to obliterate the face that had seen and understood the picture of a pretty college friend.

You are not of them! Lactamaeon screamed out of Yr, trying to protect her.

All the other mothers are proud of their young girls! The Collect was saying in the acid, mocking tone it took when things were worse than usual.

Walk out of this with that famous doctor of yours! the Censor roared. *Do you think you can go telling secrets and be safe forever? There are other deaths than death – worse ones.*

Now it is time to hide and be hidden . . whispered Idat, rarely seen god who was called the Dissembler.

From the endless-sounding embroilment, the flashing-by of gods and faces of the Collect Deborah saw, like a cartoon, flat and unforeshortened, the figure of McPherson walking down the hall of the ward. *I'm going to call him – to get help,* she said to all of it. *Go ahead,* Anterrabae laughed. *Try.* And he passed by with a whiff of the smell of his burning. *Fool!*

McPherson was passing by. Soon he would be gone. Deborah got closer to him but couldn't speak. Gesturing a little with a hand, she tried to get his attention, and he saw her out of the corner of his eyes, arrested by the intensity of her look and the strange, almost spastic motions of her hand, twisted by tension into an odd position. He turned.

'Deb? . . . What's the matter?'

She could not tell him. She could do no more than gesture feebly with her body and hand, but he saw the panic she was in. 'Hold on, Deborah,' he said. 'I'll be back as soon as I can.'

She waited and the fear mounted as her other senses closed to her. She could only see in grey now and she could barely hear. Her sense of touch was also leaving, so that the reality of contact with her own flesh and clothing was faint. The mumbling out of Yr went on, and after a while the smell of people in the heavy ether-and-chloroform stench of the Pit made her think that she should try to see them. Everything was white – it must be nurses or the winter snow.

'Deborah. Can you hear me?' It was McPherson's voice. Someone in the background was saying, 'What's the matter with all of them tonight?' McPherson was still trying to talk to her. 'Deb – don't be afraid. Can you walk?'

There was not much direction to the walk. She shambled and had to be taken, leaning on someone, to the end of the hall where the open pack was waiting. She collapsed on it almost gratefully, not feeling the first cold shock of the wet sheet. . . .

A long time later she came up clear again and after a period of breathing and listening to herself breathe, she gave a long sigh. A voice beside her said, 'Deb? Is that you?'

'Carla?'

'That's right.'

'What happened?'

'I don't know,' Carla said, 'I'm a stranger here myself, but the ward is sure going nuts tonight.'

'Going!' They laughed a little.

'How long has it been?' Deborah said.

"You hit just a little after I did. Helen's in the next room and so is Lena, and Lee Miller is having hysterics.'

'Who's on the night shift?'

'Hobbs.' The tone of dislike was plain. 'I wish it was Mc-Pherson.'

They talked for a while, letting the real world in slowly, being pleased to talk to each other but not daring to admit that they were, in a small sense, friends. Carla told how she had listened to one of Helene's hours with her doctor. The sessions were held on the ward because of Helene's violence. 'Silence is murder,' Carla said. 'Old Craig just couldn't stand all that silence. He began to talk himself and soon he was getting louder and louder and more and more upset. Any minute I expected Helene to say, "Calm down, doctor; I'm just here to help you." When he came out of there, he looked . . . like one of us!'

Deborah, fully conscious, began to stretch, feeling the now familiar bone-ache of restricted circulation in her feet and ankles. She could see the motionless mummy-hump of Carla in the bed near her.

'Deborah . . . Deb . . . I know what it was – what happened to us.'

'What?' Deborah said, wondering if she really wanted to know.

'Doris Rivera.'

Somewhere inside Deborah an awful ache rose, a recent but now familiar ache which she had begun to identify with Yri words – an ache hiding the ancient and fearsome English word: Truth.

'No, it wasn't.'

'Yes, it was,' Carla said, gaining conviction. 'She got well and went out and she's working, and we got frightened because we might someday . . . have to be "well" and be in the world; because there's a chance that they might open those doors for us, on . . . the world.' Carla's voice was cut with the knife of her panic.

Inside the motionless white casing Deborah's heart had begun to pound and her stomach to heave. She began to tremble hard and the tremor took her whole body. My God, she thought, I am now what I was in the world – a motionless mountain whose inner part is a volcano.

'Go to hell!' she cried at Carla. 'Just because your

71

mother was insane and killed herself, you think you have more reasons to be crazy than I do!' She heard the sharp intake of breath from the other bed. The spear had gone home, but her cruelty had given her no protection. She pushed her head hard against the ice pack pressing like reality at the back of her neck.

At that moment the lights went on over them and they blinked, trying to shield themselves from the glare.

'Just checking,' Hobbs said. He came and felt Deborah's pulse at the temple. 'She's still pretty high,' he said to the attendant who had come in behind him. 'This one, too,' he said as he straightened up over Carla. They left and the light went out.

In shame, Deborah turned her head away from Carla's bed.

'Is the meat done?' Carla said bitterly. 'No, give it another twenty minutes.'

'We are not of them,' Deborah murmured, and the comfort of Yr in this new context seemed almost shocking. 'Carla . . .' The words were coming hard. 'I'm sorry for what I said. I did it for me and not against you. I didn't want to hurt you – to make you sicker.'

There was quiet for a while; the only sound was their breathing. Then Carla's voice came, not rancorous or arch, although Deborah was listening for rancour. 'My sickness . . . is a glass that's full and running over, and your little drop is lost by now in all the overflow.'

'What you said about Doris Rivera maybe . . . is true.'

The bone-truth hurt, but a little less this time.

'I know.'

Deborah began to fight the reality, the pack, the questions. She struggled against her restraints, half-crying.

'What's the matter?' Carla said in the darkness.

'You could have hurt me – and you didn't!' And because Deborah could not understand why Carla had spared her, she lay shaking and gritting her teeth in cold, bare terror.

72

10

THE BLAUS SAT at dinner. Esther was tired, Jacob angry. There had been another report, and Jacob had read it. It was general and noncommittal as usual, but it seemed to him to say that certain hates, violences, and terrors that had been deep inside his well-beloved daughter had erupted. She had been transferred 'to greater protection'. What it meant to Debby he did not know. His inner eye saw only that high, barred, and screened place; his inner ear heard only the madhouse scream which had come from high up, where 'the violent ward' was, to torment night after night of his sleep. To that porch, to that screaming they had taken his Debby. Esther had known that she couldn't keep the truth from him forever. She had equivocated and hidden the reports and misread them as long as she could. Now Jacob knew also and all she could do was to try to calm him, using over and over the carefully neutral words of the new ward administrator.

'They say that she's better in some ways,' Esther explained, but Jacob didn't believe her and she wondered if she believed herself after all.

At the table, they tried to forget the report for Suzy's sake, but they both returned to it to worry it again and again this way and that, speaking in a kind of code over and around the head of the happy daughter, who sat chattering at her meal, knowing and not knowing why the heaviness was all around them like a fog, seeming to hide them from one another. It was Debby. It was always Debby. For a moment she wondered if, were she far away and sick, *she* could ever make them suffer so palpably. She realized suddenly that she would be afraid to try; she would lose – almost certainly. Fear of wanting to prove that failure once and for all, guilt at foreseeing such a failure, and anger at

Debby who had all the love, made Suzy turn from one parent to the other and say, 'All right! She's not lying in a ditch somewhere. She has doctors and stuff! Why is everybody always crying over poor, poor Debby!' She left the table angrily, but not before she had seen the pain in her parents' faces.

Carla sat next to Deborah in the dayroom, elaborately smoking her cigarette. In conformity with the revised regulations of a hard-starch new head nurse, patients wishing to smoke were required to do so in the hall or dayroom, individually 'specialled' by a nurse or attendant. For two weeks, cries of 'Cigarette! Cigarette!' had echoed and re-echoed from the hall and rooms, and the staff was beginning to look haggard.

Carla had come from the end dormitory, saying, 'Cigarette, please,' up to the barred ward door, and then turning to Deborah with a wink, 'If you can't join 'em, fight 'em.' They had sat down, waiting for time to pass.

In the first days on D ward, Deborah had been able to dramatize herself in her own mind simply by thinking: the insane asylum – the violent ward. It conjured huge and flaming pictures in her mind. The reality had offered a promise of more physical safety, but to experience the reality was to suffer a boredom as endless as the illness itself. The number of cracks on the cold corridor floor was nineteen, the wide way, and twenty-three the long way (counting the seam). When Deborah was in the world of the ward, she walked with the moving frieze up and down the corridor, around where it widened and was called 'the hall', into and around the dayroom, out to the nursing station, past the front bathroom, past the banks of seclusion rooms, past the dormitories (where wandering was not allowed), past the back bathroom, and around the other side of the corridor to start again. When she was not real enough to walk, she lay on her bed. The ceiling was nineteen holes by nineteen holes in its soundproofing squares. Sometimes she stood with the stone women near the nursing station, waiting for something to happen, or not to happen. The boredom of insanity was a great desert, so great that anyone's violence or agony seemed an oasis, and the brief simple moments of companionship seemed like a rain in the desert that was numbered and counted and remembered long after it was gone. Deborah and Carla were enjoying such a rain as Carla nursed her cigarette.

'When I get around to it, I'm going to do your portrait,' Deborah said, watching the smoke of Carla's cigarette. From Deborah's statement Carla understood that she had managed to steal both pencil and paper and hide them. They were behind the cold-water pipe in the front bathroom. The back section, where the tubs were, was always kept locked unless it was being used and it could be used only in the presence of the attendant. Deborah began to explain this and Carla caught the suggestion in it.

'It takes paper to do portraits,' Carla said.

'True.'

'What kind of a picture would it be?'

'Water-colour. I would use lots and lots of water.'

Carla understood and smiled. 'If you get to do it, you'll need something to lean on.' By this Carla meant that she had a book and that it was hidden in an accessible place.

At the times when they were capable of it, the patients took great pleasure in the codes and secrecies of prisoners or nuns or mental patients or members of remote and tiny clans who knew every moment of each other's day. Speaking past the alien faces of the attendants, they were beginning, now and then, fragments of an allegiance. Helene would move with Deborah or Carla sometimes, and then, frightened, withdraw into violence. Lee, the veteran of the ward, spoke the most. Although there was no cohesiveness or loyalty or generosity, at least they had secrets.

'I wish I could do that portrait now,' Deborah said, wishing aloud that she had the forbidden things. Paper was allowed, but pencils and pens were considered weapons and were not allowed on the ward unless used in the presence of a watching attendant.

'Do I need a hairwash?' Carla asked vaguely. In the code,

she was suggesting that they both ask to be allowed to wash their hair. Carla would ask first and get the back bathroom with the nice big sink. Since policy was that unless there were three on duty in the bathroom, no more than one patient could use the sinks at one time, Deborah would have to go to the front bathroom where she might be able to get the attendant to unlock the tubroom door and be distracted long enough for Deborah to get to her treasure.

'My hair feels dirty,' Deborah said. 'If you don't like it, you can lump it.' She was saying 'thank you'.

The plan went well and by lunchtime the forbidden pencil was resting in a sling made of discarded rubber bands hooked to the underside of the fourth bedspring of Deborah's bed. Then there was to wait for the lunch trays. Then there was to wait for the end of lunch. Then there was to wait for change of shift. Then there was to wait for supper. Then there was to wait for the sedative line. Then there was to wait for bed.

Dr Fried was off at a convention of some kind, so there were not even the therapeutic hours to break the days. Deborah could have put in for the craft shop and gone there when the people from 'D' went in the morning, but she didn't. She had given up 'doing things'. Sometimes she sketched a little, sitting on the floor and shielded by the bed of the Wife of the Abdicated. She attended the denunciations of the Collect, the tyranny of the Censor, and the witty calumny of the gods and the blandishments of Yr, but after the hours of punishment or propitiation there was time to wait through, endless time, marked off by meals and sleep, a word or two brushing by, an anger, a story, or the raging delusion of another patient – all experienced disinterestedly and remembered only as part of the frieze of the sick around the walls of the ward. Sometimes there were frightening dreams; or great volcanoes of waking terror; or fears congealed with hallucinations of sound, odour, and touch; but mostly there was only looking at the clock that was masked like the face of a fencer standing forever *en garde* over the door of the nursing station.

Esther had written another letter to the hospital, asking if she might visit Deborah on her new ward, and if she might see the ward doctors and Deborah's doctor also. The reply she got was the usual mystifying, placating one about the patient doing as well as could be expected. If she wished, she might have some time with Deborah's doctor. The ward administrator did not deal directly with patients' families, and visits to Ward D were not permitted. If there were any matters to be discussed, there would be time made available with the social worker, Mrs Rollinder. . . .

Esther took the long train ride for the single appointment with Dr Fried. She was glad that Jacob's work kept him from insisting that he drive her. At the hospital she found that her presence gave her no easier way around the doctors, whose written rules she had hoped somehow to circumvent. Dr Fried was gentle but noncommittal. She tried to ease Esther's fear about the D ward; she seemed hopeful still that this was a 'phase of the sickness'. Esther talked to the social worker and got the same answers, but more impersonally and coldly. The no-visiting rule stood.

After her visit, she rode home to lie to Jacob and the family. She would tell them that she had seen Deborah and the ward and the doctors and that it was all, all fine. They would want to hear this and they would want desperately to believe it, and so they would let her lie to them, at least for a while. She had carried an armful of magazines with her for Deborah. They had not even let her give them, and she noticed absentmindedly as she sat looking out of the train window that she still had them. She began to thumb through them idly; the lie she had to tell to Jacob and the pain she had to keep to herself seemed to be reflected in everything she saw. She tried to escape to the pictures in the magazine, but there was no refuge there either. As she looked, tears closed over her eyes and blurred the grimly gay models in the advertisements:

COLLEGE IN THE FALL
CLASSIC STYLE FOR THE CAMPUS

And on the next page:

OUR NEW YOUNG DEBUTANTES
WHITE, WHITE, WHITE FOR HER
FIRST PROM

There were forget-me-nots scattered all over that page, and Esther set her jaw hard against those flowers, waiting for the tears to stop filling in her eyes. Deborah's classmates would be looking at these pages, substituting their own faces in place of the models, as they looked forward to graduation and college. Friends of Esther's with daughters were already giving and taking the names of colleges like calling cards. They were getting the lovely outfits ready to be worn, and the diaries to be filled. She still met these mothers, her friends, and spoke to them, and their children's problems seemed only a little smaller in scope than Deborah's. 'Marjorie is so shy; she just doesn's seem comfortable with her friends!' 'Helen takes everything as if it were life and death – she's so intense.' Esther listened to these descriptions with her cold lie in front of her, and recognizing a little breath of Deborah in this sigh or that. Her little idiosyncrasies were like theirs. She, too, was shy; she, too, covered her fear with precocity and cynical wit; she, too, was intense, but would she ever come back to a world like theirs? That hospital – could it – could it have been a mistake all along?

When she got home, she saw Jacob and then the family, smiling and poised, and she parried and equivocated with fluency and conviction. She thought herself greatly successful, until Jacob said, 'Wonderful – I'm glad they think she's made so much progress, because next time you go, I'm going with you.'

'How did you destroy your sister?' Dr Fried asked Deborah who was huddled on the couch, shivering in Yr's cold through the heat of Earth's August.

'I didn't mean to – she was exposed to my essence. It's called by an Yri name – it is my selfness and it is poisonous. It is mind-poisonous.'

78

'Something you say that destroys? Something you do, or wish?'

'No, it's a quality of myself, a secretion, like sweat. It is the emanation of my Deborah-ness and it is poisonous.'

Suddenly Deborah felt an explosion of self-pity for the miasma-creature she was, and she began to elucidate, drawing larger and larger the shape of herself and the virulence of her substance.

'Wait a moment—' The doctor put up a hand, but the joy of self-loathing had taken Deborah as fully as if it had been love, and she went on and on, decorating and embellishing the foulness, throwing the words higher and higher. When she was finished, her shadow was immense. The doctor waited until Deborah could hear her and then said flatly, 'So, you are still trying to throw dust in my eyes?'

Deborah parried, defending and nursing the unrecognizable image she had made, but the doctor said, 'No, my dear – it just doesn't work. It's an old invention, this camouflage, and it was not invented by your Eeries, either.'

'*Yeeries.*'

'I wonder. No. To hide one can forget, or pretend to another happening, or distort. They are all just good methods of getting away from the truth that might be bitter.'

'Why not hide, then, and be safe?'

'And be crazy.'

'Okay, and be crazy. Why not, after what they did to me!'

'Oh, yes. You remind me cleverly of what I had left out. Another camouflage is to blame it all on someone else. It keeps you from having to face what they really did to you, and what you did to yourself and are still doing.'

Part of what Deborah had said about the evil emanation was actual and true to her, but the glorifying of it had put its reality far away for a while, and the monster-girl she now saw was a stranger to her. The doctor pressed her to continue about the destruction of Suzy, and she did, telling of the early jealousy and the later love that had been so racked and guilty. Deborah's illness had been oncoming for a long time. She described how she felt about it; that everyone she knew was tainted by it through her – Suzy more than anyone because Suzy was loving and impressionable.

'Do you make her have hallucinations or smell things that are not there? Do you make her doubt her own sanity or reality?'

'No,' Deborah said. 'The illness is not seeing or hearing things – the illness is underneath those. I never gave her symptoms. The illness is the volcano; she will have to decorate the slopes herself.'

'Are you still cold?' the doctor asked.

'Yes, ever since these rains began to fall and the icy fogs settled. On the ward they never turn the heat on.'

'Well, in the outside – the world – it is August. The sky is clear and the sun is very hot. I am afraid that the cold and the fog are inside you.'

The tumour woke, angered that there were other powers contending for her allegiance, and it sent a sharp bolt through its kingdoms to remind them that it was still supreme. Deborah doubled up, gasped with pain, and began to tremble. *I warned you*, the Censor said. The heavy smell of ether and chloroform came to her and she heard her heart pounding. 'I tried to kill my sister when she was born,' she said. She was surprised that the information did not come out any louder than her own voice. No cannon boomed.

'How did you do this?'

'I tried to throw her out the window. I was almost ready to throw her when mother came in and stopped me.'

'Did your parents punish you?'

'No. No one ever mentioned it again.'

She felt a slow, fearful gratitude to her family, who had lived with a monster and treated it like a person.

'After the operation . . .' the doctor mused.

'We were in the sunny house where we had moved for that one year. No matter what they gave me, you see, no matter what they did for me—' She was near tears for a moment, until the sickness remembered that tears were human. *You are not of them*, Yr said, and the tears drew away as suddenly as if they had never approached.

'Did you just think about killing her?'

'No! I had her in front of the window all ready to go.'

'And your parents never spoke of it or asked you about it?'

'No.' Deborah knew that they must have taken the naked fact and buried it hurriedly somewhere, like carrion. But she knew well how the stench of a buried lie pursues the guilty, hanging in the air they breathe until everything smells of it, rancid and corrupting. Yr had a region called the Fear-bog. Lactamaeon had taken her there once to see the monsters and corpses of her nightmares accumulating there from year after year of terrifying dreams. They had swum through the almost solid ground.

She had said, *What is that awful stench?*

Shame and secrecy, Bird-one, shame and secrecy, he had answered.

Deborah began to laugh, so that the doctor leaned towards her. 'What is it? Take me along with you.'

'Pity,' Deborah said, 'pity. Somewhere there is a thief who has heard that people bury and hide their gold and jewels. Can you see the expression on his face when he comes on what I have buried!' For a moment they both laughed.

11

WHEN THE EVENING shift came on, Helene placed herself in front of the nursing station and began stamping her feet heavily. The noise soon brought an attendant out.

'What's the matter now, Helene?'

'Case closed,' Helen said. 'I'm stamping Mr Hobbs' case closed.'

She was smiling archly, so that the attendant's face tightened. It was supposed to be a big secret that the night before Mr Hobbs had gone home after his shift, closed his doors and windows, turned on the gas, and died. In the nun-prisoner-pigmy confinement of Ward D everyone knew, even the unknowing.

As lunatics, crazies, screwballs, nuts, the patients felt no responsibility to be decent and desist from speaking ill of the dead. Where deformity of the body was regarded with a certain mercy, death and its conventions were heaped with scorn. Helene had once said, 'A nut is someone whose noose broke,' for they had all wanted to kill themselves, they had all tried suicide more or less diligently, and they all envied the dead. Part of their illness was that they saw the whole world revolving around themselves, and so what Hobbs had done was to stick out his tongue at them from a place where they could not get at him to slap his face for it.

The evening shift was here, and the patients were all waiting to see who would be taking Hobbs' place. When those at the head of the hall saw, they carried the news back.

'It's a Nose – a new one – a new Nose,' and there was an almost palpable groan. Noses were Conscientious Objectors who had selected to work in mental hospitals as an alternative to prison. Lee Miller had originated the name 'Nose' a long time ago by saying, 'Oh, those conchies; I hate them. They won't fight, so the government says, "We'll rub your noses in it for you! It's either prison or the nuthouse!"' Helene had laughed and someone else had said, 'Well, they're the noses and we're *it*.'

Now Carla only murmured, 'I like being somebody's punishment; it makes me feel needed,' and she laughed, but with a bitterness that was rare for her.

The Noses usually came in pairs. 'I suppose we should call one of them a Nostril,' precise Mary said, rubbing the blood from invisible stigmata. The patients laughed.

'Maybe he'll be all right,' Carla said. 'Anything's better than Hobbs.'

They watched the new staff member go his first long and hard walk down the hall. He was terrified. They saw his terror with feelings caught between amusement and anger. Constantia, in the seclusion section, began to scream when she saw him, and Mary, hearing it, said, 'Oh, my God, he's going to faint!' laughing and then hurt: 'She's only a *person*, you know.'

'He's afraid he'll catch what we have,' Deborah said, and they all laughed, because Hobbs had caught it, and died from it too.

The expedition neared them.

'Get up off the floor, will you please?' the head ward nurse said to the group of patients sitting against the walls of the hall and corridor.

Deborah looked at the Nose. 'Obstacle,' she said.

She meant that she and the other patients with feet stuck out before the terrified man were like the contrivances in the obstacle courses that men must run through in their military training; that she and they understood their substitution as 'the horrors of war', and that they would try to fulfil the Army's desire that this man's training be rigorous. But the nurses neither laughed nor understood, and passed by with another admonition about getting off the floor. The patients all knew that it was merely form. Everybody always sat on the floor and it was only when guests came that the nurses, like suburban wives, clucked at the dust and wished that 'things were neater'.

Constantia was beginning to work herself up into an all-night howl, when the ward door opened and McPherson let himself in. Deborah looked hard at him, saw everyone suddenly go easier, and said meaningfully, 'They should have changed the lock.'

She was thinking that McPherson's key-turn and incoming was of a completely different order from the one which had preceded it – as different as if there had been different doors and different locks. She felt obscurely that the words had somehow done her injury, and so she went over them, seeking the culprit.

'They ... should ... have ... changed ... the ... lock.'

McPherson said, 'I don't like this key business anyway.' Carla looked around, as Deborah had just before, knowing that no one understood, but with McPherson, not understanding carried no penalty of scorn or hatred. She sat back quietly.

They were all glad that McPherson was there, and because feeling this meant that they were vulnerable, they had to try to hide it. 'Without those keys you wouldn't know yourself from us!'

But McPherson only laughed – a laughter at himself; not at them. 'We're not so different,' he said, and went into the nursing station.

'Who is he kidding?' Helene said. There was no malice in her statement; she was merely hurrying to rebuild the wall that he had breached. She turned and disappeared into her limbo, and because McPherson's after-image still hung in the air there were no catty remarks about her fade out. But when the procession of magi passed by once more, bearing with them the Nose, rigid and clamp-jawed with fear, no one could withhold the cruelty which seemed to each her true and natural self. Helene shuddered as he passed; Carla looked blank; Mary, always inappropriately gay, trilled laughter, saying, 'Well, Hobbs' bodkins, here comes another gas customer!'

'Let's call him Hobbs' Leviathan, because he may be a whale of a lot worse!'

'Their religion doesn't permit them to commit suicide,' Sylvia said from her place against the wall.

The ward was suddenly silent. Sylvia had not said anything at all for over a year and her voice was so toneless that the sound almost seemed to come from the wall itself. The silence hung in the ward as everyone sought to make sure that there had really been words and that they had come from the frozen and mute piece of ward furniture that was Sylvia. They could all see each other checking for symptoms – did she say it or did I only hear it? Then Lee Miller broke from inaction and went to the closed door of the nursing station. She pounded on it until the nurse opened the door and looked out in annoyance, as if confronted by an unfamiliar salesman.

'Call the doctor,' Lee said tersely. 'Sylvia talked.'

'The ward report is not finished,' the nurse said, and closed the door. Lee pounded again. After a while the door opened. 'Well . . . ?'

'You'd better get that doctor, because if you don't, it will be your fault and not mine. Adams will come – she always does. She came last time at three in the morning when Sylvia talked!'

'What are you all excited about, Miller?' the nurse said. 'What did she say?'

'It doesn't matter and it wouldn't make sense to you because it was part of the conversation.'

'About what?'

'Oh, Christ. *Please!*'

Standing between Sylvia and the excited Lee Miller, Deborah saw how stupid any fragment of the conversation would sound. Sylvia had extinguished her brief, faint light. Lee had an aura of dark light around her, the Yri sign for one who was *tankutuku* – Yri for unhidden – open to the elements and far from shelter. Lee had put herself in this horrible state for someone else, who would never praise her for it or feel gratitude. Yri had a word for this, too; used rarely, it was *nelaq,* eyeless. Deborah now wanted to thank Lee for being eyeless and unhidden. Yr praised Lee, but Deborah could not speak the necessary words.

She had to do something. Lee was all alone in that hideous place called 'Involvement' or 'Reality' and no one could help her. Locked in a motionless body – as motionless now as Sylvia's – mute in English, Deborah began to tremble. In fear she made another headlong dash for Yr; the deeper the better, but the flaming Anterrabae laughed. *How dare you cast with the world! You will be punished, you traitoress!* The way to Yr closed before her.

No! No! If you do that I will go insane! she cried to them.

You admire the nelaq tankutuku, do you? Well then, there is the world. Take it!

A black wind came up. The walls dissolved and the world became a combination of shadows. Seeking for the shadow of firm ground on which to stand, she was only deceived again when it warped away like a heat mirage; she looked towards a landfall and the wind blew it away. All direction became a lie. The laws of physics and solid matter were

85

repealed and the experience of a lifetime of tactile sensation, motion, form, gravity, and light were invalidated. She did not know whether she was standing or sitting down, which way was upright, and from where the light, which was a stab as it touched her, was coming. She lost track of the parts of her body; where her arms were and how to move them. As sight went spinning erratically away and back, she tried to clutch at thoughts only to find that she had lost all memory of the English language and that even Yri was only gibberish. Memory went entirely, and then mind, and then there was only the faster and faster succession of sensations, unidentifiable without words or thoughts by which to hold them. These suggested something secret and horrible, but she could not catch what it was because there was at last no longer a responding self. The terror, now, could have no boundary.

When she came from the Punishment she was looking at her fingernails. They were blue with cold. It was the summer of a certain time and there was sunlight outside, and greenness, but she dared not use her mind to fix the time lest the Punishment return and take it away again. She got up from somebody's bed, where she found herself lying, pulled a blanket from it, and, still chattering with the cold, walked into the hall. She didn't recognize anyone, but at least she knew to a reasonable extent that she existed and that she was looking at three-dimensional solids, called people, who moved in an element called time. She went up to one of them and asked an irrelevant question: 'What day is it?'

'It's Wednesday.'

'Oh, then, what day was it?' The person didn't understand, and since she was too confused to pursue the point, she walked away. Behind her the three-dimensional solids were complaining about the heat. They fanned the air of their time in front of their faces.

She felt nauseated by the freezing cold, so she went back and lay down on a bed, desperately grateful that she recognized it as hers.

You see what it is ... Anterrabae said genially. *We can really do it. Don't toy with us, Bird-one, because we can do it up, down, and sideways. You thought all those descriptions were metaphors: lost one's mind, cracked-up, crazed, demented, lunatic? Alas, you see, they are all quite, quite true. Don't toy with us, Bird-one, because we are protecting you. When you admire the world again, wait for our darkness.*

Later, Dr Fried asked her what she had found out since their last session.

'I found out about being insane,' Deborah said, and remembering with awe the immensity and power and horror of it, she shook her head. 'It really is something. Yes, it sure is something.'

The struggle between the new Nose, Hobbs' Leviathan, and the patients went on. His rigid fundamentalist beliefs made him see insanity as a just desert for its victims, as God's vengeance, or as the devil's work, and sometimes as all three at once. As the days passed, his fear waned and the time of his righteous wrath was at hand. He saw that he was suffering persecution for his faith.

Against his loathing, the sick fought in their sick way. The literate rewrote the Bible or ridiculed its passages to make him horrified. Constantia made flagrant sexual advances to him. Helene took the towel he brought her with a little curtsey, saying, 'From Paraclete to Paranoid. Amen, amen.' And Deborah made a few pointed observations about the similarity between psychotics and religious fanatics. McPherson sensed the anger and violence blowing like a wind over the ward and wondered what he could do about it. There was not enough staff anyway. The two other new conscientious objectors were doing well on different wards, and one of them was showing signs of ability at working with mental patients. He didn't like the new man on Ward D, Ellis, much himself, but he was sympathetic towards him. Ellis was not suited for the work at all; he feared and hated the patients, and looked upon the government which had punished him as the early Christian martyrs must have looked upon the Roman procurators. Because of this, Ellis had to drag the dead Hobbs after him in the nickname the patients had given him. The worst of it was that Ellis' religion could not see suicide as anything but a sinful horror, monstrous in nature.

So, Ellis dragged a dead and stinking whale, and McPherson mused that there was no hunter in the world as clever or merciless in placing barbs in a weak place as these sick people. Sometimes he wondered why Hobbs had been attacked and never he; why Ellis, now, and not he. Never was Helene's tremendous store of knowledge used to damn him; never did the hard-faced Deborah Blau set her knife-edged tongue against him. He felt somehow that it might just be more than luck, but he did not truly know how or why he escaped the bitterness and unhappiness that vented itself all around him.

Now he watched the patients as they stood, waiting for dinner, waiting for darkness, waiting for sedatives, waiting for sleep. Blau was standing near the barred and screened radiator, staring out at something beyond the wall. He had once asked her what she was looking at and she had answered him from her otherness, 'I'm the dead, reckoning.'

Constantia was out of her seclusion room, but in seclusion still, muttering quietly in a corner. Lee Miller was clenching and unclenching her teeth; Miss Cabot from the dormitory, insisting, 'I'm the Wife of an Assassinated Ex-President of the United States!' Linda, Marion, and Sue Jepson, and all the rest were doing what they usually did. Yet there was a lingering sense of dangerous unrest – more than the sum of the parts of unrest. Ellis came out of the nursing station where he had been writing up the medication reports. The badgering began.

'Thar he blows – it's Hobbs' Leviathan!'

'Get thee behind me, Satan!'

'Hobbs committed suicide and the army committed *him*!'

'He got a commission, but not the kind that gives you eagles on the shoulder.'

'With his commission they give bats in the belfry!'

'What's the latest from Hell today, preacher?'

'Don't ask him now. Let him look over his holdings first.'

There was a radio built in behind a heavy mesh screen in the wall. It was supposed to be on only during certain hours of the day and tuned only to certain innocuous semi-light music, but now McPherson went to the screen, unlocked it, and turned the radio on good and loud. Into the ward poured the tinny sounds of romantic love-dance music, pathetically, even hilariously, incongruous in the heavy urine-and-disinfectant atmosphere that permeated the ward. When the announcer's moist voice bade them 'Good night from the Starlight Roof,' Carla replied in a parody of romantic wistfulness, 'A farewell flutter of my restraints, delicately, good night . . . good night . . .'

The whole ward erupted into laughter and relaxed, although the mind-scent of tension still hung in the air like the ozone smell after a lightning bolt. Something had been narrowly averted.

After Deborah had been given her sedative, she got into her bed, waiting the familiar wait, the gods and the Collect reduced to a somnolent undertone. McPherson came into the dormitory and stopped by her bed.

'Deb,' he said gently, 'lay off on Mr Ellis, will you?'

'Why me?' she said.

'I want all of you to let him alone. No more jokes. No more references to Hobbs.'

'Are you going to tell everybody?' (The guarded vying-for-favour and the guarded suspicion of all the world's motives and representatives overcame prudence and forced the question.)

'Yup,' he said. 'Everybody on the ward.'

'Even Marie and Lena? (They were acknowledged to be the sickest on the ward, even by the patients.)

'Deb . . . just lay off.'

For a moment she felt that he was using her. He was the only one who could get away with calling the patients by nicknames without sounding strained, but it sounded strained now.

'Why me? I thought you normal ones had agreed that we were out of it – your conventions and routines. I'm not nice

89

and I'm not polite and I know more about Hobbs than you do. He was one of *us*! The only thing that separated him from us was three inches of metal key he used to fondle for assurance. Ellis is another one. I know all about him and his hate.'

McPherson's voice was low, but his anger was real, and Deborah felt it coming from a place in him that he had never shown before.

'Do you think the sick people are all in hospitals? Do you girls think you have a corner on suffering? I don't want to bring up the money business – it's been overdone – but I want to tell you right now that lots of people on the outside would *like* to get help and can't. You ought to know mental trouble when you see it. You don't bait other patients. I've never heard you say anything against one of them.' (She remembered what she had said to Carla and the stroke of guilt fell again for it.) 'Lay off Ellis, Deb – you'll be glad for it later.'

'I'll try.'

He looked down hard at her. She could not see his face in the shadow, but she sensed that it was in repose. Then he turned and walked out of the dormitory. Deborah fought the sedative for a while, thinking about what he had said and how. It was tough but true, and under the anger of it ran the tone – the tone rare anywhere, but in a mental ward like a priceless jewel – the tone of a simple respect between equals. The terror she felt at the responsibility it bore was mingled with a new feeling. It was joy.

12

S OMETHING IN A session not long ago keeps coming back to me,' Dr Fried said. 'You were discussing being sick as if it were a volcano and you said of your sister that she would have to decorate her slopes herself. Do you know what you tell us now? Can you really not see that the gods and the devils and the whole Yr of yours is your own creation?'

'I didn't mean that at all!' Deborah said, backing away, and still hearing the Collect chanting years of people: *Snap out of it; it's all in your mind.* 'Yr is real!'

'I have no doubt that it is real to you, but there is also something else that you seem to be saying – that the sickness stands apart from the symptoms which are often mistaken for it. Are you not saying that, although the symptoms bear on the sickness and are related to it, the two are not the same?'

'That's right.'

'Then I want you to take me back into that past of yours again, before the slopes were decorated, and share with me a look at the volcano itself.' She saw the look of terror, and added, 'Not all at once; a little at a time.'

They had gone over the Great Deceits, and also the many little ones that are inevitable in life, but which, because of Deborah's feelings and beliefs, seemed to be pointing the way to doom as meaningfully as if they had been arranged as part of a plan, a secret joke that everyone knew, but no one admitted knowing. After months of therapy, Deborah began to learn that there were many reasons why the world was horrifying to her. The shadow of the grandfather dynast was still dark over all the houses of the family. She went back often again, hearing grandfather's familiar voice saying, 'Second in the class is not enough; you must be the first.' 'If you are hurt, never cry, but laugh. You must never let them know that they are hurting you.' It was all directed against the smiling sharers of the secret joke. Pride must be the ability to die in agony as if you did it every day, gracefully. Even his pride in her was anger. 'You're smart – you'll show them all!' He had sharpened her word-wit on his own, cheered the cutting edge of it, called women cows and brood-bitches, and slapped her half-roughly because she would grow up wasted, a woman. She would have to take on the whole world of fools and ingrates, and, even though she was a woman, win his battle: the ancient, mystical battle between a crippled immigrant and a long-dead Latvian Count.

In the place and time where Deborah was growing up,

American Jews still fought the old battles that they had fled from in Europe only a few years earlier. And then there were the newer battles, pitched as the Nazis walked through Europe and screamed hatred in America. There were Bund marches in the larger cities, and flare-ups against synagogues and neighbourhood Jews who had ventured out of the ghettos. Deborah remembered having seen the Blau house splashed with paint and the dead rats stinking beside the morning paper that told of Czech Jews running for the Polish border only to be shot by the 'freedom-loving' Poles. She knew much of the hate and had been attacked once or twice by the neighbourhood bullies, but the grandfather would say triumphantly, as if he saw in this an obscure kind of proof, 'It's envy! The best and the smartest are always envied. Walk straight and don't let them know if they touch you.' And then, as if the hate were peering through the joke, he would say, 'You'll show them! You're like me. They're all fools, the rest of them – you'll show them some-day!'

What she had to 'show them' was a harbinger, a deceiver, a seducer: her own precocity. The hint that she would some-day be 'someone' seemed to make the old man right. For a long time she used her bitter wit as a weapon to startle and amaze the adults in her armed truce with the world, but it never fooled the people of her own age for a single moment. The young knew her and, wise in their own fear, set out to destroy her.

'It was a willing soil then, to which this seed of Yr came,' the doctor said. 'The deceits of the grown-up world, the great gap between Grandfather's pretensions and the world you saw more clearly, the lies told by your own precocity, that you were special and the hard fact that you couldn't get to first base with your own contemporaries no matter how impressive your specialness was.'

'The gap between the carefully brought up little rich girl with maids and imported dresses and the – and the—'

'And the what? Where are you now?'

'I don't know,' she said, but she was speaking from a place in which she had been before. 'There are no colours, only shades of grey. She is big and white. I am small and there are bars between. She gives food. Grey. I don't eat. Where is my . . . my . . .'

'Your what?'

'Salvation!' Deborah blurted.

'Go on,' the doctor said.

'My . . . self, my love.'

Dr Fried peered at her intently for a while and then said, 'I have a hunch – do you want to try it with me?'

'Do you trust me with it?'

'Certainly, or there wouldn't be this science at all, where the two of us work together. Your own basic knowledge of yourself and truth is sound. Believe in it.'

'Go ahead then, or psychiatry will disappear.' (Laughter.)

'Your mother had trouble with a pregnancy when you were very small, did she not?'

'Yes, she miscarried. Twins.'

'And afterwards went away to rest for a while?'

The light struck the past and there was a seeming sound of good, strong truth, like the pop of a hard-thrown ball into a catcher's glove. Connect. Deborah listened to the sound and then began to tumble over her words, filling the missing features of the ancient nightmare that was no more other-worldly than the simple experience of being left alone.

'The white thing must have been a nurse. I felt that everything warm had left. The feeling comes often, but I thought it could never have been true that I ever really *was* in such a place. The bars were crib bars. They must have been on my own crib. . . . The nurse was distant and cold . . . Hey! Hey!' The now-friendly light struck something else and its suddenness made the small, prosaic connexion seem like a revelation full of greatness and wonder. 'The bars . . . the bars of the crib and the cold and losing the ability to see colours . . . it's what happens *now*! It's part of the Pit – it's what happens *now, now*! When I am waiting to fall, those bands of dark across my eyes are the old crib bars and the cold is that old one – I always wondered why it meant more than just something you could end by putting on a coat.'

The rush of words ended and Dr Fried smiled. 'It is as big, then, as abandonment and the going away of all love.'

'I thought I was going to die, but at last they came back.' She paused in the flight and another sudden question took her, as if it had been there forever. 'Why doesn't everybody have black bands? Surely everyone is left alone sometimes, maybe for a week or two. Parents die, even, but the children don't go nuts and have mourning bands going up and down their retinas.' It had come to her as another deeper proof that she was mismade somehow, that the fault was as elemental as her genes, a bad seed. She expected the doctor's sympathetic demur, a familiar and comforting lie with which she could light her own way back to Yr. Instead the words were strong.

'The memory may not change in form, but years of underlining give it a weight that can become tremendous. Each of the many many times you are called to remember the cold of abandonment, the bars, and the loneliness, this experience says deep inside you, "You see? That's the way life is, after all." '

The doctor rose to mark the session's end. 'We have done very well this time, seeing where some of the ghosts of the past still clutch at you in the present.'

Deborah murmured, 'I wonder what the price will be.'

The doctor touched her arm. 'You set the price yourself. Tell all of Yr that it dare not compromise you in this search of ours.'

Deborah pulled her arm away from the doctor's hand because of some obscure fear of touching. She was right, for the place where the hand had paused on her arm began to smoke and the flesh under the sweater sleeve seared and bubbled with the burning.

'I'm sorry,' the doctor said, seeing Deborah's face go pale. 'I didn't mean to touch you before you were ready.'

'Lightning rods,' Deborah answered, looking through the sweater arm to the charred flesh, and seeing how terrible it must be when one was the grounding path for such power.

The doctor, lost under the leap of the logic, could only look past the shaking body of the patient before her to where the hunted spirit had flashed for a moment in gladness and now was gone. 'We will work hard, hard together, and we will understand.'

'As long as we can stand at all,' Deborah said.

13

TIME GROUND ON. Deborah was flung and rebounded like a tennis ball in play from stage to stage in Yr, from earth to nowhere, from sunlight to black window, over the divisions that demarcate the time of the sane, trying, in passage, not to be cruel to Mr Ellis. She freed him from Hobbs' name, she was obedient if not cheerful, and she bore his martyrdom – her own existence – as well as she could. A new group of nursing students had come and gone, some comforted that the mentally ill could no longer strike fear in them, some running in terror from the whip of subtle similarity between the mad-women's uttered thoughts and their own unuttered ones. Another group had come and was being broken in on Constantia's spontaneous nudity, Helene's graceful and bone-breaking violence, and Deborah's locked eyes. A young nurse had said too loudly, 'That kid looks through me as if I'm not here at all.' Trying to give comfort, Deborah had later whispered to the nurse, 'Wrong *not*.' She was saying that it was not the pretty nurse who was not there but the ugly patient, and still the wrong-coming words only made the frightened student more alarmed, and Deborah saw again the uncrossable expanse between herself and the species called 'human being'.

Deborah was standing in the small seclusion room forward of the hall. Her lunch tray had been brought by a nurse, who fumbled with the keys (her difference), and was pale, remembering perhaps the secret bedlam horror-nightmares of her own keeping. Those, at least, Deborah shared, believed, understood. She whispered her comfort and saw the nurse get hard in the face with fear, and turn, stumbling over her own feet to hang on the fraction of the edge of her balance.

Deborah put out a hand almost instinctively, since clumsiness had made them kin, and the hand got to the nurse's arm and held her for a second. Balance caught the young woman and swung her towards vertical again and she pulled her arm away, strong in her fear, and tottered out of the room.

Suffer, Deborah said to all the assembled ones in Yr, the Yri metaphor for greeting. *I am a conductor of lightnings and burnings. Passes through me from doctor, flows to nurse. Here I have been copper wire all the time and people had been mistaking me for brazen!*

Anterrabae laughed. *Be witty*, he said, shedding hair-sparks in his unending, unconsuming, fiery fall. *Outside this room, ward, hospital, such as that and that even, when her shift is through, laugh, walk, breathe, in an element that you will never understand or know. Their breath in and out, blood, bones, night and day are not of the same substance as yours. Your substance is fatal to them. If they are ever infected with your element they will die of it or go insane.*

'Like the Pit?'

Exactly so.

Deborah cried out in horror at her power to destroy. She fell on the floor, moaning softly. 'Too much power, too much hurt. Don't let anyone hurt like that – not like that! Not like that . . . like that . . .'

Then she was standing above herself, dressed in her Yri rank and name, kicking the herself that was on the floor, kicking her low in the stomach and in the tumourous place that gave like a rotten melon. When the ceremonial creak of leave-taking sounded, the sky was burdening itself with darkness outside the barred window. She looked out, finding herself erect and in front of the window and saying quietly, 'Let me die, all of you.' If they would all come together against her, she knew that she could not live. There was no joy or happiness or peace or freedom worth this suffering. 'End me, Anterrabae, Collect, all you others. Once and for all, crush me against the world!'

The light was put on from the outside and the key grated in the lock. 'Just checking,' the change-of-shift nurse said gaily, but when she saw Deborah's face, she turned back to the one behind her. 'Finish the ward check and get a pack set up.'

Deborah did not know what look she was carrying in front of what self, but she was greatly relieved. Help was coming by virtue of some of the misery which was apparently leaking through the mask. 'Out at the eyeholes, maybe . . .' she murmured to the people who came after a while.

When she rose again, it was in the darkness. She came like a great whale from the benthic depths – another element with other rules and climates. The earth came back to a night outside another window than the one which had measured the early dusk, and there were now two beds, and full, starred darkness beyond – the glass barred, bars screened, screens tightened. It was a beautiful night, with the stars piercing clear, even behind the triple-masked window. There was a low sound from the other bed. 'Who's that?' Deborah asked.

'Our Lady of the nose-itch,' Helene answered. 'Venus de Milo with nose-itch.'

'Were you ever in a pack and had a hair get in your eye?' Deborah asked, remembering the struggles she had had sometimes with hairs or fluff or itches, little devilish mites of annoyance that seemed to be the whole world when you could not reach up and push them aside.

'I *am* a hair in my eye,' Helene said coolly, 'and so are you.'

So Deborah lay quietly, resting from the eternal apocalypse. She could see clearly through her mind, and for a while she thought about Helene, lying like a twin in the other bed. Athough Helene was bitter and usually angry, Deborah respected her intellect and also that she, too, in her thorny and unconceding way, had ceased her persecution of the martyred Mr Ellis. Most of the time Helene was out of contact and not to be reached; sometimes a bitter sentence or two broke like glass, sudden and brittle, and sometimes an attack as hard as it was surprising, but Deborah knew in the quiet, unspectacular way of her clear moments that Helene, as desperately ill as she was, had the unknown quantity of strength or will or *something* that it took to get well. Helene, she knew, could make it. Because of this, her feelings towards Helene were a texture of envy, respect, and fear.

Once, she had been cruel to Helene; she had told her that she thought she could get well and had seen the terror build in the muscular body. Deborah had not realized fully her own tormenting then. Helene had told her in a fine and reasonable voice that if she, Deborah, didn't move away and fast, she, Helene, would break every bone in that dung-stinking head. Deborah had complied.

The light went on and both of them groaned softly at the revelation of the lurid spectacle of themselves and each other after the beauty of the star-darkness. Ellis came in alone, and walked swiftly to Helene's bed to take her pulse. Normally the nurses and attendants spoke as they entered, in order to introduce slowly the presence of the world, of which they were representatives, to those who might be mid-hung and confused, and usually they waited for their presence to be acknowledged even by an eyeblink. The suddenness of Ellis' coming was too much in so vulnerable a place; when he went for Helene's head to capture her temple-pulse and force from it a number for his report, she pulled hard away from his hand. Movement of the head was a person's whole repertoire in pack; Ellis grabbed Helene's face and held it with one hand while he tried to catch the bird-pulse with the other. Again she fought away. Then he straightened a little, not angry, only deliberate, and began to hit her in the face. The blows landed sure and hard. She spat up at him, a diffused and angry spray, and Deborah, watching, saw what would be to her forever after the symbol of the impotence of all mental patients: the blow again, calm and accurate and merciless, and the spitting back again and again. Helene did not even reach him, but after every attempt he met her at the end of his arm with full force. There was no sound except the pursing sputter of the now dry lips, her laboured breathing, and the blows falling. They were both so intent that they seemed to have forgotten everything else. When he had slapped her into submission, he took her pulse and Deborah's and left. When he went out, Helene was coughing a little on her blood.

The next day Deborah became her own Yri enemy – a voluntary sharer, an eyeless-and-utterly-naked, which Yri called *nelaq tankutuku*. She went to the nurse and asked to see the ward doctor when he came to sign the orders for the week.

'Why do you want to see him?' the nurse asked.

'I have something to tell him.'

'What is it?'

'That a pacifist is one who uses his open hand.'

Nurse gave way to ward nurse. The theme again. Ward nurse to head day nurse; the theme again. The cloud was beginning to darken under the ceiling, lowering towards Punishment, but Deborah had to tell the doctor somehow and get it off her own conscience that she had been a witness and thus, in some obscure way, a sharer in the experience of both victor and victim. The nurse was sceptical and Deborah had to plead, with the cloud pressing closer and the wind coming up. At last she got permission to see the ward doctor. She told, sparely and dryly, what she had seen, trying for the world's semblance of sanity so that he would believe her. She did not use the expense of the telling to show him how important it was, nor did she speak of Ellis' propensities, which she knew were secret simply because he had the keys and the patients didn't. When she got finished, the doctor sat looking at her, watching her hair grow. She knew from long experience that he did not see the cloud, feel the dark wind, or sense the Punishment. He sat in another season – springtime, maybe – beneath a separate sun whose rays ended at the periphery of her eyesight, her reality, and her kingdom.

At last he said, 'Why doesn't Helene tell me this?'

'Helene left right after it happened.' She was about to add that it was like Helene to blank out and leave her holding the bag, her way of getting even for the time when she had told Helene that she saw the possibility of wellness in her. She saw that this was unwise, but the realization stopped her mind on it, like cloth caught on a nail, and she could say no more.

'We are interested in stopping any brutality going on around here, but we can't take something without proof. You were in pack because you were upset, you know. Something perhaps you believe you saw . . .'

'Ask Ellis at least. With his Soul . . . he's going to have trouble with it anyway if he has to lie.'

'I'll make a note of it,' the doctor said, making no move towards his ubiquitous notebook. He was clearly giving her what Lee Miller called Treatment number three: a variety of the old 'fine-fine', which went, 'Yes, yes, of course,' and was meant to placate without changing, silence without comprehending, and end friction by doing nothing. As she looked at him, Deborah thought about her sedative order. She had wanted an increase in her sedation and she knew that if she asked now he would give it to her. But she didn't want to buy sleep with Helene's swallowed blood, and she let him go, murmuring, 'Chloral hydrate generosity, and charity in cc's.' She watched the worms that were dropping out of the cloud. The doctor left. Never mind; she would tell Dr Fried, The Fire-Touch, about it.

Furii, or Fire-Touch, was the new Yri name for Dr Fried; it recalled the fearsome power that had seared Deborah's arm with an invisible burning.

'Did you tell the ward doctor this?' Furii asked.

'Yes, and he gave me the Number Three With Smile: "yes-yes".' She felt ridiculous in her honourable abstinence from the heavier sedation that she had wanted. She wished that she had at least got something from what was bound to be so costly.

'You know,' Furii said, 'I am not connected with the running of your ward. I cannot break into ward policy.'

'I'm not saying that policy should be changed,' Deborah said, 'unless the policy is beating up patients in pack.'

'I have no say in discipline of ward personnel either,' Furii said.

'Is Pilate everybody's last name around here?'

At last Furii agreed to mention it in the staff meeting, but Deborah was not convinced. 'Maybe you doubt that I saw it at all.'

'That is the one thing that I do not doubt,' the doctor said. 'But you see, I have no part in what is to be done on the wards; I am not an administrative doctor.'

Deborah saw the match lighting dry fuel. 'What good is your reality, when justice fails and dishonesty is glossed over and the ones who keep faith suffer. Helene kept her bargain about Ellis and so did I. What good is your reality then?'

'Look here,' Furii said. 'I never promised you a rose garden. I never promised you perfect justice . . .' (She remembered Tilda suddenly, breaking out of the hospital in Nuremburg, disappearing into the swastika-city, and coming back laughing that hard, rasping parody of laughter. 'Sholom Aleichem, Doctor, they are crazier than I am!') '. . . and I never promised you peace or happiness. My help is so that you can be free to fight for all of these things. The only reality I offer is challenge, and being well is being free to accept it or not at whatever level you are capable. I never promise lies, and the rose-garden world of perfection is a lie . . . and a bore, too!'

'Will you bring it up at the meeting – about Helene?'

'I said I would and I will, but I promise nothing.'

Because Helene had left her standing alone with the burden of witnessing, Deborah found herself going, without a conscious choice, to Lee Miller, the one who went *tanku-tuku* for the forgotten words of Sylvia. Lee could not allow anyone to be behind her, and she didn't like to stand against the wall the way the others did, so she had to keep circling relentlessly to 'keep everyone properly placed'. Without allegiance or loyalty, but because of a mysterious sense of fitness, Deborah began to follow Lee, the ptolemaic sun circling her planets.

'Get away, Blau!'

That, too, was fitting; by her speaking to Deborah she was admitting, Deborah thought, that they were actors in the same event and related to one another.

'Get away, Blau!'

Deborah came on after, bearing the chains of the relationship.

'Nurse! Get this bitch out of here!'

The nurse came. 'Get off the hall, Deborah, or stop following.' The nurse was a third actor, but not *tankutuku*. The gravity bond dissolved; Deborah moved away again.

By the light of my fire, Bird-one, Anterrabae said, *see how carefully, how carefully they separate you from small dangers: pins and matches and belts and shoelaces and dirty looks. Will Ellis beat the naked witness in a locked seclusion room?*

Deborah slid down the wall to an accustomed place on the floor among the other statues, watching the pictures in her mind – simple pictures, explicit and terrifying.

In the evening, Lucia, a new patient with a certain prestige for her violence and the nine years she had spent in one of the roughest hospitals in the country, suddenly said to the small group of perpetually cold ones who were huddled around the radiator enclosure, 'It's different here. I been lotsa joints, lotsa wards. My brother, too; lotsa wards. What's here ... there's more scared, more mad; pissin' on the floor and yellin' – but it's because of the maybe. It's because of the little, little maybe.'

She went off again, leaping in her long ostrich run down the hall, laughing in order to negate the immense, fearful power of her words, but they had been given and they were hanging in the air like the zoo smell of the ward itself. Everyone was afraid of the hope, the little, little Maybe, but for Deborah, coming at that moment, the words had a special ring, so that she looked out into both worlds and saw the imminent things, the lowering cloud and the worms that were dropping from it, and the law, blowing like a shred in the black wind.

'Never mind the Maybe; it's an administrative problem.'

14

ESTHER AND JACOB sat together in the office, waiting, Dr Fried saw, for reassurance and for peace. She wanted to tell them bluntly that she was not God. There were no sure promises and she could not be a judge of what they had done or not done to their daughter to bring her to this battlefield.

'Is it wrong to want a child like anyone else's?' Jacob asked. 'I . . . I mean is there a cure, really, or will she stay here and have to be placated and comforted . . . always?' He heard how cold his words sounded. 'It isn't a question of love – sick or well – it's only that we have to expect something, even to hope for something. Can you tell us what we may hope for?'

'If you want to hope for a college diploma and a box of dance invitations and pressed roses and a nice clean-cut young man from a fine family – I don't know. This is what most parents hope for. I don't know if Deborah will have these things someday or if she will even want them. Part of our work together is to find out and come to terms with what she really does want.'

'May we see her?'

Dr Fried had known that the question would come, and here it was. It was the one she didn't want to answer. 'Of course, if you decide to see her you may, but I would not advise it this time.' She tried to make the answer very, very calm.

'Why not?' Jacob said, moving loudly against his fear.

'Because her feeling of reality is quite shaky now. The way she looks might alarm you a little, and she knows this and is afraid for you . . . and for herself also.'

Jacob sat back dazedly, wondering why they had ever done this thing. The old Deborah as she was might have been sick as they all said. She had been unsure and wretched, but she had been theirs – unsure, to be guarded and planned for; wretched, to be cheered and mothered. At least she had been familiar. Now, the picture that this doctor made was of someone unrecognizable.

'Let me say that the symptoms are not the sickness,' the doctor was saying. 'These symptoms are defences and shields. Believe it or not, her sickness is the only solid ground she has. She and I are hacking away at that ground, on which she stands. That there will be another, firmer ground for her after this is destroyed she can only take on faith. Imagine it for yourself for a moment and you can see why she doesn't pay attention to her grooming; why she gets so frightened and the symptoms proliferate.'

Dr Fried tried to describe the feelings of someone who had never known real mental health in her life. 'We who have never experienced this sickness firsthand can only guess what horror and loneliness there must be. You know, she is now being called upon to suspend all the years of what she has known as reality, and to take another version of the world on faith. Deborah's sickness is now a desperate fight for health.'

'The world we gave her wasn't so horrible,' Jacob said.

'But she never took your world at all, don't you see? She created a robot that went through the motions of reality, and behind it the true person drew further and further away.' Knowing that people feared the unknown person behind the familiar robot, she let the matter rest.

Jacob said quietly, 'I still want to see her.'

'No, Jacob – it's better—!'

'Es – *I want to see her!* It's my right.'

'Very well,' the doctor said affably. 'I'll call and have her brought down from the ward and you may see her in the visitors' room.' She went to her phone. 'If you should want to see me again afterwards, please have the attendant on duty call me. I will be here until four.'

She watched them leave and walk rigidly towards the

hospital building. The Families. 'Make him well,' they say. 'Make her well,' they say, 'with good table manners and a future according to our agreed-on dream!' She sighed. Even the intelligent, the honest, the good, find it too easy to sell their children. Deceits and vanities and arrogances that they would never stoop to for themselves they perpetrate on their children. Ach! Another sigh escaped from her, because she had never given birth or nursed a child, and because she wondered suddenly if she, too, would not connive or be ambitious, buy dreams and wish them impossibly on a Deborah if the Deborah were her own. She thought a moment longer, then turned and went to the phone, and got through at last to D ward.

'She was just taken down to visitors, Doctor,' the attendant said.

'Oh, well, then, never mind. I just hoped . . .'

'Doctor?'

'Just that there was time for her to comb her hair.'

In the car driving home Esther and Jacob were silent. They were waiting for the truth to become plain to them, but because everything they had seen contradicted everything they felt to be true, they were mute in their confusion. They trusted Dr Fried. She had not been hypocritically calming, but she had given them hope, and it was hope for which they were most desperate. But their daughter had been almost unrecognizable. She had not frightened them with mumbling or violence, but with a subtle and terrifying kind of withdrawal. She had not inhabited her body.

As they left the visitors' room Jacob had said only, 'She's very pale—'

And Esther, striving to catch what she was feeling, murmured, 'Someone . . . someone beaten to death from the inside.'

Jacob's anger had risen against her and he had turned away. 'You always talk too much! Can't you just let it be?'

On the way back to Chicago, all they knew was that it was past time for Suzy to be told the truth.

Dr Fried continued to chase, corner, and urge her recalcitrant patient through the circles of loving and hating. Deborah kept fleeing away to Yr's darknesses, dissembling, and throwing up dust to hide in. She longed for blindness and ignorance, for she now realized that if she herself saw or recognized anything, it would have to be exposed for discussion, however shameful, fearful, or ugly it might be; although to Deborah the reason for this necessity was as mysterious as the lower places of Yr itself.

'I have let you get away from your father long enough,' Furii announced during one session. 'When you speak of him, it is with fear and hatred – and with something else.'

The deeper secret, towards which Furii reached with her world hooks, lay beneath common injustices: the beating over a trivial thing, the simple misunderstanding at a crucial time. Part of the secret was that Deborah was like her father. They shared a sudden, violent temper, long smoulderings that erupted in incongruous rages. And because she recognized the similarity, she feared him and herself also, and she felt his love for her was blind, that he never knew or understood her for a single moment. And there was something else beyond his understanding.

'I was scornful of him sometimes,' she said.

'I know you are remembering something.'

'He was always frightened of the men – the men lurking to grab me from dark streets; sex maniacs and fiends, one to a tree, waiting for me. So many times he shook warnings into me. Men are brutes, lusting without limit. Men are animals ... and I agreed in myself. One time he was scolding me for having seen an exhibitionist on the street. Because I had attracted the man's attention my father somehow connected me with having done something. He was full of rage and fear and he went on and on as if all such men were bound by laws like gravity to me alone. I said to him, "What do they want with me, broken into and spoiled already. I'm not good enough for anyone else." Then he hit me very hard because it was true.'

'Was he afraid, perhaps, of the commands of his own passions?'

'What? He was a father—' Deborah said, beginning to know the answer before she refuted it.

'He was a man first. He knows his own thoughts. Do all others have such thoughts? He knows they have. Do all others have so good control as he has? Surely they cannot.'

Deborah pondered the almost-lust that was almost apparent so many times. It was full of guilt and love intermingled; it had badgered and confused her, making of her a secret accomplice in all of the heinous crimes of the maniacs which he was forever describing. In his fear he saw her as having the same hunger and guilt as they did – as he did. He had spoken of the diseased parts of these men and Deborah knew that her shame-parts too had been diseased. Always in her dreams what she fled from and then turned to face at last was the eternally horrifying familiar face of her father and herself.

'Is it so fearful now?'

'No ...' And then, thinking how great the shadow had grown in the Fear-bog, and that it was only him and a few unspoken, briefly hinted thoughts of her own that had been so cloaked in guilt that their true shapes had disappeared, she said, 'No, not fearful – good. I was not only ... only to him a daughter who was making him embarrassed all the time. Part of the yearning was the human ... human. ...' Deborah began to cry.

She was well into it when the terror caught. Furii saw it coming, strangling out the sobs.

'Quickly!' she said. 'It may try to make you pay, that sickness of yours, for our having outdistanced it. Quickly I tell you that you have touched insight, which is truth and love and forgiveness; that these are part of the reality of which you have been so afraid. Are they not wonderful and thrilling, these things?' She saw the light drawing away. The voice that came next was coming from Yr.

'Well ...' From far across the barrier, '... you did it. I

cried. I forgave my mother and father really. Now I guess I go home.'

'You are not so stupid and neither am I,' Furii said earnestly, trying to speak across the widening space. 'There are many secrets to come and you know it. You are now parting with food that sustained you – all the secrets and the secret powers – and no other nourishment has yet appeared to replace it. This is the hardest time of all, harder than even your sickness was before you came here. At least *that* had a meaning for you, as awful as the meaning was sometimes. You will have to trust me enough to take on faith that the new food, when it comes, will be richer.'

They spoke more, Furii eliciting from her the many small scraps of supporting evidence from years of living. Deborah was exhausted, but the stubbornness was still in her, helping her to yield and cast with Furii and her world while she awaited the last collision which would leave her insane forever.

'There is more – much more,' Furii said. 'We will go until we see it all. When it is over, you can still choose Yr if you really wish it. It is only the choice which I wish to give you; your own true and conscious choice.'

'I could still be crazy if I wanted to?'

'Crazy as a fruitcake . . . if you wanted to.'

'Nutty as a fruitcake.'

'Ah, yes, I remember. I hear also someone say "bats". What is "bats"?'

'It means bats-in-the-belfry. It means that up in your head, where the bells ring, it's night and the bats are flying around, black and flapping and random and without direction.'

'Oh, I will have to remember that one! The Americans capture the feeling of mental illness quite accurately sometimes.'

'And if I should want it – if I should need it . . . afterwards . . .'

'You have no experience to know what mental health is, but I don't think that you will need or want to have bats in the steeple. Still, the answer is yes. If you need it or want it afterwards, all your choices will still be there.'

On the ward there was a barely covered excitement. Two packs had been set up in the small seclusion room and were waiting to be occupied; the hall seemed to be all white and khaki, with nurses and attendants walking fast from here to there, yet still waiting.

'What's up?' Deborah whispered to Lee, the one most likely to know and to tell it.

'Miss Coral's coming back again,' Lee said. 'She was here before your time. Thank God. It's been dull as beans up here.'

Just before lunch was due to be brought up, the heavy elevator went rattling down and everybody in hearing gave a little jump. After a while they heard it coming back up and stopping outside the double doors of Ward D. A group of white uniforms filled the translucent screen of frosted glass, and then the key turned and the ward administrator appeared in his magnificence. He was followed by two attendants (for feet) and two attendants (for head) carrying, under heavy restraint, a tiny, white-haired old lady. Behind them flowed assorted secondary personages of procession: receiving-ward day nurses, acolytes, the regular clergy, novices, postulants, and others.

'*That* is Miss Coral?'

'All ninety pounds of her,' Lee said. There was a ringing string of beautifully balanced, varied, and intricate profanity as the bundle moved down the hall, past the set-up packs (surprisingly), and into the Number Four seclusion room beyond.

For a while there was silence and then the bearers began to drift back down the hall. Deborah was about to turn again to her post at the dormitory window when she saw the last of the attendants joining the others. His coming was absurd, frightening, interesting, funny, non-Newtonian; he was flying. He was prone on the air, his expression utterly blank, as if he felt obliged to live out his life as a trajectory.

But he did not come to rest; he fell and it was the heavy, clumsy sound of his falling that stopped his companions and spun them around. Deborah breathed heavily with disappointment. It was only a man after all.

He was not hurt in the flight nor in the fall, but he was nearly run over in the stampede of staff that rushed back to subdue the source of his propulsion. The patients followed to watch and heckle. Miss Coral stood at the open door. Her tiny being was like electricity. *That hair has been burned white*, Deborah said quietly in Yri. The three men who went to move Miss Coral were pitiful against the sharp motions of her fighting body; she literally shook them off, her blank and expressionless face staring straight ahead. When more attendants leaped into the mêlée there was less for her to do, and she stood still because they were working against one another. Helene, sensing a challenge to her reign as at least the most feared on the ward, ran into the deserted upper hall, removed the hasps from the hinges of the nursing-station door; tore the door off with its own weight and hers, flung it into the hall, and followed it with everything that came to hand. Sylvia, planted like a poorly made statue against the wall, found that she could not bear the tension of Helene's violence and suddenly exploded, diving at Helene in the broken ruins of the door, trays, medicine, cutlery, and towels. Someone rang the emergency bell, and it took twelve extra people to still the riot and put Helene and Sylvia in pack. Apparently the orders for Miss Coral had been forgotten by the ward administrator, because the door was simply closed after her and that was that.

'Well,' Lee said as Deborah passed her in the hall, 'It beats anything we've had up here for a while, you must admit that.'

'I sure wish I could have made it to that narcotics cabinet,' Deborah mused. 'I never knew a little old lady was strong enough to sail a grown man.'

'She was here two years ago. I saw her throw a bed once. Not push it; throw it. She's also the best-educated one of all of us.'

'Better than Helene?'

'Hell, yes! She speaks four or five languages and is some sort of mathematician on the outside. She tried to explain it to me once, but, as you know, I stopped in the eighth grade.' Looking around, she began to circle again, impatiently trying to get the world properly placed.

Four days later, Miss Coral's door was left open, giving her access to the ward. When, after a few hours, she came hesitantly to the threshold, she found Deborah sitting on the other side.

'Hello,' Deborah said.

'Hello. . . . Aren't you rather young to be up here?' the voice was old, but not harsh, and the vowels were spread wide in diphthongs the way the Deep South spoke them.

'I'm sorry I'm young,' Deborah answered with a bitterness that was half pose. 'We have the right to be as crazy as anyone else.'

The second part was more like a plea, and to her surprise the superbly inhuman fighter smiled softly and said, 'Yes . . . I suppose that's true, though I never thought of it in those terms before.'

The crude hunger that had made Deborah sit at the door for upwards of four hours would not allow her to be civil or patient.

'Lee Miller says you know languages and mathematics. Is that true?'

'Oh, is she still here? Too bad,' and Miss Coral clucked.

'Can you really speak them?'

'Heavens, no! They only taught us to read and write a language in those days and it was only to read the classics.'

'Do you remember the languages?' She looked to Deborah like an Anterrabae who had stopped falling, with the lightning-blue eyes and the static-stiff white hair that only needed rekindling to ignite the whole firebrand. She looked at Deborah for a while. 'What is it that you wish?' she said.

'Teach me.'

The rigid lines seemed to melt, the body slackened, and water rose in the hard eyes and overwhelmed them for a moment. 'I'm ill,' Miss Coral said. 'I've been very ill, and I forget. I could be inaccurate sometimes because of the years ...' (Deborah was watching her sustain an invisible brutal beating, trying to stand up) '... and the sickness ...'

'It doesn't matter.'

'I'm tired now,' Miss Coral said, backing away again into the bare room. 'I will make a decision and inform you of it later.' She slammed the knobless heavy door behind her.

Sitting on the floor in the door-draught, Deborah could hear the muffled sounds of the battle: curses and cries, falling and blows. An attendant passed her. 'I thought I opened that door – what's going on in there?'

'Coral *vs* Coral – divorce action. Fighting over custody of the child.'

'Blau, you saw her come out. Did she close that door herself?'

'Maybe she should talk to somebody,' Deborah said.

The attendant turned away and went slowly to start the chain of permissions. Deborah sat down in front of the door again and emptied her pocket of all its treasures. She found two cigarettes which she had picked up after a forgetful student nurse. They were only half smoked. She went to Lee Miller's bed and put them under her pillow as an offering of thanks. Sylvia's debt had been repaid.

It was quite a while before the ward nurse arrived. Sitting by Miss Coral's door, Deborah was sensing the inexorable guilt of relatedness; her substance had spread through the ward reflecting anguish on everyone. For every such battle as raged behind this door she was symbolically responsible. Yet she also remembered Carla saying that her sickness was like an overflowing glass, and Deborah's drop or two could hardly matter. Was she responsible or not?

Being unable to decide, she let the question go. After a while the sounds from inside the room stopped and Miss Coral's voice, dead-level with exhaustion, called through the door.

'Young woman – young woman – are you still there?'

'Are you calling me? Is it me you want?' Deborah called back when she could speak.

'Yes.' Then Miss Coral said:

> *'Inter vitae scelerisque purus*
> *Non eget Mauris jaculis neque arcu*
> *Nec venanatis gravida sagittis,*
> *Fusce, pharetra.'*

'What is that?'

'Tomorrow,' Miss Coral said. 'And the spelling, too.'

15

DEBORAH and Miss Coral met in loose moments between the closings of their separate worlds. Deborah had entered upon a dry and barren era. The smell of her burnt-up self was always in her nostrils – charred flesh and hair, clothing, and the rubber and leather of shoes. She lost her ability to see colour and the black bars limited the scope of her vision to a small, vertical strip of grey. Nevertheless she learned. Her pockets and secret hiding places became crammed with scraps of paper carrying the words, sentences, and poems of Miss Coral's remembered classics in Latin; Greek alphabet and vocabulary; and bits of the stolen honey of the licentious middle ages.

'It was too sinful in our day,' Miss Coral told Deborah shyly. 'The medievals were beasts, supposedly, and their Latin, degenerate; but the books went around the school dormitory at night and not all of it was lascivious. Strangely, it is they, the singing madmen, that I most remember ...' and she recited Abelard and Scottus. 'Perhaps in "folly and darkness" I resembled them ... We are here, after all ... And she was caught in a paroxysm of weeping and rage.

A conventional teacher could never have made a moment's headway against the defensive anger of Miss Coral's pupil, but Deborah felt no threat in the small bits of gentle teaching, for her tutor's manner was limned with her own pain and despair, and precluded the sour superiority that Deborah sensed in most teachers. Miss Coral was a fellow inmate, and Deborah's genuine hunger, at last divorced from her deceptive precocity, forced her to reach out and take all that Miss Coral had to give.

In line, waiting for sedatives: 'That *De Ramis Cadunt Folia*. . . . I did okay until I got to the part about *Nam Signa Coeli Ultima*.'

'Well, you know those words. . . . I remember you had them in other poems.'

'I know what they mean, but . . .'

'Oh, yes, that *Signa* is "sign", but here it is astrological, and would mean more like "house" or "ascendancy".'

Waiting before trays:

> '*Morpheus in mentem*
> *trahit impellentem*
> *ventum lenem,*
> *segetes maturas,*

. . . I don't remember the rest.'

From poems they went to bits of poems, to sentences, to phrases, building Deborah's knowledge on familiar words in their changing grammatical forms. Miss Coral worked with her memory and Deborah with her hunger and the forbidden pencil.

At last Miss Coral said, 'You have all the Latin and Greek I know. I'm sorry about the grammar – I've lost so much, but at least you will come across familiar landmarks when you read the classics; you have quite a number of bits and pieces all copied down on those papers of yours.'

Indeed, the scraps of paper were becoming an embarrassment, cramming her pockets and stuffed under the bedsprings. She realized that it was time to ask for the special privilege of a notebook. It took a week or so to get up the nerve, but finally she took her place among the 'petitioners' who waited for the ward doctor to come on his rounds. There seemed to be quite a few this time, even without counting those who were there habitually:

Lee: 'Hey, I want double sedatives tonight.'

The Wife of the Assassinated: 'Let me go home! I want to go home!'

Mary (who has Dr Fiorentini): 'I've contracted a social disease from the socialists!'

Mary (who has Dr Dowben): 'Murder and fire! There's a fire!'

Carla, who was going to go to the movie in town, needed special permission, being a 'D' patient, and money. Miss Coral, starting at the bottom of the *via dolorosa,* was there to ask for some basic ward privilege.

The doctor arrived on the ward, and the requests and answers flew back and forth. When Deborah asked for the notebook, he looked at her quickly, measuring her.

'We'll see,' he shot back over his departing shoulder, and went his way.

That afternoon Dr Adams came on the ward to see Sylvia. When she left, she was missing a copy of *Look Homeward Angel* that she had been carrying with her. Later in the day one of the student nurses looked in vain for her lecture notebook. The written pages turned up two days later in the elevator outside the Disturbed Ward, but the half of the book which was blank had disappeared.

Deborah began to bother Helene for remembered poetry, and Helene obliged by giving her some of *Hamlet* and *Richard III,* dredged up, to her own amazement, from some distant but still-living source. Greek words were dutifully copied and then Latin; *Look Homeward Angel* became an agony under Deborah's mattress, but she read and reread it until Dowben's Mary got hold of it and ate it, leaving only the binding. Carla had read the novel once and for a while they talked about it.

'If I can learn these things . . .' Deborah said, '. . . can read and learn, why is it still so dark?'

Carla looked at her and smiled a little. 'Deb,' she said, 'who ever told you that learning facts or theories or languages had anything to do with understanding yourself? You, of all people . . .' And Deborah understood suddenly how the precocious wit, though it had supported her sickness and was part of it, acted for her independently of the troubles that clouded her reality.

'Then one may learn, and learn, and be a schizo.'

'At least it may be so in Deborah,' Helene said caustically.

Deborah put her notebook behind the dormitory radiator and lay down on her bed. She stayed there for the next three months, getting up only to be let into the bathroom or to be taken off the ward to see Dr Fried. The darkness seemed complete. Phases of Yr came and went, the Collect met and dispersed, but outside the sessions with Dr Fried she did not fight any of it. Carla sometimes came in and talked to her, telling the ward gossip or the little happenings of the day. Deborah was incapable of saying how much these visits meant. They were sometimes the only human contacts she had for days at a stretch, for her lying mask gave forth looks that hurried the attendants away; they would give the tray or put out the clothes and leave without a word or a nod. Because she began to have bad dreams and loud, hard awakenings, she was moved out of the noisy and populous front dormitory and placed in a small room in the darker back hall with two more of the living dead. The coming of daylight shut their mouths and cut off their vision a foot or two beyond their eyes, but their dreams burst from them in screaming shards that shattered the brittle crust of drugged sleep for which the other patients fought. It was considered better to have the three of them waking one another than to have the whole ward upset, so they were immured together and left to themselves. Some of the nights seemed like imitations of the dramatic-fantasy Insane Asylum that Deborah still carried somewhere from her childhood store of nurses' threats. Often she would wake with one of the room-mates standing over her, arms upraised, or the other hitting her in a sleep-blind anger. One night she thought suddenly of her father and that other facet of his love, which was human need, and to the fat one, whose pounding had awakened her, she broke the mould of silent terror. 'Oh, Della, for God's sake go back to bed and let me get some sleep.'

Della turned away and Deborah found herself happier

than the mere success of her command would warrant. One night Helene herself – an angry, brutal Helene – played the apparition. Thinking that it was only one of the room-mates, Deborah snorted in what by that time had become standard form.

'Get away, damn you. Beat it!'

'I'm insane,' Helene said, menacing closer in the darkness. 'I'm insane . . .'

Deborah recognized the voice and knew the tremendous strength of violence in Helene, but now laughter came welling up as naturally as if she had always had it as a friend.

'Do you think you could compete with my smallest nightmare on its dullest day?'

'I could be capable of anything . . .' Helene said, but Deborah thought she heard more hurt pride in the tone than savagery.

'Listen, Helene. You are bound to the same laws that I am, and there is nothing that you can do to me that my own craziness doesn't do to me smarter and faster and better and good night, Helene, go back to bed.'

Without a word, Helene turned and went back across the hall, and Deborah for the first time permitted herself to speak a small word of praise for the good light in her own mind.

During the dark months spent lying on the bed, she sometimes thought about the half-mythical person, that Doris Rivera, who had been in these rooms, had suffered these fears, had seen the subtle disbelief in those around her that she would recover, and yet had gone out, well, and taken the world.

'How can she stand it, day after day – the chaos?' Deborah asked Carla.

'Maybe she just grits her teeth and fights every minute, waking and sleeping.'

'Does she have a choice? Can she be sane by willing it?' Deborah asked, seeing Doris in her mind as a listless frozen ghost bending her every energy to the Semblance.

'My doctor says we all choose, really, these different ways.'

'I remember . . .' Deborah murmured, '. . . the years I

lived in the world. . . .' She thought of the Censor again (*Now take a step – now smile and say, 'how do you do.'*). It had taken extravagant energy to afford a Censor for the Semblance. 'I gave up because I just got tired – just too tired to fight any more,' she said.

Furii had told her that sanity had to do with challenge and choice, but challenge as Deborah knew it was the shock-challenge that Yr created for her in snakes dropping from the walls, people and places appearing and disappearing, and the awful jolt of the collision of worlds.

Furii had said, 'Suspend experience; you may not know what it is like to feel, even remotely, what mental health is. Trust our work together, and the hidden health deep inside yourself.'

But in the shadows a huddled, skinny shape waited for her thoughts to come to it; Doris Rivera who had gone into the world.

Finally, one afternoon, Deborah, for no reason that she knew, got up from her bed and walked the length of the hall to the ward door. She had come out. Her greyed vision was still severely limited, but it seemed to matter less.

Miss Coral was sitting on the floor near the door, smoking a carefully attended cigarette, and seeing Deborah she smiled her completely disarming little-old-lady smile.

'Why, welcome out, Deborah,' she said. 'I've been remembering, if you still want to share it.'

'Oh, yes!' Deborah cried, and went to the nursing station, borrowed one of the 'official' numbered pencils and a sheet of paper, and spent the time until dinner racing after Miss Coral and Peter Abelard and thick gusts of Medea. It had never occurred to her that Miss Coral would be happy to see her, or that Carla, when she saw her on the hall, would smile and walk to her. 'Well, hi, Deb!' It was brave of Carla to do this right off. It showed trust and a very touching loyalty, since it was usually far safer to wait to see, in anyone's change, how the change ran before coming over and showing recognition. Deborah could think of no special reason for Carla's courage and generosity. She wondered for a moment if it might not be that Carla was simply glad to see her. Could there be a world, really, beyond her walled eye?

Suffer, victim, Anterrabae said gently in the metaphoric Yri words of greeting. In obedience to him and his command the range of her vision grew, and with it, something like a potential for colour, although the colour itself was still not present.

'I'm glad you got out today, Deb,' Carla said. 'I was going to come in and tell you: I'm set to move down to B ward tomorrow.'

You will not listen, will you, Bird-one? Anterrabae said softly. *They plant the seed and call it forth in rich soil. Sun and water and food are all given. They coax it forth from its casing, crying, 'Join us; join us.' Sweet singing and the feel of warmth. The first green beginnings come, and they stand over the shoot with a dropper full of acid ... waiting.*

The awful truth began to dawn on Deborah that Carla had become her friend, that she liked Carla, and that the scarred befriending part of her still had the power to feel.

The Censor began to roar with laughter, and Anterrabae fell faster away. He was teasing her with his great beauty; his teeth were fire-struck diamonds and his hair curled with flames. Deborah became aware that she had neither commented nor moved one plane of the mask.

'Oh,' she said, and then because she wanted it, to make herself suffer, and the only way she knew how was by telling the truth, she said, 'I'll miss you.'

The terror of the statement brought a cold sweating through her and she began to shiver with it. She got up and went to huddle with those of Dante's third circle before the fickle mercy of the radiator.

The next morning when Carla was ready to leave, she said another short good-bye. 'I'll be around. You could even get privileges to come and visit me down on "B".'

Deborah turned a puzzled face towards Carla, for with the help of Yr's codes and magic she had excised the feeling of loss and friendship, and the reality of Carla's presence. So Yr was still strong; its queen and victim still maintained a shred of power over the world's will to make her suffer. She went through the day almost gaily, and got Miss Coral to remember Lucretius' hooked atoms, and gave a hard wit-parry and thrust home to Helene that brought the fleeting mixture of envy, respect, and terror that was Helene's form of response. It was the first time since Deborah had come up on 'D' that she had put on her disguise, consciously striven for in her fear of Carla's leaving. Doris Rivera had got up and gone; Doris Rivera was semi-legend, and Deborah had mentally cast her as a sort of ghost, unable to live, unable to die, a figure of desperate and pathetic endurance; for Deborah could not imagine meeting the world again on any other terms than those. But Carla, she knew, was alive and responsive, and she was on her first step into the nightmare that people called 'reality'. The eye of destruction was drawing closer to where Deborah waited, just out of its sight. Soon it would turn to her. She was eased in her illness now enough that the disguise of normality was gone. And the eye would focus on her and the hand would pick her up and set her out in the wilderness of reality, without even the thin coat of defences she had spent her life making and this year in the hospital destroying.

Overhead, in the dimension of Yr, Lactamaeon, tauntingly beautiful, was free in his open sky, enjoying the shape of a great bird. She had once been able to soar with him in that great sweep. *What do you see?* she called to him in Yri.

The cliffs and canyons of the world; the moon and the sun in the same bowl, he answered.

Take me with you!

Just a moment! the Censor intervened with his rasp-voice. Deborah never actually saw the Censor because he was not of either world, but had a part in both.

Yes ... wait. Idat, the Dissembler, unmale, unfemale, joined him. While they discussed the matter elaborately, parodying the now familiar psychiatric manners and terms, Lactamaeon found a chasm, dove into it with a high eagle-scream of triumph, and was gone.

Somehow, in the interim, it had come to be evening. Miss Coral came up to Deborah, saying, 'I guess that the secret of enjoying hospital food is to be too ill to notice it.'

'Mary still has some of those candy bars, doesn't she? Ask her and maybe she'll give you one.'

'Oh, but I can't ask. I never could ask for anything. I thought you knew that. When I have to ask, something happens to me and I . . . well, I start to fight.'

'I didn't notice,' Deborah said, wondering if she ever looked at anyone or noticed anything about the world.

'I wanted to tell you something,' Miss Coral said almost shyly. 'I've found a tutor for you – someone who reads classical Greek fluently – a real Greek student, and if you ask him I know that he'll be glad to help you.'

'Who is it? Someone here – a patient?'

'No, it's Mr Ellis, and he's here now, on the evening shift.'

'Ellis!' Deborah realized that the episode with Helene and the bitter cost of witnessing and going Unhidden had been before Miss Coral's time – that since McPherson had spoken to her she had not talked to Mr Ellis at all and that somehow his sneering and scorn, while still as plain as Anterrabae's fire, had faded into a part of the undertone of the ward. He spoke little now, and had little to defend. He was no longer new on the job, no longer being tested by the patients and he was now looked upon by them and himself as merely a custodian of things, some of which were still alive. Perhaps he had been spoken to about beating patients; perhaps not. There might be or might not be those who rose from packs during his hours less convinced of the world than they had been when they went in.

'If you want to learn,' Miss Coral continued gently, 'it's he who holds the key—' She laughed a little at the allusion. 'You have all the Greek I can give you.'

Down the hall Deborah could see Ellis unlocking the bathroom for The Wife of the Abdicated. He did not look at his charge or speak as he stood back and let her by him. Without expression he moved back on the corridor, not looking at anything or anyone. As he passed Deborah, the tumour wrenched inside her, doubling her over hard so that she found herself on her hands and knees. The dark sweat took a while to pass, but it was Castle, the new aide, and not

Ellis whom she found watching her shaking the dizziness away.

'What's the matter, Blau?'

'Your spatial laws are okay,' she said from the sweat, 'but God – watch out for the choices you give us!'

16

FOR WEEKS ESTHER BLAU had worried and fretted over having to tell Suzy about her sister's illness. Who had not heard all the old-style high melodrama of insanity; of the madwoman in *Jane Eyre*, of Bedlam, of the hundreds of dark houses with high walls and little hope, of lesser dramas in lesser memories, and of maniacs who murdered and passed on the taints of their blood to menace the future? 'Modern Science' had given the official lie to much of this, but beneath the surface of facts, the older fears remained in the minds of the well no less than of the sick. People paid lip service to new theories and new proofs, but often their belief was no more than the merest veneer, yielding at a scratch to the bare and honest terror, the accretion of ten thousand generations of fear and magic.

Esther could not bear the thought of Suzy replacing the familiar image of her sister with the wild-eyed face of the strait-jacketed stereotype chained in an attic. She realized now that it was this stereotype that she and Jacob had begun to imagine the first time they heard the grating of the locks, when they saw the barred windows, and when they shuddered to the screaming of a woman from some high gable. Still, Suzy had to know; it was past time. The little sister was growing up and they could no longer talk around her; it wasn't fair to keep shutting her out from the source of their deepest concern. But the telling would have to be done in some sure way, safely and expertly. They wondered if Dr Lister could tell Suzy. But Dr Lister refused; it was Esther's job and Jacob's, he said.

'Wait a little longer,' Jacob said. Esther knew that 'wait-a-little-longer' was only one of the doors he used to slip quietly into inaction. Close your eyes and it won't exist; everything will be fine-fine-fine. It was a lie. So they fenced back and forth with it and at last Esther won her way. That evening, when they were finished with dinner and Suzy had gotten up to do her practice on the piano, Esther called her back.

'This is serious . . .' To her own ears her voice had an odd mixture of gravity and embarrassment. Sitting stiffly, she began to tell her younger daughter that Deborah's 'convalescent school' was a hospital; her doctors, psychiatrists; her illness not physical but mental. After they had eased into the icy subject, Jacob began to add, modify, explain this part and that, presenting as fact much of what he himself had been uncertain about.

Suzy listened with the complete impassivity of a twelve-year-old, her face giving no sign or flicker by which the parents could detect how she was hearing the words they were wringing out of themselves. When they had finished, she waited a while and then spoke slowly.

'I always wondered why those reports seemed to be more about Debby's thoughts than about her body, like pulse or temperature.'

'You read the reports?'

'No. I hear you quoting things to Grandma sometimes, and once you read to Uncle Claude part of it, and it sounded kind of funny to be about the usual kind of sickness.' She smiled a little, no doubt remembering something else that had puzzled her. 'It all fits now. It makes sense.'

She went into the next room to practise her piano lesson. A few minutes later, she came back to where Esther and Jacob were still sitting at the table, stunned, over their coffee. 'It's not like she's Napoleon or something . . . is it?'

'Of course not!' Then they spoke a little stiltedly and painfully about the optimism of the doctors, the advantage of early treatment, and the strong force of their patience and love all weighing in Deborah's favour.

Suzy said, 'I hope she comes home soon – sometimes I

miss her a lot.' And then she went back to the duty of Schubert.

They sat for a long time shocked at the difference between the expectation and the happening. Esther felt weak with the sudden easing of the tension.

Jacob said slowly, 'Is this all? ... I mean is this all there is or didn't she really hear us? Will she be back, when the shock wears off, with the look on her face that I have been afraid of for all these months?'

'I don't know, but maybe the cannon blast we were fearing was only what we heard.'

Jacob took a long draw of his cigarette and let his anguish leave his body with the exhaled breath.

'English is a wonderful language,' Furii said, 'to have such expressions. You look like what they call "down in the dumps".'

'English is no better than Yri.'

'To praise one thing is not to damn another.'

'Isn't it? Isn't being wrong courting death?' (The sharp sword of precocity had been comfortable in her hand; she had honed its edge herself. To be queen of Yr [and its slave and captive] was to be right and only right.)

'But you made costly mistakes, didn't you?' Furii asked gently. 'You identified the wrong girl at the camp.'

'I was wrong a hundred times. But as long as I was ugly and ruined and beyond hope, and of a substance that was poisoned and poisoning, I could still appear to be right. If I was wrong – even a little – then what was left?'

She saw the weak and wound-licking ghost of old vanity in what she was saying and laughed. 'Even in Pernai – nothing – I had to have a little something.'

'And so do we all,' Furii said. 'Are you ashamed of it? To me it is one sign that you are a member of Earth at least as much as of Yr. Do you believe that your substance, as you call it, is really poisonous?'

Deborah began to tell her about the Yri laws governing the ultimate substance of each person. People were differentiated by this substance, which was called *nganon*. *Nganon* was a concentrate which was defined in each person by nurture and circumstance. She believed that she and a certain few others were not of the same *nganon* as the rest of Earth's people. At first Deborah had thought that it was only she who was set apart from human kind, but others of the undead on D ward seemed to be tainted as she was. All of her life, herself and all her possessions had been imbued with her essence, the poisonous *nganon*. She had never lent her clothes or books or pencils, or let anyone touch any of her things, and she had often borrowed or stolen from other children at school or camp, delighting, until their stolen *nganon* wore off them, in the health and purity and grace of the possessions.

'But you told me that you used to bribe the children at camp with the candy that your mother sent you,' Furii said.

'Well, yes. The candy was in a box, all cellophaned and impersonal. Being unopened it had no essence, and it takes about a day or so before the Deborah-rot sets in. I gave it right away almost as soon as I got it.'

'And so you bought a little popularity for a few hours.'

'I knew I was a liar and a coward. But by that time the Collect had begun to come stronger and stronger, and "liar and coward" were standard comments.'

'And this feeling was threaded through with the precocity that you had to maintain, and with your grandfather's saying always how special you were.'

Deborah had pulled away her mind and the doctor looked up with a kind of sharpness in her eyes, catching Deborah at the edge of something.

'*Anterrabae* . . .' Deborah called in Yr.

'Where are you now?' Dr Fried interjected.

'*Anterrabae!*' Deborah said aloud and in Yri. '*Can she bear the great weight?*'

'What is it now, Deborah?' the doctor asked.

She moaned to the god, then turned to the mortal in desperation. 'Anterrabae knows what I saw – what I have to speak of . . . If only I had not seen it; if it had been hidden, that special thing . . . that thing.'

When she began to shiver with the cold of an ancient

parting, Furii gave her a blanket, and she lay on the couch rolled up in it and shaking.

'During the war . . .' she said, 'I was a Japanese.'

'An actual Japanese?'

'I was disguised as an American, but I was really not an American.'

'Why?'

'Because I was the Enemy.'

It seemed to Deborah an ultimate secret, and Dr Fried was forced to ask her to speak louder time and time again. She began to explain that because she could go into Yr or rise out of its incredible distances without visibly changing, Yr had given her, as a gift for her ninth birthday, the power to transmute herself in form. For a year or so she had been a wild horse or a great bronze-feathered bird. She quoted to Dr Fried the Yri incantation which had once freed the bird-self from the illusion of the ugly and hated girl:

> '*e, quio quio quaru ar Yr aedat*
> *temoluqu' braown elepr' kyryr . . .*'
> (Brushwinged, I soar above the canyons of your sleep
>   singing . . .)

When she was this great soaring creature it seemed as if it was the earth ones who were damned and wrong, not she, who was so complete in beauty and anger. It seemed to her that they slept and were blind.

When the Second World War had come, making of the names of Pacific Islands another language of hell and magic to Americans, the Collect had said to her, 'They hate these Japanese as they have always hated you,' and Anterrabae, in the urbane falling-smile, *Bird-one; you are not of them.*

She had remembered hearing the fragment of some speech on the radio. 'Those who aren't with us are against us!' And the Collect had cried out, *Then* you *must be this enemy they fight!*

On a certain night before falling asleep, Deborah had been reborn as a captured Japanese soldier. From behind the mask of an American-Jewish girl with a past of an American suburb and city, the elliptical eyes of the Enemy looked for the day of his unmasking. The tumour's impossible, in-sistent anguish was his war wound, and his mind, versed in a strange language, rang with dreams of escape. He did not hate his captors – he never wished that they would lose the war, but the world now offered meaning to the irreconcilable oppositions in Deborah, the ruination of her secret and fe-male parts, the bitter secrecy of her wound, and the hidden language. Captivity and secrecy and the glory and misery of Yr's declaration *You are not of them* were somehow justified.

On the day that the war in the Pacific was over, Anter-rabae caused Deborah to break a glass and step on the pieces with her bare foot. There was no pain, and the doctor, winc-ing himself as he picked the slivers out, was awed and a little puzzled at her 'soldierly' stoicism.

At last I am brave enough for the damn doctors! Deborah said in Yri to Lactamaeon.

You are captive and victim, Lactamaeon said. *We did not want you to escape.*

'You hid this presence from everyone around you,' Furii said. 'Did you hide it also from Yr?'

'It had no place in Yr; it was part of the Earth dimen-sion.'

'And so the Censor had the care of keeping it secret. Is that not so? I have trouble to understand the place of this Censor in your kingdom.'

'The Censor is supposed to protect me. In the beginning he was put at the Midworld barrier to keep Yri secrets from coming out in Earth's conversations. He censored all my acts to keep Yr's voices and rites from reaching the Earth's people. Somehow he became a tyrant. He began to order everything I did or said, even when I was not in Yr.'

'But this Censor, and Yr itself, was still only an attempt to understand and explain reality, to build a sort of truth where you could live. Well,' the doctor concluded, 'I am sure there is much to see here and to study. You are not a victim now; you are a fighter with me, for the cause of your good, strong life.'

When her patient left, Dr Fried looked at her desk clock.

It had been a long, exhausting session, though the clock showed the time had been no longer than usual. The intensity of her listening, of her sharing, had been so great that she wondered if she could face an afternoon of the cries and agonies of the other patients and the studies and bitter questions of the psychiatric students. What was it today, again? She looked in the appointment book on her desk. Oh, yes, the seminar. But there was, miraculously, an hour before she had to leave. For three weeks her Schumann records had lain on the record cabinet unopened. Beethoven was calling from her memory. Why was there always so little time? She stretched and walked into the living room, teasing herself by humming little bits. Schumann or Beethoven? How does the *doctor* feel today?

She took the package down and opened it, and as she did so, she began to think about a patient whose doctor had come for her advice on a seemingly insoluble problem. No. No more patients now. She got the machine ready and put the first record on the spindle. Schumann's sweet, gentle music filled the room. She listened and her mind shifted to German and the poetry of her youth. She sat back in the soft living-room chair, closed her eyes, and rested. And then for the twelfth time that day, the phone rang.

On Deborah's way back to the ward the dreaded cloud lowered, and the rumble of the Collect and Censor and Yr began. Terror at what was coming made her try to break through her silence when she was back on the ward. Seeing the head nurse leaving, she went after her, but she could not speak; the door closed and the day shift was gone. The evening shift came on and the menacing moved closer, hovering to engulf her. Just before the wave broke, Deborah went to the ward nurse who was overseeing the evening spoon-count.

'Miss Olson . . .'

'Yes?'

'It's going to hit – please – it's going to hit harder than I can stand up under. I should be in a pack when it hits.'

The nurse looked up; it was a keen and penetrating look. Then she said, 'Okay, Miss Blau. Now go and lie down.'

The wave broke as hard as she had foreseen, with a tremendous gust of ridiculing laughter, but the fleeing of her senses was not complete. The Censor's voice, like a cinder on which Deborah's teeth were grinding, was loud in her inner ear: *Captive and victim! Don't you know why we have done this? The third mirror – the ultimate deception is still to be given! You came to this hospital – it was in the plan. We let you trust that doctor. You opened your secrets more and more. This is the final one. Now you have given enough of your secrets, and you will see what she will do – she and the world!* And the cinder-laugh crazed Deborah's teeth to splinters in her mouth.

Her face was wooden as she walked to the pack and lay down on the cold sheet, but when the full punishment came, she was already under heavy restraints, fighting and thrashing in the bed that would not give an inch. . . .

When she came clear it was a long time later. She looked around, seeing. The newly cleared vision was like a blessing. The other bed had its white hump, but she did not know who was making it.

'Helene?'

Silence. It had been a long time. The circulation in her feet had nearly stopped altogether, and her heels, where they had made the long hours of contact with the wet sheets, were beginning to burn. She lay back and pulled hard with her whole body, trying to get the weight off the tightly bound ankles. When she had to let go, she rested, trying to save the clarity that was permitting her to see down into her mind. It had been longer than four hours; the attendants would come soon and take her from the now painful 'fighting clothes'. But they did not come. The pain became intense. She could feel her ankles and knees swelling against the sheets and the downward pull of the restraints, but even their heavy ache did not neutralize the sharper, burning pain of the blood-starved feet. Pulling to relieve the weight of the bones inside the legs, Deborah succeeded only in striking hard cramps into both calves. When she found she could not ease the knotted muscles, she waited on, gritting her teeth. And still they did not come. She began to whimper.

'Miss Blau . . . Deborah . . . what's the matter?'

The voice came from the other bed, but she could not recognize the voice.

'Who is that?' she asked, frightened of another kind of deception.

'It's Sylvia. Deborah, what is it?'

Deborah turned her head and her wonder penetrated through the pain. 'I didn't know you saw me or knew my name,' she said. She had always thought of Sylvia as everyone else did, as a useless piece of ward furniture. She now felt ashamed of having taken her at her own silence.

'Sick, but not dead,' Sylvia said. 'Are you all right?'

'God . . . it hurts. How long have we been in?'

'Five hours – maybe six. We were packed together. Try yelling and maybe someone will come.'

'I can't . . . I never could,' Deborah said.

Time went on, and the intensity of the pain unlocked Deborah's voice. For a while she called loudly, hoping that Yr would not hear it as a scream of cowardice and punish her with it forever. And still no one came, and finally she stopped. Sylvia laughed a little, low in her throat.

'I forgot that the yelling of lunatics is lunatics' yelling.'

'How can *you* stand it?' Deborah said.

'I probably have better circulation than you. I don't hurt at all, usually, but if your feet are tied just a little too tightly, or if you have trouble with your blood – Ah – the night-kitchen light has gone out. Three o'clock, then.'

Deborah had never reckoned time by the routine of the hospital, or the day-and-night changes and personal idiosyncrasies of the staff, and she was amazed at the perception of one who had always, but for one moment months and months ago, seemed far closer to the dead than to the living.

'How long have we been in, then?'

'Seven hours.'

And still they did not come. Deborah's face was full of

tears that she could not wipe away. Burning in the pain-flaming darkness, Anterrabae fell, crying, *Deception! Deception! The time is now!*

And still they did not come. She realized that the fragile trust had opened her wide again for the cold wind and the cold knife. She groaned against the white-hot stabbing that was moving into her legs. 'God, they build their tortures cunningly!'

'You mean the restraints?' Sylvia asked.

'I mean the *hope*!' As she spoke, the mirror of the final deception, the Awaited Death Oncoming moved towards her. '*I see you, Imorh,*' Deborah said, speaking for the first time aloud in the presence of a stranger the language of Yr.

When they came at last she was very quiet and they were cheered.

'Now you're all calmed down.'

She could not walk, but the late night shift was not too busy and they let her sit for a while until the swelling went away, the colour returned to her legs, and her feet could carry her. Before leaving Sylvia in the hard light and her unrolling, Deborah turned, wanting to repay her for the mercy that had wrenched her from silence. She walked towards Sylvia's bed, watching the eyes of the others grow wary.

'Sylvia . . .'

But Sylvia was furniture again – a statue or a manikin, familiar only in form and alive only to the seeking finger at the pulse-place.

Sure doom was not as difficult to bear as the little Maybe had been. Deborah had expected the last deception for so long that its coming was almost a relief. Before she went to the doctor's office, the Collect and gods and all of Yr massed together on its horizon. 'I will not go easily,' she said to them, 'not this time. I will not be brave and obliging. No more games. No more being a good sport. I will not play the Game, and go to this death as if I didn't know what it was.'

When she saw Furii with her familiar smile of greeting, a current of doubt moved in and away. Maybe she doesn't

131

know, Deborah thought. But the thought was foolish and a dream. The last Change was death or worse; it had been said years ago, and last night, the first help she had asked for in English had been given easily, easily, and was only in scorn. She had surrendered her separateness, trusting, on the cold bed. They make a good score of it. Her ankles and feet still ached from their joke. Dark against the fireworks of the pain was that shadow: the always known Oncoming. By what other hand could the end be so sure and so complete, if not by this fire-touch woman who was now sitting before her?

'Well?' she said.

'Well?' Furii answered.

A sudden rage came. 'I know that this has to be played in a certain way, and there is a game that the victim is not supposed to break through. But I know about the game and the end of the game. Why make me foolish as well as dead! All right! I am foolish. The deception and the last change is here, so throw it and be done!'

'Where are we now?' Furii said, shaking her head a little, very carefully unexcited. 'You tell me about the Japanese soldier and about having been set apart and special. I try to make you secure that in giving such valuable secrets to our view you do not risk my faith in you for a moment. Then you come the next day and make our work part of the great deception and change.'

'They knew when I was ready,' Deborah said. 'When I could ask for help, they knew that I trusted and they were ready with the stone to break the flowerpot.'

'Somehow the old hospital of the past and this present hospital have joined their natures in your mind. I will not open your trust and then betray you.'

'Haven't you got any mercy?' Deborah shouted. 'Everyone is so afraid of getting blood on the living-room floor. "I can't stand to see suffering," they say, "so die outside!" It has started already and you still say trust and everything is fine!'

'When I look at you now in this bad shape I can hardly say "fine-fine". What happened between yesterday and now?

If you say that the last change has started, just tell me . . . tell both of us how.'

Slowly, the doctor let Deborah come closer and closer to speaking the truth. Slowly, bit by bit, Deborah told her about asking for the pack. 'It has a kind of humour in it, too,' she said bitterly. 'It was like what sane people do when they see a rattlesnake. They scream for help, run for safety, lock the doors, crawl under the bed, and then, when the snake is caught, they faint. I got all ready for the onslaught, but I forgot that I was standing on *their* ground and all they had to do was to dissolve it under me.' She told about the long time calling out, and the pain and laughter from Yr, and she took a righteous pride that was almost gleeful in answering Furii's questions.

'Are you sure it was that long?'

'Absolutely.'

'Now, you did call for help . . .'

'You were never a mental patient, were you?'

There was no smile at all, and Furii, as grave as Deborah had ever seen her, said, 'No . . . I am sorry, too, because I can only guess at what it must be like. But it will not stop me from being able to help you. Only it makes it your responsibility to explain everything fully to me and to be a little patient with me if sometimes my perceptions are a bit slow.'

She went on and the quizzical look returned. 'I think now, though, that you are a little too happy with yourself for this trouble you have. I think you are giving up too easily, so let me say again that I will not betray you.'

At last Deborah had her tinder.

'Prove it!' she shouted, remembering with what good cheer the teachers and doctors and counsellors and family had dispensed deceit and misery over the years.

'A hard proof, but a valid one,' Furii said. 'Time.'

17

IN THE SAME kind of restraints as those in which Miss
Coral had arrived, and with the same thrashing and profanity, the safari brought its new tigress to captivity, and,
as before, the ward was laced with tension. Such arrivals
always mirrored this patient's anguish, threatened that one's
violence, and blew like a shifting wind over those to whom
any change was a symbol of death. Outwardly there was
little acknowledgement of the presence of new patients;
many came to 'D' and many went from it, but the fighting
ones always bound the ward with a special kind of panic.
Now Lee Miller, proud of her veteran's status on the ward,
watched with faintly amused tolerance until she looked into
the face of the tigress proceeding down the hall. Then, recognizing it in the swarm of attendants, she turned, went to
her bed, and lay down.

Later, when Deborah went to Lee Miller and asked her
who it was (knowing that certain patients usually learned
by grapevine days in advance who was coming, Name, Age,
Occupation, Religion, whether Married or Single, Previous
Hospitals, Shock treatments – what kind and how many –
Other Treatment, and Remarks), Lee replied, 'Why ask
me?' and pulled her blanket over her face.

Deborah was reduced to seeking out an attendant.

'It's a re-admission,' the attendant said lightly. 'Isn't much
written. Her name's Doris Rivera.'

With a sick feeling Deborah moved back against the wall
and the attendant went by her. Fear and anger, fear and
vindictive joy, fear and jealousy rose in her. She began to
gag with the surfeit. The great Doris Rivera had broken her
back on the wheel of the world. It was proof of something.
Suddenly, the envy burst out of her mouth in a great gust of
bitter laughter.

'So much for Rivera, the North Star! Who did she think
she was, anyway!'

'Napoleon!' Lena shouted, and grabbed the heavy ash-tray she was using and threw it, missing Deborah and hitting the wall beside her.

The attendant said, 'Come on, now, Lena,' but there was no force in it.

Later, Deborah heard her in the nursing station saying, 'Damn that Blau bitch! Mommy and Daddy are shelling out plenty on that bitch who isn't fit for saving.' Someone else demurred, but it was only for form's sake. Deborah turned slowly and walked past the doors of the seclusion section to the front of the closed box where Doris had been taken.

'That's where you are, Presumptuous!' she said to the person behind the door. Who was she to have tried, challenging them all? And how dare she have failed under the grinding of the world! But there also came a long surge of pity, which was also pity for herself, and an answering terror, which was also terror for herself. So they come back; the ones who are too stubborn to accept that their *nganons* are poisonous and who are beaten to ruins. They come back, and slowly, they get up off the ward's floors, shaking like the loser in a prizefight, and after a while stagger back towards the world again and again, and come back, not on the canvas, but in it. How many times will it take before they die at last?

And you, Bird-one, Lactamaeon said, smiling a little. *Darkness and pains and hard fear and mindlessness, and yet your heart is still going and your pulse still makes you a part of the census.*

Why? she shouted at him in Yri.

Because your keepers are sadists!

Throughout the day, everyone was busy seeing Doris. Doctors and nurses rang the keys of their authority in her locked door. Packs and sedations, consultations and coun-sellings kept the ward excited and angry. A multitude of little sisters were consumed with envy for the attention given to a sibling who had come home to violate their sovereignty. Dowben's Mary stood outside the door groaning wordlessly as the members of the parade emerged, and Lee Miller sat in her place on the hall muttering angrily, 'So you've botched the job, Doc. Pick up the marbles and go home ... She's lost. Doctors never know when they're beaten.'

By the time Doris herself appeared, very pale and haggard, a few days later, she had a whole hall of secret enemies. Deborah appraised her in the light of the myth which she and Carla had made. Doris was very thin and she had greying hair, but even exhausted and dizzy with sedatives, there was an abundant sense of life thrumming through her. In whatever manner she had taken the world for this long, it had not been on her knees.

She saw Deborah looking at her with the merciless eye of the whole ward.

'What are you gawking at?' she said in a hard, honest voice. 'You don't look like a fashion model either.'

'You were here before,' Deborah said, blurting out unexpected words to answer the unexpected remark.

'So what?'

'How come you are back?'

'It's none of your goddam business!'

'But it is!' Deborah shouted. Before she could explain, the anxious cordon of attendants flanked Doris and led her away. Deborah was left with the anger strong in her ears and the question still held unasked.

Yr began to rumble and the Collect prepared its brittle laughter. '*I will, too!*' she said to the phalanx of her other dimension. She went to the closed door of Doris' seclusion and pounded on it.

'Hey! Was it too tough – is that why?'

'No! I was too tough, and a lot happened,' the door shouted back.

'Like what?'

'Like none of your goddam business!'

'But they talk about getting well – and going out. Everybody does, and—'

She had been heard. The attendants moved to nip trouble in the bud. 'Get away from that door, Deborah. You have no business there,' the white blurs said.

'I was talking to Doris,' Deborah insisted, not knowing

if any of her questions would be answered, but feeling that she had to ask that door – even if it gave no answer – if she would be forced to take the Censor back, and the semblance of sanity, and all the other lies and horrors, in order to live in the depthless, colourless world outside.

'Okay, Blau ... come along.' Their voices were warning her: pack or seclusion or both if she didn't come along.

'Hey, you!' the door said. 'Listen – leave her there. Maybe I can answer the crazy bitch's questions. I won't know until she asks them.'

'Rivera, this isn't your affair,' the attendant on one side said righteously. 'Blau ...'

'All right—' Deborah said. 'All right.'

That afternoon, Dowben's Mary tripped and fell and her shoe flew off and Deborah caught it. She threw it back to Mary and for a while four or five of the patients began to play catch with it, sending it around corners and into the dormitory. On a high catch, Deborah came down hard on her ankle. The next morning the ward doctor examined it and said that he thought it was broken.

'Our X-ray machine is out of whack,' he said. 'She'll have to be taken to St Agnes'.'

And so, two uniformed students, terrified that she might escape, took Deborah in a taxi to the hospital. At St Agnes', set apart in a private room and guarded inside and out by two sets of nurses, Deborah alternately laughed and swore. Other nurses and aides kept creeping by the door to her room. 'Is that the mental patient in there?' (Whispered outside, as though she were a movie star or a carrier of the plague.) Heads turned, eyes turned as she made her way down the hall to X-ray. (Elaborate disinterest – 'If I look, will she look?')

The students who accompanied Deborah felt very important and did not fail to tell the others in the X-ray room that their duty was the 'disturbed ward'.

'Are they *violent*?'

Perhaps the reply was a wink; Deborah did not hear any

answer. Suddenly she saw herself as they must be seeing her: lank hair, dirty, flabby from inactivity, wearing an old ward bathrobe over her own miserable pyjamas (they had thought that she might stay at St Agnes', and dressing was a nuisance), the Crazy Look maybe. She could never tell what the mask might look like. And then it struck her: here it was – what Doris Rivera had faced and what Carla might soon face – the World. She fainted.

Looking up at the avid faces outside the X-ray room only a few moments later, Deborah realized how much she would hate to have a broken ankle and have to stay where she was so much more insane than she was on the 'violent' ward of a nuthouse. She sat up.

'How do you feel?' her own nurses asked (as if they were the only ones with sufficient knowledge to approach her psychologically). It occurred to Deborah that if she frightened them all enough, they would let her go back, ankle or no.

'It's one of my attacks' – she tried to look ominous – 'coming on.'

'Well!' the doctor said very heartily, 'that's a nasty sprain she has there – but nothing's broken!'

A long sigh of release from everyone; out the door she limped with a bound-up ankle and two nurses to lean on and into the waiting cab and fast-fast to highway to road to smaller road to gate and into the back door of South Building (Wards B to D) and up in 'the meatwagon' to 'D' and home and Thank God! Thank God!

In the evening, at night wash-up, she limped into the big bathroom and looked at herself in the steel plate that served as a mirror. The self-hate of hundreds upon hundreds of patients had been vented on it and tempered steel cannot endure such an onslaught. Even the weaponless had found weapons to scratch it and dent it and no inch of its surface was clear. '*E nagua*,' Deborah said to it; the formal Yri for: 'I love you.'

'Off to the physical hospital . . .' she told Furii, '. . . I never wished you used straitjackets until yesterday. I would have

138

loved to make the picture complete. I'm a fool, though; I didn't even think about frothing at the mouth until I was well away!'

'You are trying to hurt yourself now,' Furii said. 'What happened?'

When Deborah told her, she sighed.

'It goes very slowly, this prejudice,' she said, 'but it is getting better. I remember how much worse it was before the Second War and really how much worse before the First. Be patient about this. Because you know so much more about mental illness than they do – you are freer to be understanding and forgiving.'

Deborah shifted her gaze. Again, there was Furii's subtle, all-pervading message to cast with the world, to help it, even while sick and estranged.

'I can't help anyone, don't you see! Don't you understand anything I've been telling you? The *nganon* cries from itself!'

'What? Try to tell me what this is ... perhaps I do not understand.'

'I'm separated from the good. There's a saying in Yr, and the Censor used to torture me with it; I will translate it for you. "In silence, in sleep, before action or breath, utterly and immutably, *nganon* cries from itself." It means that the poisoned substance, the enemy-self can cry out and draw to itself all the other few poisoned ones that there are in the world. It draws them without my knowing, magically, no matter how or what I do.'

'I think you mean it has drawn one or two or three,' Furii said. 'I want you to tell of them.'

Beyond all of the forces of Yri magic, gods, and worlds, Deborah was sure that there was another proof of her intrinsic unworthiness. This proof lay in the world, in the simple, daily matters of an earthly youth. It was the seemingly magic force which attracted her to others. One had to choose or be chosen as a partner at camp, a seatmate at school, the member (in a certain order of importance) in all kinds of cliques and groups and classes. A semblance of membership in the Earth-world had to be served. Deborah had found that she could meet the demands of this membership only with the tainted, the very poor, the crippled, the disfigured, the strange, the going-insane. These pairings-off were not planned or thought out even secretly; they came about as naturally as the attraction of magnet and metal, yet many of the fragments which had been drawn together thus knew why in their hearts and hated themselves and their companions.

One summer at camp there had been a brilliant girl named Eugenia. The time before the last great change was running out, and Yr was demanding more and more of Deborah's days in service to it, and giving less and less of its comfort in return. Eugenia and Deborah found each other and they knew why and sometimes they tormented each other for it. Yet there was a sympathy, too; a knowing without needing to be told what suffering there could be behind the simplest act, an understanding of how hard the Semblance was to hold up before the world. Above all there was need for surface companionship – to walk to the dining room together, to the ball field together, to the lake together, to comfort each other without the words being utterly lies or only lip service to the Semblance. Although they needed walls between themselves and the others, they most needed – just sometimes, with just someone, to break through that sound-proof plate-glass partition that was the Semblance, and for a little time, to say things as if the whole world were not the Collect.

After a while the camp accepted them as friends of each other and wrote them out of its anger and hard judgements. Deborah had known, of course, that Eugenia was different, alone, bitter, and unquiet, but she had tried to shield herself from the thought that Eugenia was a carrier of the poisoned *nganon*. One day Deborah had managed to slip away in order to be quietly in Yr on the Plains of Tai'a where she could fly if Yr allowed it. She had many hiding places at the camp where she could find an hour or so of peace before the world started to call and look for her. One of the best of these was the deserted shower-house, but when she went there on this day, she sensed that someone else was there. She began to sing to warn the one who could not see her. Too many times she herself had been intruded upon while laughing or speaking Yri aloud, and had had to bear the torments of the Censor for it. Now, there was a frantic scrambling in one of the stalls and the sound of Eugenia's voice.

'Who is it?'

'Deborah.'

'Come here.'

Deborah went to the shower. Eugenia was standing naked in the stall of the dry shower. She was sweating heavily. As Deborah came towards her she held out a heavy leather belt. 'Here,' she said. 'Beat me.'

'What?'

'You know what I am. I don't have to lie to *you*. Take it. Use it.'

'What for?' Something awful was coming.

'You're running away, and pretending you don't understand. You know what it's for – it's for *me,* and you have to —'

'No—' Deborah began to back away. 'I can't. I won't.'

Eugenia's need filled up the space between them. Sweat was running from her face and beading on her shoulders and arms. 'Don't forget what I know about *you*! I'm going to make you beat me with this belt, and you will ... because ... you ... *understand.*'

'No—' Deborah moved farther away. It flashed through her mind that perhaps her *nganon* had reached Eugenia and combined with Eugenia's own waiting virulence to bring this about. Deborah might be Ruin – *Pernai* shackled and shod in destruction – but it was for herself alone; she had never asked anyone else to partake of it. Then it suddenly came to her that Eugenia's *nganon* might be more virulent than hers. Even so, to witness was to share; to share was to be responsible. Her *nganon* had called to Eugenia's, thus opening, thus causing ... Deborah went to Eugenia, took the belt, threw it down, and ran from the showers. She never looked at or spoke to Eugenia again.

'Then the one who is a friend – anyone who likes you or is

attracted to you – is ruined, if not by you, then by closeness to you . . .'

'Yr puts it as a joke, but you say it more to the point. Yes, that is true.'

'Is it true of your mother and father and sister?'

'Men are not poisoned by female poison. I think that they are broken in some other way. I never thought of it before, but I see men here. They have whole wards of them, just like us.'

'Indeed so,' Furii said. 'It is true for women though? You still have this fear of contaminating?'

'I have been slowly contaminating them for many years.'

'And the results of this?'

'I think that my sister will be insane.'

'You still think so?'

'Yes.'

The phone rang and the doctor rose and went to the desk to answer it. There were few hours when the phone didn't ring at least once, and during one amazing session there had been five calls. Furii shrugged in a little helpless sign of apology and spoke for a few moments. 'Now . . .' she said, sitting down, 'where were we?'

'In the bell-clanging world,' Deborah said acidly.

'Some of the calls I cannot stop – they are long distance or made specially from doctors who have no other time. I free us from as many of them as I can.' She looked at Deborah with a little grin. 'I know how hard it is to succeed with a "great famous doctor". There is always such a desire to even up the score a little, even if it is with your own life, to keep her from an imaginary "perfect record". I tell you I have many failures, too – *in spite* of my being in such great demand. Will we work together?'

'We were talking about contaminating.'

'Ah, yes. I'm curious,' Furii said. 'If this incident in the showers had happened to you now, would you be as frightened?'

'No,' and Deborah laughed because it seemed ridiculous.

'Well, why not?'

'Well . . .' Deborah came into a sort of sunshine. 'I'm crazy now. As soon as you admitted that I was sick – as soon as you admitted that I was so sick that I had to be in a hospital, you proved to me that I was saner than I had thought. You know, saner *is* stronger.'

'I don't quite understand.'

'I had known all those years and years how sick I was, and nobody else would admit it.'

'You were asked to mistrust even the reality to which you were closest and which you could discern as clearly as daylight. Small wonder that mental patients have so low a tolerance for lies. . . .'

'You look as though you are seeing this for the first time,' Deborah said, still in the light. 'Is it true? Did I bring you something?'

Furii paused. 'Yes, in a way you have, because though I knew other reasons why lying is bad for the mentally disturbed, I never saw it in this particular way.'

Deborah began to clap her hands, smiling.

'What is it?' Furii said, seeing that the smile was not bitter.

'Oh, well . . .'

'You are happy to give then, as well as to be given?'

'If I can teach you something, it may mean that I can count at least somewhere.'

'I weep,' Furii said. 'I weep big crocodile tears for your Yri gods.' And she imitated the hypocritical down-pulled mouth of form-sorrow. 'They are wasting the time of a real human being who will someday recognize it and break their houses down and send them away.'

'You make me see a pinnacled white cloud . . .' Deborah said, 'but behind it is still the same Furii of the fire-touch and the lightning bolt,' and she trembled to think of having to endure without Yr.

Later, they began to explore the secret idea that Deborah shared with all the ill – that she had infinitely more power than the ordinary person and was at the same time also his inferior. The poisoning *nganon* had been such an idea for Deborah, but she saw into the intricacies of it coldly, with her reason and not as a truth of the spirit. One evening, as she sat in the hall waiting for the sedative call, she looked at Miss Coral, sitting like an ancient owl on one of the heavy chairs, and at Lee and at Helene, who had just come walking towards them.

'Can you read my thoughts?' she asked them.

'Are you talking to me?' Lee said.

'To all of you. Can you read my thoughts?'

'What are you trying to do – get me sent to seclusion?'

'Go to hell,' Helene said pleasantly.

'Don't look at me,' Miss Coral said, with the genteel horror of a countess visiting an abattoir, 'I can't even read my own.'

Deborah looked around at the figures decorating the walls of the hall. They were always waiting, always seeming never to have moved or changed.

'If you're seeking objective reality,' she muttered to herself, 'this is one hell of a place to start.'

18

IT WAS SPRING, the season of passion and impatience. The terrible vacuum caused by the rushing by of time made Jacob feel empty inside. He sat at the grammar-school graduation exercises of his younger daughter, heard the singing and the speeches, the prayers and the promises, and felt the emptiness deepen as if it would never end. He had told himself that this was Suzy's day and that Deborah was to be no part of it. But against his conscience, his wishes, his promises to Esther and himself, he could not get the thought of Deborah out of his mind. Why wasn't she here with them?

It was the second spring that she was gone, and how much closer was she to the modest, obedient, womanly being that his heart cried out to have as a daughter? No closer. There had been no improvement at all. The young girls began to file out of the auditorium, all innocence and white dresses.

Jacob turned to Esther, who, for Suzy's sake, was dressed stunningly in what the family called her 'coronation clothes'.

'Why can't she come home for a while. We'd go to the lakes?' he whispered.

'Not now!' Esther hissed.

'She's not committed there by law!' he whispered back.

'It may not be good for her.'

'It may be good for *me*; *me*, once in a while!'

In the evening they took Suzy out to a fancy restaurant. She had wanted to go to the class party, but Jacob, feeling that time and beauty and all his days of them were slipping away, had wanted this one evening at least. Because he wanted it so badly, it was a failure from the start. Suzy was subdued, Esther, saddened because the present daughter was being stinted again for the absent one. Jacob knew that the symbol breaks when it is too heavily weighted, but he could not help himself. The whole evening had a forlorn quality to it.

Esther, trying to sound natural by naming the name, said, 'Debby wanted to come to your graduation – and if she could, she would have sent something.'

Suzy looked at her quietly and said, 'She was here. I saw you talking about her when we were getting our diplomas and again when we were getting ready to march out.'

'Nonsense!' Jacob said. 'We didn't talk about anyone.'

'It's okay, really, even if you didn't really talk out loud; it was that look you get . . .' She thought of describing it, in case they didn't know how it showed on their faces, but the words that came were so painfully embarrassing that she could not say them.

'Nonsense!' Jacob said again, waving it away. 'A certain look – nonsense !'

Suzy and Esther caught each other's glance. He was hiding again. Be merciful to him, Esther said with her mind. Suzy looked down at her white graduation dress. She fussed with a button for a moment. 'You know the girl who stood in front of me when we got the diplomas? Well, her brother is a real dream—'

Although those in the hospital wondered how springtime could come in spite of their particular pain, it came and was triumphant. It made the patients on D ward angry that the world which had murdered them did not suffer for its sins, but, on the contrary, seemed to be thriving. And when Doris Rivera tied up her hair, put on a suit and a shallow smile, and left again for the world, it seemed to many as if she were in league with the springtime against them. The Wife of the Abdicated had a theory:

'She's a spy. I knew her years ago. She takes it all down and the opposition gives her money for it and later when it's published it becomes indigenous.'

'We must be charitable,' Dowben's Mary said because she was Saint Teresa. 'We must be charitable even though she has every social disease it is possible to have. Not to mention infections in private places put there by men of no social standing. Not to mention schizophrenia of a dirty, filthy nature.' She had gotten very loud and her tone had the hard, familiar edge of terror.

'You mentally ill are so amusing,' Fiorentini's Mary said.

There was a fight.

The whole ward, it seemed, had fallen into a whirlpool of anger and fear and fights broke out with wild and pointless spontaneity.

'There are so many patients in seclusion,' a new student mused.

'When they get a few more, they will start to double them up,' Deborah answered.

'Yes ... yes ...' the student agreed (Number Three with Smile, fleeting). Deborah turned away and had another try for the clock with her shoe.

'I'd like to stop *that* smile.'

'Your face alone should be sufficient,' Helene said.

'At least you can be superior to *me*!'

And there was another fight.

'You get these times on the ward,' the old attendants assured the new ones. 'It's not usually this wild.' But the new ones didn't believe them. In all of the new groups of student nurses there was the usual fear, but for the latest group there was a particularly poignant one. Two nurses from the previous group had 'cracked up' shortly after having left their psychiatric affiliation and were now themselves patients in mental hospitals. 'What you see,' it was rumoured, 'can drive you crazy.'

And so the four new students assigned to D ward stood in a tight, scared little clutch, the only beauty, youth, and health present, and in the spring of the year. Never did the bearers of poisonous *nganons* feel their separation so much as on this day. Helene and Constantia would fight the new enemies until their strangeness wore off, and Deborah would obliterate them in her own way until they faded into the ward's daily anonymous pattern. She would not see them except as blurs of white. She would seldom hear them unless they spoke of her or gave specific orders. This protection against their newness and beauty was more successful than fighting. Although it was not a conscious act, she was grateful for it. It was not only the beauty and sprightliness of the students that hurt, but their strangeness, which made Deborah feel self-conscious in her craziness.

One afternoon, sitting on the floor near the nursing station and measuring the stare of the enemy clock, Deborah heard two of the students talking.

'A new one from B? Where'll they put her?'

'I don't know, but she really must have blown if she's coming up here.'

'Remember what Marcia told us – they do better and then they do worse. I hope she's toilet trained at least and knows where to put her food!' And they giggled.

The giggle was a reflex of anxiety and Deborah knew it, but when they brought Carla up later, all sprung inside and with the beaten look that Doris Rivera had had, Deborah was bitterly angry at the white unseens for having laughed. They had not been talking about some nut, but about Carla, a Carla who was good all the way to the bone; good enough even to be kind when Deborah had struck her at the core of her pain.

No one, seeing Deborah and Carla, would have known

147

that they were friends. It would be an imposition, incomprehensible to the sane, for Deborah to greet Carla, who was in distress and who would be sorry later if a greeting drove her to violence or even rudeness. Deborah did not look at Carla; she only waited behind her stone mask until she would see the secret sign from Carla that meant recognition.

When the sign was given, they moved towards each other, appearing as elaborately unconcerned as they could. Deborah smiled very slightly, but then a strange thing happened. Into the flat, grey, blurred, and two-dimensional waste of her vision, Carla came three-dimensionally and in colour, as whole and real as a mouthful of hot coffee or coming-to in a pack.

'Hi,' Deborah said, on a barely rising tone.

'Hi.'

'Can you smoke?'

'No privileges.'

'Uh.'

Later Deborah passed Carla outside the bathroom, waiting to be let in by an attendant.

'Supper on my bed, if you want.'

Carla didn't answer, but when supper came, she brought her tray to the back dormitory where Deborah was now staying.

'Okay?'

Deborah moved aside so that Carla had the choice place, on the foot of the bed where it was level. ('Hello, hello, my three-dimensional and multi-coloured friend. I am so glad to see you.') Aloud she said, 'Doris Rivera was back, but she left again.'

'I heard.' Carla looked up at Deborah and by another miracle, perhaps like the one which had made her clear to Deborah's eyes, she seemed to see through the mask. 'Oh, Deb – it's not so bad. I had to come back because I tried too much at once, and because part of what I did was against my father . . . and for lots of other reasons. I'm not giving-up; I'm just tired, that's all.' Her eyes filled with tears, and Deborah, frozen with confusion and terror in the presence of her friend's grief, could only wonder what there was in that awful, chaos-ocean of the world that made the drowning ones go back to it, still pale and choking, for another try and another and another.

Why do they think they can float like others when the surface tension of their nganons was broken by the first drowning? Deborah cried to Lactamaeon.

Idat only knows, he said. *For some, nothing is impossible.*

Deborah's inner muscles tightened with fear. *Then you think that her nganon is not intrinsically evil, but is . . . is circumstantial?*

Yes.

But I am a friend of hers. If she is not of my substance, I will poison her!

Exactly so.

Can a thing go so against the Laws? Even the Law says, 'nganon calls forth itself'. Did I call forth a different essence, and if so, why?

Perhaps as a punishment, Lactamaeon said. *Occasionally others are damned by you to punish you.*

Deborah looked from the god and saw Carla still crying. It was part of the Deceit, it seemed, to believe that one knew the code, that after years of suffering to find a way to out-guess it, the final step gave way and there was the old chaos, anarchy, and laughter.

She was my friend! she cried to the departing gods. *She seemed not to be hurt . . .*

You are not of the same substance; the nganons are not the same. You will be her murderer, they said.

When Carla finished crying, Deborah's body was still at the other side of the bed, but her self was not with her body.

For some unfathomable reason, one of the students attached herself to Deborah. Busily and with the gratuitous, meddling cheeriness of her dedication, the student followed her, a white blur and a blurred voice in the grey background, whenever Deborah poked her face out on the 'public' part of the ward.

You must be sicker than you think, Deborah said to herself in Yri. *These people usually take the worst ones to throw*

149

to God. God is their dog and Deborahs are so many bones. Therefore shall my name be Bone.

It seemed very funny indeed in Yri, and she laughed aloud and then she made the symbolic Yri gesture with her hands and the mimicry of laughter, mutely, as it was in Yr.

Who laughs there? Anterrabae joked with her.

It is I, the God-Bone-Thing! she answered, and they laughed until she felt the torment of the earth easing inside her. *What will happen to that one's dear glory when God smells what her offering is?* And they laughed again.

And the surprise on the face of the sweat-bone student storming Heaven? And there was more laughter, but it ended in sorrow because Deborah knew that she was not strong enough to ask the student not to track her and bother her with solicitous noises.

The spring went on and although Deborah gave and gave to Furii the secrets and fears and passwords of the passages between her worlds, she was surrendering them only to hasten her own capitulation to a total deceit that was as sure as the Juggernaut or the falling of Anterrabae. She did not lose the chill feeling of detachment before the doom and for a while she even posed a little in drama of that doom, making a high art of dying beautifully.

Furii threw up her hands. 'Not only sick, God help us, but adolescent, too!'

'Well?'

'Well, there is no help for it – you must do what you have to, parodies and all. Only please help me to see which is the sickness against which we pit our whole strength, and which is the adolescence that is only another sure sign that you are one hundred per cent Earth-one and woman-to-be.' She looked at Deborah keenly for a while and then smiled. 'Sometimes the work gets so intense – all the secrets and the symptoms and the ghosts of the past to be met – one forgets how arid and meaningless this therapy can all seem before the world comes to be real to the patient.'

Deborah looked at the doctor's littered desk. Looking away to it had often been a relief; on it lay a paperweight, whose odd shape resisted definition and eased the eyes and the mind from the tension of those hours. She was going to it now because, though it was familiar, it could not hurt. Furii saw her looking at it.

'Do you know what that is?'

'Agate?'

'No, not agate. It is a rare kind of petrified wood,' Furii said. 'My father took me on a trip to Carlsbad when I graduated from what you call the high school. There the strangest sorts of rocks and formations are made, and he bought this for me as a souvenir of the trip.'

Furii had never once said a personal thing about her own past or self. Early in their time together, when the first trust was coming and Deborah had wrestled with her understanding and had forced herself to stay *tankutu* (unhidden) while Furii's questions probed, Furii had risen at the end of the hour and had broken off a large and beautiful blossom from a cluster of cyclamen in her flowerpot. She had said, 'I don't ordinarily break flowers, but this you have earned. I don't often give presents either, so take it.'

It had been worth the cost of the two terrible punishments from Yr that Deborah had received for accepting flowers from the Earth, although when she had come clear from the second, it was days later and the beautiful flower had long since wilted and died. Now Furii was giving a second gift, a little piece of herself. Its delicacy meant more than a small respite from the probing or an unsaid message to 'take heart'; it said, 'I will trust you with one of my memories as you have trusted me with yours.' Once again, adolescence or no, it made of Deborah an equal.

'Did you like the trip?' she said.

'Oh; it was not exciting or "fun" such as young people have now, but I felt so grown-up, and it was an honour to be with my father, just the two of us in the adult world.' Her face had the memory-shine of the old happiness. 'Well!' She put her hands on her knees with finality. 'Back into the salt mines. All right?'

'All right,' Deborah said, getting ready to bear inwards again.

'Oh, no; wait. There is something else. I want to tell

151

you now so that you can get used to the idea. I am leaving for my vacation early this summer because of a conference in Zurich. Then comes my vacation and then I go to join in a symposium for some writing which had been long put off.'

'How long will it be?'

'I plan to leave on June twenty-sixth and be back on September eighteenth. I have arranged for you to have someone to talk to while I am gone.'

In the sessions that followed Furii talked about the colleague's qualifications, the possibility of resentment at what might seem a rejection, and the fact that this new doctor was not going to go deeply into the work, but would be there to stand for the world in the battles between Deborah and her censors, collects, and the forces of Yr. It was all deft and sure, but Deborah sensed the *fait accompli*, the oiling of the ancient wheels on which one was broken.

'I know lots of doctors here,' Deborah said wistfully. 'Craig; and Sylvia's doctor, Adams – I've seen her at work and I like her. I talked to Fiorentini once when he was on call at night, and then, the best one is Halle. He says he was the one who saw my parents when I was admitted. I've talked to him and I trust him . . .'

'Their schedules are all full,' Furii said. 'Dr Royson will see you.' The gears were oiled, the wheel ready; her acceptance would merely be form.

'My third rail,' Deborah said.

'What is that?'

'A free translation of an Yri word. It means: I will comply.'

19

DEBORAH WORKED AGAINST time, wishing to resolve everything before Furii left. She asked for and got a transfer to B ward – still locked, but not 'disturbed'. Paper and pencil and books and privacy were possible there, but it was like a tomb compared to the rampant craziness of 'D'. Because she had been a 'D' patient, the others on 'B' were afraid of her, but she knew a few of them and there were some good nurses who reminded her of McPherson by mentioning him. The therapeutic hours infused with the desperate urgency created by Furii's leaving, and if the insights were not brilliantly lit, they were at least hard-worked and honest.

'I leave you in good hands,' Furii said on the last day. 'You know the B-ward administrator well and there is Dr Royson to talk to. I hope you have a very good and profitable summer.'

Because Yri law wove into the world's laws, Deborah knew that Furii was gone forever. As she had excised the love and memory of Carla from her feelings when her friend had left 'D' for the first time, now Deborah forgot Furii as if she had never been and never would be again. From the silent self-conscious hall of B ward, she went to see the New One.

She found Dr Royson sitting stiffly in his chair in one of the offices on the main floor. 'Come in,' he said. 'Sit down.'

She sat down.

'Your doctor has told me a lot about you,' he said. Deborah turned her mind for something to reply, thinking only: How stiffly he sits; I told her I would be fair ... I told her I would try as hard with this one. ...

'Yes,' she said. He was not a friendly person. She understood and set out to try the first directions. 'You're from England, aren't you?'

'Yes.'

'I like the accent,' she said.

'I see.'

This is one-by-one from the jawbone! Anterrabae groaned a little scornfully.

After a short silence the doctor said, 'Tell me what you are thinking.' It seemed to come like a demand.

'About dentistry,' Deborah said.

'And what thoughts do you have about dentistry?' he said in his unchanging tone.

'That it can be more expensive than we think it will be,' Deborah said. She caught herself and tried again. 'I'm out of Novocain because Furii took it away with her.'

'Who is that? Who took it away?' He jumped on it as if it were some prize.

'The doctor – Dr Fried.'

'You called her something else – what else did you call her?' The same demand, like a pickaxe.

'Just another name.'

'Oh, the Secret Language,' and he leaned back. Comfortably on safe ground, it looked to her. It was in the book on page ninety-seven. It was All Right. 'Dr Fried told me that you had a secret language.'

Withdraw! Anterrabae said. He used the poetic Yri form and in her heartsickness it seemed newly beautiful – *Te quaru*: be as the sea and ebb and leave only a moment of the sandshine. *But I promised her,* Deborah insisted to the firelit falling god in the black place.

She is dead, Lactamaeon said on the other side of her.

'Tell me one of your words in that language,' the outside voice insisted.

'*Quaru,*' she said absently.

'What does it mean?'

'What?' She came to look at him suddenly and at the brutally hard lines of his disapproving face. He even sat austerely.

'What does it mean, that word you spoke? What was it?'

'*Quaru* ...' she repeated. She was flustered with the confrontation, and she heard her own voice tell the gods, *But I promised* ... 'It means ... well, it means wavelike, and it can imply something more of the sea, sometimes the coolness, or that soft, swishing sound, too. It means acting the way a wave acts.'

'Why don't you merely say wavelike then?' he said.

'Well ...' She was beginning the black sweat that was prelude to the Punishment. 'You use it for anything that is wavelike, but it gives the sea-connotation with it and sometimes that can be very beautiful.'

'I see,' he said. She knew that he didn't.

'You can use it for the way the wind is blowing some-times, or beautiful long dresses, or hair that is rippling, or ... or leaving.'

'It also means leaving?'

'No, ...' Deborah said. '... there is another word that means leaving.'

'What word?' he demanded.

'... It depends on whether one has the intention of coming back ...' she said miserably.

'Very interesting,' he said.

'There is also a saying—' (She had made it up that minute to try to save herself and them.) 'It is: don't cut bangs with a hatchet.'

'Cut *bangs*?' he said.

An Americanism, perhaps, so she tried again. 'Don't do brain surgery with a pickaxe.'

'And what does that signify to you?' he said, perhaps for-getting that if she could speak truly to the world, she would not be a mental patient.

'It suffered and died in translation,' she said.

There followed a long silence between them, and though she tried at the next hour and the next and the next, his humourless and automatic responses brought down the muteness like a night. He worked hard to convince her that Yri was a language formulated by herself and not sent with the gods as a gift. He had taken the first words she gave him and shown her the roots of them from scraps of Latin, French, and German that a nine- or ten-year-old could pick up if she tried. He analyzed the structure of the sentences and demanded that she see that they were, with very few exceptions, patterned on the English structure by which she, herself, was bound. His work was clever and detailed and sometimes almost brilliant, and she had many times to agree with him, but the more profound he was the more profound was the silence which enveloped her. She could never get beyond the austerity of his manner or the icy logic of what he had proven, to tell him that his scalpels were intrusions into her mind just as long-ago doctors had in-truded into her body, and that furthermore, his proofs were utterly and singularly irrelevant. At the end she marshalled all of her strength, and with as good a clarity as she could give him, she said, 'Please, Doctor, my difference is not my sickness.' It was a last cry and it went unheard.

Now, with Furii dead and the warmth of Earth's summer contradicting Deborah's own season, whose sun was a grey spot in an empty universe, there could be nothing else but muteness. She stopped reacting at all and her surface became as dead as the moon. As time went on, her motion ceased also and she sat like a fixed display on her bed. Occasionally, inside, Yr would present her with its alternatives and she would ride with Anterrabae in the hot wind of his fall or soar for a second with Lactamaeon on the rising columns of air over the Canyons of the Sorrow in Yr, but these times were all too rare and took incessant ceremonial tolls. Now even Yr seemed far and not to be apprehended.

She named the new doctor Snake-tooth, drawing the implication of the name from the hot summer-dry shaking of rattles, a senseless but evil sound, and she would think of it as she sat rigid and mute before him hour after hour. Slowly a volcano began to form beneath her still and mask-like face, and as more days dragged by, voices and counter-voices, hates, hungers, and long terrors began to seethe within its stony depths. The heat of them grew and mounted.

At a certain time Idat, the Dissembler, came to her in the shape of a woman. Idat was always veiled when she came so, but she was beautiful and never came without reminding her queen and victim of her beauty and saying also that she, Deborah, might someday aspire to being simply ugly. On this visit, the veil was lowered slightly, and Idat all in white.

Suffer, Idat. Why do you flow white?

Shroud and wedding gown, Idat said. *Two gowns that are the same gown. Behold! Should you not dying, live; and living, die; surrender, fighting; and fighting, surrender? My road will give all opposites at the same time, and the same means for the opposite ends.*

I know you from the veil outward, Idat, Deborah answered.

I mean that men set backfires, one to kindle yet quench the other.

Is it applicable also to stone?

With my help, Idat said.

Deborah perceived that by burning she could set a backfire that would assuage the burning kiln of the volcano, all the doors and vents of which were closed and barricaded. And by this same burning she could prove to herself finally whether or not she was truly made of human substance. Her sense offered no proof: vision was a grey blur; hearing merely muffled roars and groans, meaningless half the time; feeling was blunted, too. No one counted matches on B ward and what Yr wished her to obtain was always clear to her vision, freed from the blur. She soon had the matches and a supply of cigarettes picked up here and there. With five of them glowing, she began to burn her surface away. But the volcano only burned hotter behind the stone face and body. She lit the cigarettes again and put them out slowly and deliberately against the inner bend of her elbow. There was a faint sensation and the smell of burning but still no abatement of the volcano. Would it take a conflagration then, to create a backfire?

Sometime later a nurse came in to tell her something. Perhaps she smelled the burnt flesh, for she forgot what her message was and left, and soon a doctor was there. Deborah saw through her mask, with relief, the picture of the face of Dr Halle. That it was summertime somewhere else and that the picture was in fact a living being, she accepted on faith, like facts too remote to be worth debating – the number of miles in the earth's circumference, or the statistical variations of waves of light.

'What do you mean by a backfire?' he was saying.

'It seems necessary,' answered a representative of the volcano.

'Where?'

'On the surface.'

'Show me.' The words were careful but not critical or hypocritical.

The sleeve was now stuck to the burned place, but she

pulled it off before he could cry the civilized 'Don't!', instinctively wincing a little and thrusting his hand out as if she were made of real flesh.

After he looked, he said, a little sadly she thought, 'I think I'd better take you up to "D".'

'Whatever.'

'Well' (and with a hint of a gentling), 'you'll be one of my patients there. I've just taken over the administration of that ward.'

She gave the Yri hand-gesture of compliance with the slightly upward tilt, meaning that whether or not there was darkness, at least she felt safer because Halle could be spoken to and never gave the Number Three with Smile. He took her, with his usual decent lack of fuss, back to the D ward. When they stood inside the double-locked doors, someone from Yr said, *Look at him. See? He feels safer now.*

Poor man, she answered.

'You've made pretty much of a mess there,' Dr Halle said, studying the burned place. 'It'll have to be cleaned up and it's going to hurt.'

A student, delighted to be 'medical' again, was standing by with an impressive tray full of medical metal. Dr Halle began to scrub and clean the burn. A faint sensation followed his instruments, but there was no pain. For his concern and the time he was taking, Deborah wanted to give him a present. She remembered Furii and the gift of the cyclamen.

She is dead, though, Anterrabae said.

But you can give him a flower, Lactamaeon whispered.

I have nothing tangible.

Furii gave you a memory of hers, Lactamaeon said. She thanked Lactamaeon with the Yri thanks: *Go warm-shod and well lighted in the mind.*

She tried to think of a truth to tell the doctor as a present. Perhaps it might be the one about seeing – that even when seeing every line and plane and colour of a thing, if there was no meaning, the sight was irrelevant and one was just as well blind; that perhaps even the famous third dimension is only meaning, the gift which translates a bunch of planes into a box or a madonna or a Dr Halle with antiseptic bottle.

'I'm being as gentle as I can,' he was saying.

She looked at him sharply to see if he was trying to burden her with the responsibility of gratitude. No. She wondered if he was immune to her poisonous *nganon*. She decided that her gift would be a reassurance that he could touch her and not die.

'Don't worry,' she said graciously, 'the time of contact is so short that there is no chance of infection.'

'That's why I'm using this,' he said, swabbing away. As he was bandaging, she realized that he had not understood, so she decided to tell him about the meaning of the third dimension of sight. It came out in a single blurted sentence.

'Vision isn't everything!'

'No, I guess not,' he said, finishing up. Then, as if he had caught something, he said, 'Do you have trouble with your eyes?'

'Well ...' Deborah was embarrassed by the suddenness of the truth. '... when I get upset ... I usually have trouble seeing properly.'

Oh, really? How interesting, the Collect said sarcastically.

'Shut up! I can't hear myself think!' Deborah shouted at them.

'What?' Dr Halle turned. Deborah looked at him in horror. Her words to Yr had pierced the barriers of the earth's hearing. The clamour from the Collect built higher until it was an overwhelming roar and the grey vision went red. Without warning the full Punishment fell like an executioner's hand and the testimony of light, space, time, gravity, and the five senses became meaningless. Heat froze and light hurled tactile stabbing rays. She had no sense of where her body was; there was no up or down, no location or distance, no chain of cause and effect....

She endured outside of time and beyond exhaustion, and then she came up in world's daytime, a pack, a strange doctor.

'Hi.'

'Hi.'

'How are you?'

'I don't know. How long . . .' But she realized that he could not know when she had started down. 'How long since I have been up here?'

'Oh, three days or four.'

She became aware of aching in her hands and little aches along her arms and shoulders. She became terrified. 'Did I hit anybody? Did I hurt anybody?'

'No.' He smiled a little. 'You were having quite a go at the doors and windows, though.'

In revulsion and shame she tried to turn away, but a neck cramp caught her so that she began to cough and had to turn back towards him to work it away. 'I don't know you. How come you are here?'

'Oh, I'm on call today. I stopped in to see if you were okay.'

'Good God!' she said in awe. 'I must have torn the place down. They never call a doctor unless somebody's killed himself.'

He laughed a little. 'That's not true for me; I'm a new doctor. Can you come out? Do you feel ready?'

'I don't know,' she said.

'Well, we'll give you another half hour. Don't worry about that aching. A lot of it is just tension. Well – so long.' She heard his key busy in the lock and the inexpertness was strangely moving.

When she returned to her bed on 'D' – it was one which she had had before in the front dorm – she found it surrounded by woe. In the shuffle of comings and goings, the Wife of the Abdicated had been moved two beds down and Deborah was now between Fiorentini's Mary and Sylvia, still mute and vacant about the face. The Punishment had exhausted Deborah and she lay on her bed watching the world's shadows draw long, shading the world's time towards evening.

Mary lay resting on the next bed. After a while she said gaily, 'Kid, I never knew you had it in you. You can really fight!'

'I didn't hit anyone . . .' Deborah said, feeling a little sick at the mention of it and wondering if she had, in spite of what the young 'new' doctor had said.

'Oh, but the talent is there; the talent is definitely there!' Mary laughed her laugh like breaking glass, an imitation of mirth from one who had never understood it. 'But, you are insane of course, out of your mind – didn't know what you were doing.' Again she used a light voice, a parody of an actress in a sophisticated comedy.

'Yes,' Deborah said quietly, 'but I can't figure out why I came out of it . . . why it stopped . . .'

'Well, really, every *case* like you ought to realize that *that hell*' – and she began to shake with shudders of high, shrill laughter – 'can't last any more than you can stand it. It's like physical pain – tee-hee-hee –there's just so much and then, no *more!*'

'You mean that there is a limit to the thing?'

'Well, *more* would be *obscene*, my dear, simply *obscene!*' and the high, young-girl giggle broke again into a sharp, back-bristling laughter.

Deborah wondered if Mary were right and if, in the nightmare of no laws, there were at least boundaries. The light faded and the dormitory grew dim. Perhaps there was mercy even in Hell. Her vision cleared a little and the softened lines of the beds and the walls and the bodies of the breathing dead around her took on the faint glow of the summer dusk. The overhead lights went on and with them came the knowledge that Mary, agony and all and with her awful laughter, had reached out with what little help she could summon, if only to say that there was, indeed, a limit. Even poisonous persons could, if they threw all their courage and energy into it, help one another. Carla had done it, Helene had done it, Sylvia in her death as furniture had done it, and now Mary had offered from herself a fragment of hard wisdom.

Deborah remembered her first meeting with Mary and laughed. She had said, 'I'm Deborah,' and pointed to her bed, 'over there.' Mary, with her omnipresent mirthless grin had replied, 'I'm Bedlam as seen by Walt Disney.'

In the evening Deborah felt a need and got up to scout the ward for fuel for another backfire.

20

For Deborah, the backfires became the only way of easing the pressure of the stifled volcano inside her. She continued to burn the same places over and over, setting layers of burns on top of one another. Cigarette butts and matches were easy to obtain, although they were supposedly guarded with great care; even D ward's precautions were no match for the intensity of her need. Because the effects of the burnings lasted only an hour or so and because she could only bear the building up of pressure for three or four hours, she had to have a large supply of used cigarettes and the matches to relight them.

For a few days the wounds remained secret, even though she had to change the site of the burning when they began to infect and drain. She was amused but not surprised at how oblivious the nurses and attendants were. The wounds drained and stank and no one noticed. She thought: It's because they don't really want to look at us.

At the end of the week, the new doctor came up to the ward again. 'You look a lot better,' he said, stopping by Deborah in the dayroom.

'I ought to,' she said a little acidly, 'I've had to work like hell to keep it up.'

'Well, with such an improvement, you should be ready to go back to B ward very soon.'

When she heard this, she realized that B ward, with its unprotected time and free matches, was a perfect chance for the death she thought she wanted. Then she noticed that she was terrified, and wondered why. If he was letting her die as she wished, why was she angry?

'I have some more burns,' she said simply.

He looked shocked, recovered quickly, and said, 'I'm glad you told me.'

She began to pull on her sweater, twisting it like wet laundry in her hands. *If I want to die, what am I saving myself for?* she demanded, still angry at the mental image of him permitting her to burn herself to death on B ward.

You told him because you are a coward! the Collect said. They began the old jibes again.

'How is the old sore?' the doctor said, loosening the bandaged place. She did not answer him because he was seeing for himself. The burn was stubbornly refusing to heal. 'You haven't done any more to this?' he asked, a little bit accusingly and afraid to make it stronger.

'No,' she said.

'We'll try another kind of bandage. Let me see the new burn.' He looked at the other arm. 'How many times did you burn this?'

'About eight.'

He bandaged both places and left, no doubt to scold the nurses about the carelessness of leaving dangerous, fire-making materials on the ward. The burning cigarette he left behind him in the dayroom was long enough for two series of burnings.

When the lawgivers of D ward discovered that its patients were not so safe as they had thought, they swept the ward up and down with reforms to widen still further the distance between themselves and the patients. The fork that had been introduced on 'D' a year before was now rescinded. The Age of Metal gave way to the Age of Wood and fire prevailed only within the precincts of the nursing station, the modern era. In the pleistocene beyond, *Pithecanthropus erectus* shambled and muttered gibberish, ate with its fingers and wet on the floor.

'Thanks a lot, kid,' Lee Miller said sarcastically as she walked past Deborah into the lighted place where Modern Man supplied the patients with his status-symbols – cigarette and match.

'Go to Hell,' Deborah answered, but her tone lacked conviction. Later, the Wife of the Abdicated accused her of being a spy and in league with the Secretary of the Interior, and as Deborah already knew, the Secretary of the Interior was one of the worst Enemies.

Getting matches and butts now became difficult, but by no means impossible. Modern Man was careless with the fire-tipped cylinders he burned and breathed, and waiting beside him was a fire-hungry primitive whose grey and flat world magically included the cigarette in sharp focus, colour, smell, and three dimensions of form.

But firing back at the volcano did not change its surface, its granite garment, as Anterrabae called it. And gods and Collect and Censor were wildly and inexplicably free with the Punishment. Even the logic of Yr seemed to have been erased and the laws overturned. Deborah began to believe that the volcano would erupt and explode. She remembered that the Last Deception had not yet come.

The days had long since become an Earth-form that was only a grammatical nicety. She woke up in one of them and found herself in pack, as so often before. A key turned in the lock of the door and a nurse entered. Behind the nurse, looking unbelievably different because she had not changed at all, stood Furii.

'All right,' she said, and came in. The nurse brought a chair for her, and Deborah began to wish that she might escape the woman's face and the disgust she saw in it. Furii looked all around, sat beside the bed, and nodded with a kind of awe.

'My goodness!'

'You're back,' Deborah said. The self-hate, terror, shame, pity, vanity, and despair never crossed the stone surface. 'Did you have a good time?'

'My goodness,' Furii repeated. 'What happened? You were doing very well when I left, and now, back here. . . .' She looked around again.

Deborah was afraid of the joy she felt in seeing Furii alive. She said, 'You've seen this . . . awfulness before; why are you so shocked?'

'Yes, I have seen it. I am only sorry to see you in it, and suffering so much.'

Deborah closed her eyes. She was stricken with shame

164

and she wanted to escape to the Pit, to be dark and blank, but Furii was back and there was no hiding place. Her mind held. 'I didn't know you were coming.'

'It is the day I said I would be back,' Furii said.

'Is it?'

'It is, and I think maybe you got in this bad shape to tell me how angry you are that I went off and left you.'

'That's not true—' Deborah said. 'I tried with Royson – I really did, but you were dead – at least I thought you were – and he wanted only to prove how right he was and how smart. I forgot that you would come back. . . .'

She began to thrash again, even though she was exhausted. 'I'm all stopped and closed . . . like it was before I came here . . . only the volcano is burning hotter and hotter while the surface doesn't even know if it is alive or not!'

The doctor moved closer. 'It is one of these times,' she said quietly, 'when what you say is most important.'

Deborah pushed her head hard into the bed. 'I can't even sort them out – the words.'

'Well then, just let it come to us.'

'Are you that strong?'

'We are both that strong.'

Deborah took a breath. 'I am poisonous and I hate it. I am going to be destroyed in shame and degradation and I hate it. I hate myself and the deceivers. I hate my life and my death. For my truth the world gives only lies; I tried with Royson time after time, but I saw that all he wanted was to be right. He might as well have said, "Come to your senses and stop the silliness" – what they said for the years and years when I was disappointing them on the surface and lying to them with the inmost part of Yr and me and the enemy soldier. God curse me! God curse me!'

A soft scraping sound, a breathed rasp, came after, as she tried to cry, but the sound of it was so ridiculous and ugly that she soon stopped.

'Maybe when I leave,' Furii said, 'you can learn to cry. For now, let me say this: measure the hate you feel now, and the shame. That quantity is your capacity also to love and to feel joy and to have compassion. Also, I will see you to-morrow.'

She left.

That evening Miss Coral came to Deborah holding a book. 'Look,' she said timidly, 'my doctor has left this with me. It is a book of plays and I wondered if perhaps you might not wish to read them with me.'

Deborah looked over at Helene, who was sitting against the wall. Had Helene been offering the book, she would have kicked it across the floor to Deborah, perhaps with a taunt. Did any two people even in the World speak the same language?

As she answered, Deborah could hear herself mirroring some of Miss Coral's elaborate form of speech and also her shyness. 'Which one would you prefer?' Miss Coral asked. They began to read *The Importance of Being Earest,* with Deborah doing most of the men and Miss Coral doing most of the women. Soon Lee and Helene and Fiorentini's Mary were reading, too. With the actors parodying themselves, the play was uproarious. Mary, laugh and all, was Ernest as a well-born bedlamite, while Miss Coral as Sybil reeked with magnolias and spider-webs. Oscar Wilde's urbane and elegant comedy was being presented on the nightmare canvas of Hieronymus Bosch. They read the whole play through, and then another, aware that the attendants were laughing with them as well as at them, and thinking, for all the fear it caused, that it was a good night; one which, magically, was not included in their damnation.

Esther Blau faced Doctor Fried unable to speak. Then she cleared her throat.

'Did I understand you correctly?'

'I think so, but first—'

'Why! Why?'

'We are attempting to find out why.'

'Can't you find out *before* she's all burnt up!'

Esther had read the carefully general report, but something in its tone had alerted her and she had come down again, full of foreboding, to see Deborah. She had been told that it would be unwise; she had demanded to see Dr Halle, and once in his office, she had heard the facts no words could modify or ease. Now she sat before Dr Fried, angry and frightened and despairing.

'And what can I tell her father – what lie can I tell him now so that we can keep her here where she gets sicker and more violent all the time!'

Through her fear the doctor's words sounded long and slow. 'I think perhaps that we are all letting ourselves go overboard with this burning business. It is, after all, a symptom of the sickness which we all know is there, and which is *still* responding to treatment.'

'But it's so . . . so *ugly*!'

'You mean the wounds?'

'I haven't seen the wounds – I mean the idea, the thought. How could anyone do that to themselves! A person would be in—' Esther gasped and put her hand before her mouth, and tears spilled over the rims of her eyes and rolled down her face.

'No, no,' the doctor said, 'it's the *word* that is making you so frightened. It is the old evil word "insane", which once meant "hopeless and forever", that is making you suffer so.'

'I never let myself think that word for Debby!'

The façade is broken and what is behind the façade is not so bad, Dr Fried thought. She wondered if she could let the mother know it in some way. It might be a small comfort. The telephone rang and Dr Fried answered it in her affable voice, and when she turned again to face Esther, she found her composed.

'You do think, then, that there is still a chance for her to be . . . normal?'

'I think that there is certainly a chance for her to be mentally healthy and strong. I will say something to you now, Mrs Blau, but it is not for your daughter and I will appreciate it if you never mention it to her. I am approached at least four times every week to do therapy with a patient. I have doctors' analyses also to supervise for the university School of Psychiatry, and at every session I must turn many away.

I would be worse than wasteful to give a moment's time to a hopeless case. I do not keep her one moment longer than I think I can help her. Tell them this at home. You need not keep telling lies – the truth is not unbearable at all.'

The doctor saw Deborah's mother out of her office, hoping that she had helped. Easy comfort might do for some other branch of medicine (placebo was a prescription more common than doctors themselves liked to admit), but the whole weight of her life and training was against it. And after her experiences, anything that sounded even faintly like placating would frighten Esther Blau; if she had been strengthened by this talk, the whole family would be strengthened in turn.

Dr Fried understood that Esther had outgrown her subjection to her father. She was now a strong, dominant, even dominating person. The same force in her that had tried to conquer all of Deborah's enemies, to her detriment, might be the saving force as well. If she believed in this therapy, for her daughter, she would stand against the whole family to see that it was carried out. Deborah's illness had done more than shake the portraits in the family album. Some of the family had had to question why, and had grown a little themselves because of asking. If this were true, it was a source of hope seldom mentioned in the psychiatric journals, maybe because it was beyond 'science' and beyond planning for. Outside the doors of study, Dr Fried's father had once told her, an angel waits.

Coming out of the doctor's house into the brisk autumn day, Esther looked towards the high, heavily screened porch behind which she knew was D ward. What was it like there? What was it like inside the minds of people who had to stay there? She looked away from it quickly, finding that it was blurred by a sudden overwhelming of tears.

Deborah sat on the floor of the ward having her burns dressed. She had begun to be of medical interest; the wounds refused to heal. The student nurses, delighted by so tangible a condition, worked faithfully and busily with their unguents, potions, bandages, and tape. The smokers were still angry at Deborah, holding her responsible for the new rules, and even Lee, who needed to talk, was sending scornful looks at her. While the nurses worked, Deborah watched what she had come to call the Breathing Frieze of other patients, sitting and standing, expressionless except for a look of great awe that their blood could move its ways so steadily, their hearts could beat beyond will or passion. When the nurses finished dressing the recalcitrant burns, they left the hall for a moment. Out of the corner of her eye, Deborah became aware that Helene was looking hard at Sylvia, who was standing next to her, immobile as ever. The next moment, Helene came close and struck Sylvia heavily once, and once again. Sylvia stood beneath the blows and gave no sign of being conscious of them. Challenged, Helene exploded into a whirlwind of rage. A wild creature seemed to be hurling itself against rock. Helene beat and screamed and scratched and flapped, spitting and red-faced, her hair flying. Sylvia reacted only by closing her eyes slowly. Her hands were still limp at her sides; her body, it seemed, was totally commended to the forces of gravity and inertia; she appeared to take no interest in the beating. The sudden, swift happening was interrupted by the standard six attendants required to get Helene away. Soon she was borne off drowning in a wave of khaki and white.

Deborah remained standing ten feet from Sylvia. Both of them seemed alone on the planet. Deborah remembered the time two years earlier when Helene had rushed at her to destroy the face that had witnessed, and be safe from its knowledge. Everything had been Helene – doctors, nurses, attendants, the ward's quickened rhythm, the wet sheets, and seclusion – all, all Helene, and Deborah had stood alone and shamed, because she had been too degraded to defend herself. She had stood as Sylvia was standing now, like a statue. Only her breathing betrayed her, wrenching in and out, almost as if she were snorting. Deborah was the only one who could know why Sylvia, who had failed to defend herself, needed as much attention as Helene was now getting.

I should go to her and touch her on the shoulder and say

something, Deborah thought. But she stood still. I should go because it happened to me and no one knows as I do, how it is. . . . But her feet were in her shoes and her shoes were not moving towards Sylvia, and her hands stayed at her sides and were not moving. In the name of the dark night together when she broke her silence for me, I should go. . . . And she tried to wrench free of her granite garments and stone shoes. She looked at Sylvia, the ugliest of all of the patients, with her drooling and her pale, waxy face in its frozen grimace, and she knew that if she went to give what she of all people knew was needed, Sylvia might destroy her with silence alone. A fear came up to consume the wish to act. In another moment the subduers of Helene began to come back from the battle and the chance was lost. From the subsiding fear, shame rose. It grew up over her face so that she stood for a long time stone blind and wishing for death.

Later, she stood before Furii in the office and told her what she had seen and had not done.

'I never told you a lie!' Deborah said. 'I never told you that I was human. Now you can throw me out because I have a guilt with no apology.'

'I am not here to excuse you,' Furii said, looking up at Deborah from the chair, and lighting a cigarette. 'You will find no shortage of moral issues and hard decisions in the real world, and, as I have said before, it's no rose garden. Let us bless the strength that let you see, and work towards the time when you will be able also to *do* what you see to do. We have now to work hard on the roots of this burning which you do in your anger at me and at the hospital.'

Almost at once Deborah knew that Furii was wrong about the reason for the burning and the need for it, and most wrong about its seriousness. While it had the semblance of terrible aberration, Deborah felt that this was as deceptive as the quiet slopes of her volcano.

'Do you think the burning is very serious?' she asked Furii.

'Most serious, indeed,' Furii answered.

'You are wrong,' Deborah said simply, hoping that the

doctor really believed what she had so often said about the patient trusting her own deep beliefs. There were over forty burns, inflicted over and over again on flesh scraped raw to receive them, and yet they didn't seem worth the fuss that was being made about them.

'I don't know why, but you are wrong.'

Deborah looked around the cluttered office. For members of the world, sunlight was streaming through the windows, but its goldenness and warmth were only there for her to perceive from a distance. The air around her was still cold and dark. It was this eternal estrangement, not fire against her flesh, that was the agony.

'Restricted or not,' she murmured, 'I will do penance.'

'Louder, please, I cannot hear you.'

'Selective inattention,' Deborah said, laughing at the words of psychiatry, whose private language and secret jargon had not the beauty or poetry of Yri. Furii saw, too, and laughed.

'Sometimes I think that our professional vocabulary goes too far, but we speak to one another after all, and not only to ourselves and the falling gods. Was it to them that you spoke just now?'

'No,' Deborah said, 'to you. I have decided not to be immoral, because of what happened to Sylvia. If I couldn't do what I should have done after Helene attacked her, at least I won't implicate her in my burnings, since you say that they are serious.'

'How do you mean this?'

'She smokes sometimes, but she is forgetful. She has put cigarettes down when I was there to pick them up quickly and be gone. Both Marys smoke like wild women and all I have to do is make sure that no one spots me. They are contributing to my delinquency, aren't they?'

'I suppose, in a way they are. Actually you are taking advantage of their symptoms.'

'That must not be allowed to happen,' Deborah said quietly. She wondered why Furii had left matches in her waiting room, and cigarettes, too. The nurse who had accompanied her was easily distracted; Deborah wondered if

Furii knew how trying those minutes of waiting had been.

When the time was over, Deborah got up to leave, saying, 'I am cutting my throat now myself. I won't steal burning butts from the patients unless they're left in the ashtrays or are forgotten, and I won't let you contribute either because you wouldn't want to.'

Then she reached into her sleeve and drew out the two packs of matches she had taken from Furii's table and threw them angrily on the paper-littered desk.

21

WHEN THE VOLCANO erupted at last, there was no backfire in the matchbooks that was big enough to stave it off. Deborah had not anticipated anything more unusual than dark-mindedness and howling from the Collect when she began to feel the familiar whip of fear and hear the one-tone whine of accusation from the invisible hating ones. She had been in the tubroom behind the front bathroom by herself because all the seclusion rooms were full. (Often the nurses would unlock the door for her and let her be alone in there until someone needed the toilets up front; for half an hour after the evening wash-up, solitude was almost a certainty.) It had been evening and soon it would be bedtime. She hadn't wanted to carry her hell to bed with her, kicking the effects of dose after dose of chloral hydrate that kept growing deeper in the glasses and went down like burning celluloid.

She lay down on the cold floor and began beating her head slowly and methodically against the tiles. The black in her mind went red, swelling and growing out of her so far that before she knew it she was engulfed in the furious anger of eruption.

When her vision cleared, it was only enough to see and hear as if through a keyhole. She was aware that she was shouting and that attendants were in the room and that the walls of the room were covered with Yri words and sentences. Ranged around her were all the outpourings of hatred and anger and bitterness in a language whose metaphors used 'broken' to mean 'consenting' and 'third rail' to mean 'complying'. All the words were extreme. *Uguru*, which was 'dog-howling' and meant loneliness, was written in its superlative form in letters a foot high the length of one wall: UGURUSU. The words were written in pencil and in blood, and in some places scratched with a broken button.

There was a look of horror and surprise even on the faces of a hardened D-ward staff, and it was that look which brought the full fire from her. The world's fear and hatred were like the sun, common and pervading, daily and accepted – a law of nature. Now its rays were focused in their look, waking fire. The words Deborah spoke were not loud, but they were full of hatred and they were Yri.

'Where is what you used to scratch this, Miss Blau?'

'*Recreat,*' Deborah said. '*Recreat xangoran, temr e xangoranan. Naza e fango xangoranan. Inai dum. Ageai dum.*' ('Remember me. Remember me in anger, fear me in bitter anger. Heat-craze my teeth in bitterest anger. The signal glance drops. The Game' – *Ageai* meant the tearing of flesh with teeth as torture – 'is over.')

Mrs Forbes came then. Deborah had liked Mrs Forbes – she remembered having liked her. The anger was rising steadily and too much of what Deborah said could not wait even for the Yri logic and frame of words, and went sailing off into gibberish with only an Yri word here and there to let Deborah know what she was saying. Mrs Forbes asked Deborah if she could send the others away, and Deborah, grateful for her courage in offering this, showed the two open hands and tried for form in her speech that was only going further and further into meaningless sounds.

'This word here – the biggest one – I think I heard you say it. Has it a meaning?'

Deborah groped wildly for gestures, words, or sounds to convey the impact of the volcano's eruption; the word she had written in the blood from a cut finger was the third form of anger, which she had never spoken or written before and which was more extreme than black anger or red-white anger. After moving about restlessly for a while, she threw back her head in a soundless scream, wide-mouthed. The nurse looked at her.

'Is the word *fear*?' she asked. 'No – not fear – *anger*.' And then looking at Deborah again: 'An anger you cannot control.' After a pause she said, 'Come on, we'll try seclusion until you can take care of yourself.'

The seclusion room was small, but the force of the volcano would not let her rest. It kept hurling her from one side of the room to the other; walls and floors pounded her head and hands and body. Now her lack of inner control matched the anarchic world with an Yr gone newly mad itself.

After a while they caught her up and put her in a pack. She fought with them, terrified of what she might do to them now that she had no law. English, Yri, and gibberish all flowed together. Gradually, the anger was overtaken by the fear, but the words to warn them that she was wild could not be framed, and she fought them with her head and her teeth while the restraints were being tied, trying, doglike, to bite, herself, her wrappings, the bed, the beings. She fought until she was exhausted and then she lay still.

After a while Deborah could feel the constriction of blood in her legs and feet that usually brought a familiar pain, but there was no pain. The burns, she knew, had had their raw surfaces ripped open under the bandages, but there was no pain from them either. How cold the wind was blowing above the law! ... She lay shivering, although the sheets had been close for many hours and she should have been warm. Beyond even the laws and logic of Yr she breathed out in wonder: My enemy, my virulent, plague-pouring self – and now not even control of it. . . .

'*There was a gear* . . .' she cried aloud, and it came in Yri loud and mingled with strange words which were not hers. '*There was a gear all teeth, two at least world-caught. And now nothing, nothing engages with the world!*'

You are not of them, the Censor said. It was an old phrase, perhaps the oldest one in Yr, but its context changed from comfort and pity, to anger and terror, and now to the last deceit, the final move of the game which was part of the world's secret purposes and her damnation. She now knew that the death she feared might not be a physical one, that it could be a death of the will, the soul, the mind, the laws, and thus not death, but a perpetual dying. The tumour began to ache.

Furii looked at her and said, 'Are you ill?' and Deborah laughed with the same ugliness that her cry had been. 'I mean, is something physically the matter?'

'No.' She tried to tell Furii, but the walls began bleeding and sweating, and the ceiling developed a large tumour which began to separate itself from its surface.

'Can you hear me?' Furii asked.

Deborah tried to say what she felt, but she could only gesture the Yri gesture for insanity: flattened hands thrust towards one another but unable to meet.

'Listen to me. Try to hear me,' Furii said seriously. 'You are afraid of your power and that you cannot control it.'

When Deborah could speak at last, she could only say, 'Yri . . . in the world . . . collision . . .'

'Try again. Just let it come.'

'Gears uncaught . . . *n'ai naruai* . . . uncaught!'

'It is why you need a hospital. You are in a hospital and you do not need to fear the terrible forces that seem to have been opened in you. Listen hard now, and try to stay in contact with me. You must try to talk to me and tell me what is happening in your collided worlds. We will work with all our strength to keep you from the excesses of your sickness.'

Some of the fear eased so that Deborah could say, 'It came Yri, English, nonsense. Wild . . . hitting. Anger.'

'Were you angry for all the years, in the way that anger gets when it grows old and is rotted with guilt and fear – like bad-smelling pebbles inside?'

'Much . . .'

'The suffering was not because of your anger then, was it?'

'No . . . Yri . . . on earth . . . collision. Censor . . . death

175

penalty ... the last ...' She began to tremble in a cutting cold.

'Use the blanket,' Furii said.

'Yri cold ... *nacoi* ... earth blankets ...'

'We will see if Earth warmth helps,' Furii said. She picked up the blanket and covered Deborah with it. Deborah remembered that there was no Yri word for 'thank you'. She had no word to give Furii her gratitude. It remained a mute weight inside her. Even the trembling did not lessen, so that Furii could see it and be glad.

'Tell me this,' Furii was saying, 'of the emotion you felt as you heard yourself cry out in these languages, how much was anger and how much was fear?'

'Ten,' Deborah said, thinking of the emotion by letting a stroke of it come up and engulf her once again, 'three anger, five fear.'

'That is only eight.'

'I suffer,' Deborah said, helping herself with Yri hand-motions. 'After you I suffer smarter. Now I never fill them. Two is for miscellaneous.'

Furii laughed. 'Anger some, fear quite a bit, and what are those little two miscellaneous? Relief, maybe, not to have to give everything to that wall between Yr and the world? Also, was there not something overt to remind me that I went away and left you with it all?'

Deborah felt that the last idea was only half true, but she let it sound in the judgement with the others, and she said, 'Fear ... Censor – doing the forbidden ... destroy me ... and ...'

'And what is it?'

'Then ... no. No-ness; not Yr even. Loud gibberish and just *No. No!*'

'Not even the gods for friends,' the doctor mused. She drew her chair up closer to where Deborah was huddled shivering under the blanket whose warmth stopped short of her interior climate. 'You know, Deborah, you have a gift for health and strength. Before you let go for this breaking of walls, you trusted our work together and you trusted me. Before you let the anger come, you got yourself on D ward and in the sort of seclusion that was at hand, and when a nurse was on duty, mind you, whom you liked and trusted. Not so dumb for someone who is supposed to have lost her marbles. Not so bad at all, that talent for life.'

Deborah's eyes began to get heavy. She was very tired.

'You are worn out,' Furii said, 'but no longer so very frightened, are you?'

'No.'

'The anger may come again. The sickness you have built may also come and fight you perhaps, but I have faith that you will conquer it enough to get the help and control that you need. Half of your fear is that you will not be able to be stopped, and it is this fear which makes it impossible to speak so that others can understand.'

When Deborah got back to the ward after her session with Dr Fried, she found that another holocaust had visited it.

'Your good friend . . .' Lee Miller said under her breath '. . . sweet, genteel Miss Coral.'

'What?'

'She took that bed there, and *threw* it! She picked it up and threw it at Mrs Forbes!'

'And it hit?'

'Sure it hit. Mrs Forbes is now in a physical hospital as a patient – with a broken arm, cuts and bruises, and who the hell knows what else.'

Lee Miller was angry because Mrs Forbes was one of those rare elect whom the patients themselves, consciously or not, tried to save from harm. She took time, she was intelligent and unselfish, and – most rare – she was happy in her work and the patients knew it.

'Mistake,' Deborah said, like talking wood. 'By mistake.' She remembered others: a patient who had aimed at one person and hit another, the student nurse who always seemed to be walking where fists and chairs were landing. If this one could somehow be made to fit in with the others . . .

'Maybe the dear patient was temporarily insane!' Fiorentini's Mary chimed in gaily. 'Temporary Insanity – that's a legal term. It means before and during and a while after, but they never say how long which way. Very exact, the law . . . a science, you know.' And she skipped down the hall like a seven-year-old, erupting in a new giggle and leaving the old one to grate against their senses.

'Is Mrs Forbes coming back?' Deborah asked, feeling sick to her stomach. She understood that Lee was taking out her anger at her because Miss Coral was in seclusion and not to be approached, while Deborah was standing before her, available. Deborah had not thought of herself as being anyone's friend, but it occurred to her that Lee thought otherwise.

She turned very slowly to Lee, and with overdrawn dignity, because dignity was new to her and strange and worn uncomfortably, she said, 'Okay, Lee, Carla, too.' (She was still afraid to say the word 'friend', because of its transcendent danger.)

Lee walked to the door of the nursing station and beat on it. When it opened, she asked for a cigarette, and when it was lit for her, she growled, 'What am I doing here with all these crazy people?' Deborah walked into the dorm, lay down on her bed.

The more she thought about it, the more she wanted to know why Miss Coral had hit Mrs Forbes; why one of the Good Ones? After the line-up for sedation that evening, she moved unobtrusively to the corner beyond the nursing-station door, and stood completely still with her head against the water pipes that were placed there. The hot pipe was jacketed with insulation, but the cold, though uncomfortable, was sometimes used by the patients as a listening device. If a person put the whole side of her head against this pipe and held her breath, she could hear the conversations going on inside the nursing station, even with the door closed. Deborah had assumed that the sounds were transmitted by the faucets, because the reception was better when the speakers were near the steel sink. She was not noticed where she stood; the whole ward had been darkened for the evening, and the attendants who were out on the halls were busy getting the reluctant patients to bed. Inside the nursing station the reports were being written.

178

'Over there,' a voice was saying. It sounded like Miss Cleary.

'No, there – by the coffeepot.'

The idea of having coffee anytime, now or whenever, set off a water of desire in Deborah's mouth, and she pushed her head harder against the pipe to get her mind off it. They began to talk about allotments of days off. The hall was clearing fast. If they didn't get down to it soon, she would have to move.

'Jesus, I'm tired.' (That would be Hanson.)

'You ain't the only one.' (Bernardi.) 'I don't know, but seems to me they're all getting sicker.'

'You mean crazier.'

'Tch, tch, tch. Watch your language!' They laughed.

'No, honest – the damn ward is never a day without fights, a couple more in seclusion, half of 'em in packs. Now that old Coral Allan everyone calls Miss Coral, as if she was some Southern belle – I've heard people talk about her, but I never seen it myself 'til this afternoon.'

'God! You ever think an old lady like that could lift a bed, no less chuck it?'

Deborah wanted them to talk about Mrs Forbes, and when they started to, she smiled against the cold pipe.

'You seen Lou Ann?' (Mrs Forbes' first names were Lou Ann.)

'Hudson and Carelle went down with her. Sophie's going down to see her tomorrow, and I will too, if I get off.'

Deborah ground her teeth with impatience. They were beginning to get ready to close the night on their charges. If the evidence was not given now . . .

'Hey, you seen Blau last night?'

'No – I missed that one; I was back with Whitman.'

'Oh – (laugh) *brother*.'

Deborah didn't want to hear about Blau. She had come to find out what circumstances there might be to mitigate the pain she was feeling about Coral *vs* Forbes; some reason to hold against all of her knowledge that always deceived her and ended blind and mad.

'Lord! In the bathroom and yelling all kinds of nonsense.

Filled the wall with some kind of crazy writing and come out fighting like a tiger. All the time we was packing her she was swearing in that kind of babble-talk – not anything you could understand, but you looked at her face and there was that hate. Brrrr.'

'She didn't talk at all today.'

'Well, put it in the records.'

Deborah sank down along the cold track of the pipe to the floor. She covered her face with her hands. It was hot with shame. She crawled a little away from the pipe so that she would be on neutral ground, and dissociated from the source of her knowledge. She began to cry with the incredible sounds she had made before, murmuring to all the worlds and to the collision, the one unchanging thing, 'You are not of them.' She was still heaving and holding her face when Martenson, the student nurse, came and stood over her.

'Come on now, Miss Blau,' she said, 'let's get to bed.'

'Okay,' and she stood up, still hiding in the dark behind her hands, and stumbled into the dorm and to bed. She continued to sob.

'What *are* those obscene noises?' Fiorentini's Mary chirped. 'Some new sort of homosexual perversion, I am sure. . . . Oh, you insane are all so inventive – it's because you have time to *think things through*.' She began to murmur and laugh.

The Wife of the Abdicated became disturbed by Mary's laughter and the choked-out noises of Deborah's crying and began to protest. 'Have you no respect, you filthy whores! I am the secret first Wife of Edward, the Abdicated King of England!'

'Well, Hail Columbia!' said Jenny, rarely heard, but one who liked her sleep.

'Hail Mary, Full of Grace . . .,' called Dowben's Mary, who always brought out the atheist in everyone with her endless prayers.

'Oh, Christ! Now you've started that bitch up again!'

The tumult mounted and Deborah heard it as a counterpoint to the ugly sounds that were still working inside her. The attendant came and shut them all up, and there was silence, with each soul sealed away in a seclusion to the limits of which no eye could seem to reach.

Deborah lay in bed, and her thoughts returned to the puzzle. Dust motes blown and floating all the patients were, but even so there were some things that were not done. Deborah knew very well that she could never ask Miss Coral why she had thrown the bed or how it was that Mrs Forbes' arm had been intruded upon by that bed. Beating, stealing, swearing, blaspheming, and sexual eccentricity were not sins on D ward. Spitting on the floor, urinating, defecating, or masturbating incontinently in public aroused only passing annoyance rather than horror, but to ask how or why was not forgivable and to oppose another patient's act was a sign of crudity at best and at worst a kind of assault – an attempted mayhem at the barriers which were the all-costly protectors of life. Lee Miller had cursed Deborah for the burnings which had resulted in the whole ward's restriction, but she had never asked why they had been done or expressed a wish that they be stopped. There was ridicule and anger, but never intrusion. Miss Coral could never be confronted with throwing the bed, and her friends, such as they could be, would henceforth delicately expunge the name of Mrs Forbes from their conversation in the presence of the one who had caused her to be hurt. Where then could Deborah get the answer to her question?

Through the days of wondering, Deborah's surface registered nothing, and when she spoke her words were the mangled Anglo-Yri-gibberish and there were only enough to try to answer a question or to hint at a need. The ambiguity of what she said surprised her as much as anyone. When an attendant asked her if it was her day for a bath, she tried for a purely English answer, but it emerged as, 'It never goes deep enough.'

In the bathroom: 'Blau – are you in there?'

'Here is *cutucu*.' (The second degree of being hidden.) As she struggled to translate, finding it almost impossible to span the light years of distance between herself and them, the confusion of tongues only alienated her further. She would become frightened, whatever she said next could not be translated at all, and the formless sounds would make her even more frightened. Only with Furii was there any clarity.

'They said we were getting sicker; all of us. They said I was getting sicker.'

'Well, do you think you are?' Furii said, lighting another cigarette.

'No games.'

'I do not play games. I want you to think deeply and answer honestly.'

'I don't want to think any more!' Deborah said, with her voice rising in the wind of her sudden anger. 'I'm tired and scared and I just don't care any more what happens. Work in the dark and work in the cold and what for!'

'To get you out of this damn place, that's what for.' Furii's voice was as loud as Deborah's.

'I won't tell you anything more. The more garbage I give away the more I have left. *You* can turn me off and go out with your friends or write another paper and get another honour for it. I can't turn me off, so I'm turning the fight off, and don't you worry – I will be nice and docile and nothing more will go on the walls.'

The cigarette gave a long puff before the doctor's face. 'Okay,' she said, almost amiably. 'You quit, poor little girl, and you stay in a crazy house the rest of your life. You stay on a crowded disturbed ward all your days. ... "Poor darling," the world will say, "she could have been such a nice person ... so talented ... what a loss."' The mobile features made a 'tch-tch' purse of the mouth.

'And more talented than I really am because I'm here and will never test it!' Deborah shouted because the bone-truth gave such a fine sound, even from Hell.

'Yes, damn it, yes!' Furii said.

'Well, what?' Deborah said, good and loud.

'Well, did I ever say it would be easy? I cannot make you well and I do not want to make you well against your own wishes. If you fight with all the strength and patience you have, we will make it together.'

'And what if I don't?'

'Well, there are lots of mental hospitals, and they build more every day.'

'And if I fight, then for *what*?'

'For nothing easy or sweet, and I told you that last year and the year before that. For your own challenge, for your own mistakes and the punishment for them, for your own definition of love and of sanity – a good strong self with which to begin to live.'

'You certainly don't go in for hyperbole.'

'Look here, my dear girl,' Furii said, and thumped the ash of her cigarette on the tray, 'I am your doctor and I see these years how allergic you are to lying, so I try not to tell lies.' She looked at Deborah with the familiar half-smile. 'Besides, I like an anger that is not fearful and guilty and can come out in good and vigorous English.'

They were quiet for a while and then Furii said, 'I think it is time, and that you are ready, to answer for yourself the question that you raised before. Are you getting sicker? Don't be afraid – you will not have to hang for your answer, whatever it is.'

Deborah saw herself as Noah, sending out a dove to scout the fearful country. After a time the dove came back, quaking with exhaustion. No green branch, but at least it was a return. 'Not sicker,' she said. 'Not sicker at all.'

'Not sicker . . .' Doctor Fried said at the meeting of the D-ward staff. '. . . Not sicker at all.'

The ward personnel listened politely and attentively, but it seemed unbelievable to them that the bursting stream of gibberish and the uncontrolled and useless violence was not a great change for the worse. Before, Deborah Blau had been morbid and silent or morbid and witty; she had had an immobile face and a sarcastic and superior manner. These were real signs of serious mental illness, but how she fitted the familiar form of D ward's patients. She was 'crazy', a word felt and used by most of them except in the presence of the doctors or when they thought they might be overheard. It was the penetrating but unspoken word in the air now.

'Well ... the burning business is slowing up a little ...' one of the attendants said, without much conviction.

'That would be her "new morality",' Doctor Fried answered with her little smile. 'She said that she does not wish to involve other patients in her sickness, so she must get her fires elsewhere. She has made some restrictions on the stealing.'

'Do they ... do they have considerations like that? I mean ... morals?' It was a new man asking. They all knew what the answer was supposed to be, but few of them really believed it. Only a few of the doctors really believed it and only some of the time.

'Of course,' Doctor Fried said. 'As you work here, you will often see evidences of it. There are many examples of such ethics or morals, which have moved "healthy" ones to awe over the years – the little nicety, the sudden and unexpected generosity of great cost to the patient, but present nevertheless to remind us and to kick the crutch from our complacency. I remember when I left my hospital in Germany, a patient gave me a knife to protect myself. This knife he had made in secret by grinding down a piece of metal for months and months. He had made it to save against the day that his illness would become too painful for him to bear.'

'And did you accept it?' someone asked.

'Of course, since his ability to give was an indication of health and strength. But because I was coming to this country,' she said with a gentle little smile, 'I gave the knife to one who had to stay behind.'

'She's a good speaker, don't you think?' Doctor Royson said as they left. He had come to the conference as Doctor Halle's guest and because he had worked for a while with some of the patients.

'Blau is one of her cases,' Doctor Halle said. 'Oh, yes, I forgot. Of course, you knew that.'

'Yes, I took over while she was away,' Doctor Royson said. 'How was it?'

'At first I thought it was her resentment that made the working so difficult – you know, having the regular therapist leave her – a rejection, you might say. But you know, that wasn't the case. It was something we don't like to face because we are doing medicine, and that's a science which doesn't admit of likes or dislikes. We just didn't get on. We didn't like each other. I think perhaps we were too much alike. . . .'

'Then it's no wonder you struck sparks.'

'Do you think there's any real progress in that Blau case? *She* seems to think so.' He turned a little and made a gesture towards Dr Fried. 'But . . .'

'I don't see any, but she would know.'

'She is a fine doctor – I wish I had her brains,' Royson said.

'She is brainy,' and Halle looked back at the chubby little woman who was still answering questions in the conference room, 'but after you know her a while, you'll find out that with little Clara Fried, brains are only the beginning.'

22

THROUGH THE DISTORTION of heat-watering air over the volcano, through the grey lava-flow desolation between eruptions, Deborah noticed the onset of a certain kindness towards her from the ward staff – a kindness that seemed to be more than form. A new attendant by the name of Quentin Dobshansky, one of the Good Ones, like McPherson, came to replace tired old Tichert; Mrs Forbes came back to work on Male Disturbed, in the other building, and another autumn yielded to another winter.

Winter was a hard season. The ancient and erratic heating system wheezed and clanged, overheating everyone to dullness when it was on and letting them all freeze when it wasn't.

'By what methods do they heat this place?' Lee asked, echoing eternal questions about eternal subjects. She was huddled with her coffee cup, trying to warm her hands.

'It's a system that Lucy's Abdicated First Husband the VIIIth thought up,' Helene said.

'The heating is taken care of by all the characters in the dreams we tell our doctors.'

'They don't hate us, though,' Mary chirped gaily, 'at least not me. They despise me intensely, but they don't hate me – because the Bible says not to!'

Deborah got up and went in search of warmth. Since the eruption of the volcano, the need to keep alert for backfire material had lessened, though the anguish had not. The volcano's fear-rage would still come and throw her against a wall with the force of its eruption, or send her running down the hall until she was stopped by a closed door or a wall. She was in pack every day, sometimes twice, and, once tightened in, she would let the fight explode and overcome her as violently as it would. Yet . . . yet they were all kinder, all the nurses and attendants, joking even, and giving little gifts of themselves.

'Don't you know why?' Furii said.

'No. I am exploding and they take time with me. Lots of times I feel the thing coming and I ask to get packed and they do it, although it takes time and energy, and afterwards, we sometimes even talk.'

'You see,' Furii said gently, 'when this volcano of yours broke, something else broke, too: your stoniness of expression. One sees you now reacting and living by looking at your face.'

Deborah went ice cold with the special fear that was many years old and from which she had protected herself at such great cost.

'*Nacoi . . . nacoi . . .*'

'What is it?' Furii asked.

'It was always . . . unmatching . . . what the face showed: "Why are you angry?" when I was not, and "Why are you scornful?" when I was not. It was part of the reason for a Censor and the set rules and Yri laws.'

'You are free of them now,' Furii said. 'Your face does not make enemies for you; it only shows a person reacting to what she feels. Anger and fear show also because you suffer them. But do not be frightened; no need any more to lie about anger and fear, and, best of all, enjoyment shows too, and fun, and hope also, and these expressions are not unmatching, as you call it, but are appropriate and will become more and more subject to your own conscious wish and choice.'

But Deborah was still frightened. Her facial expressions were a mystery to her, one that had never been solved. In memories whose meaning was still dark to her, she counted years and years of enemies made in ways which she could never explain. Part of it had been the look – must have been the look – some expression not hers which she had been wearing, a voice and a doer not herself and capable of turning allies into persecutors. Now that the volcano had melted her stone face it might all start over again: the *nacoi*-life to which she had no key and realities to which she could lay no claim.

The afternoon was cold and lowering, and coming back from the doctor's office she laughed at herself and at the attendant with her, shivering in the cold (real cold), while she alone, although close to the attendant's side, was also in cold (intra-regional fear) and cold (Yr-cold).

'Like to freeze you to death!' the attendant said. It was nice being spoken to in that way, so Deborah repaid the sense of equality with truth.

'You've only got one kind of cold; the kind coats can fix.'

The attendant sniffed. 'Don't you believe it,' she said, and Deborah remembered back, through a thousand falls and punishments, to McPherson saying, 'What makes you think you have a corner on suffering?'

'I'm sorry,' Deborah said, 'I didn't mean it as an insult.'

But the attendant was bitter and angry, and began to tell Deborah about how hard it was to raise children and work for long hours and low pay. Deborah seemed to hear into the attendant's mind, where the woman was saying also that the work was ugly: cleaning up messes from adult bodies and sitting in the midst of childish noises made by adult lungs and ingenuity. The woman was angry at Deborah, who was at that moment a symbol of 'the job', but Deborah felt that she was giving a confidence also. The dislike was impersonal and honest and therefore not hard to bear. At the door, whose lock and key were also symbols, the whole relationship ended; the attendant erased it as if it had never been, and her face was impassive as she walked away from her charge.

Deborah walked idly around the ward for a while. When the change of shift came on, she asked to be let into the bathtub room to be by herself for a little while. Inside, the heat was turned off, but by force of habit she went to the old radiator and sat down on its covered top. A window above it looked out over the lawn part of the hospital grounds, where there were trees and a thick hedge that concealed the wall – Deborah had named it the Preserve. The sun, ready to set, glittered beyond the hedge like a cold star, and the trees seemed bare and grey in the diffusing light. It was quiet. Yr was quiet and the Collect, for once, was silent also. All the voices in all the worlds seemed stilled.

Slowly and steadily, Deborah began to see the colours in the world. She saw the form and the colours of the trees and the walkway and the hedge and over the hedge to the winter sky. The sun went down and the tones began to vibrate in the twilight, giving still more dimension to the Preserve. And in a slow, oncoming way, widening from a beginning, it appeared to Deborah that she would not die. It came upon her with a steady, mounting clarity that she was going to be more than undead, that she was going to be alive. It had a sense of wonder and awe, great joy and trepidation. 'When will it begin?' she said to the gradual night. It came to her that it was already beginning.

The night had fully arrived when she opened the door of the bathtub room and went out on the ward again. The third dimension, the meaning, persevered in the bare lines of walls and doors and the planes of people's faces and bodies. There was a great temptation to watch – to keep seeing and hearing, sensing and revelling in the meaning and the light – the senses and planes of reality, but Deborah was the veteran of many deceits and she was cautious. She would subject this new thing to Furii's time-hunter and let it shoot its arrows.

She ate supper and found herself capable of suffering that she had to do it messily, with fingers and a wooden spoon. The food tasted. It was substantial under her teeth and afterwards she remembered having eaten it.

'Whatever this thing is ...' she muttered, '... I wonder when they will pull it out from under.' She spent the evening listening to the attendants talking to one another like lonely outpost sentinels in a strange and barren land. They wouldn't know what this thing was, but it was beginning to frighten Deborah because she didn't know what it was going to turn into. Maybe it was another part of the Game, that always recurring last laugh of the world.

When she gulped down her sedative and walked to bed she said to Yr, *Suffer, gods.*

Suffer, Bird-one, we are waiting ...

I have a question: Two natives are in a comic strip, but they don't know it, and think themselves alive. They are building a campfire on an island, which is really the back of a hippo who is standing in a river. They begin to cook their dinner. When the heat reaches through the hippo's hide, he gets up and walks away, carrying the natives with astonished faces. Then the reader of this comic strip laughs and turns the page on which are natives, astonishment, jungle, river, hippo, and fire. The question is: What can their faces show now? What can they do now?

One would have to wait in order to find out, Anterrabae said. *Who knows, this happening may be gone by tomorrow.*

You may not even have to do anything about it, Lactamaeon said. *You may not even have to think about it.*

Maybe it was just a symptom, Deborah said.

In the morning she lay in bed awake, but wondering if it would be wise for her to open her eyes. Someone was screaming in the hall, and she could hear a student close by – rustling apron and apprehension – trying to wake Dowben's Mary. Through her closed eyes the light from the morning sun was red. The lucky ones by the windows got all the benefit of the sun, but every morning the day reached out for all of them for a little while at least, and this morning it made Deborah search in her mind for something that had changed in her.

'Something happened to me . . .' she whispered to herself, '. . . something yesterday. What was it? What was it?'

'Come on, Miss Blau, rise and shine,' the student said.

'What's for breakfast?' Deborah asked, not wishing to give any of her questions away.

'Typical regional cooking.' Fiorentini's Mary chirped. 'They never say what region, but I have some ideas!'

'What kind of regional cooking do they have for people who are out of this world?' someone asked.

Then it came to Deborah what had happened last night, with the colour and the form and the meaning infusing it and the sense of life. Was it still there, waiting beyond the eyelid? She opened her eyes wide and at once. The world was still there. She got up, wrapped herself in her blanket, and went out on the hall and to the nursing station.

'Excuse me, do I see my doctor today?' She had been a thousand times a mendicant before that door, but this time it seemed to be different, although no one acted as if it were.

'Just a minute. Yes, you're down for off the ward today. Two o'clock.'

'Can I go by myself?'

The suspicion came up like a surgical mask over the nurse's face. 'I'll have to get a written order from the ward administrator. You know that by now.'

'Can I see him when he comes?'

'He's not going to be on the ward today.'

'Will you write my name down, please?'

'All right.' And the nurse turned away.

It sounded more like a maybe, but Deborah knew by now that it was not good form to seem too insistent, even though the world might be gone by the time the permission came through.

At her hour she was shy and frightened that speaking of it might end it, but after a time of groping she told Furii about the seeing and, more importantly, about the meaning and the thing that had come attached to the meaning: the slow, opening hope.

'It was not like what usually happens in Yr,' she said. 'It reminded me of you because it was just a simple statement in my mind that I was going to live, to come up alive.'

Furii gave her the familiar testing look. 'Do you believe that this is a true prognosis?'

'I don't want to say because I may have to hang by my thumbs from it.'

'No, you won't. Nothing will change for us.'

'Well . . . I think . . . I think that it may be true.'

'We prove it then,' Furii said. 'We get to work.'

They spent the time cutting ways to the old secrets and seeing facets of them that needed the new hunger for life to come real. Deborah saw that she had taken the part of the enemy Japanese as an answer to the hate of the ones at the summer camp, his foreignness and violence being an embodiment of anger. A part of the same insight opened on to the subject of martyrdom – that being martyred had something to do with Christ, the pride and terror of every Jew.

'Anger and martyrdom,' she said, 'that's what being a Japanese soldier was, and I gave the doctors the "good soldier" that they wanted. Anger and martyrdom . . . It sounds like something more . . . like the description of something I know . . .'

'What more?' Furii asked. 'It must have had many walls to have supported itself for all these years.'

'It's a description of . . . why . . . why, it's *grandfather*!' Deborah cried, having unearthed the familiar tyrannical Latvian to whom she had given such an unrecognizable mask. It was a description of him and it fitted him better than height or weight or number of teeth. 'The secret soldier that I was is a *mutu* – what Yr calls a kind of hiding image of my kinship with him.'

'Coming to see this . . . does it hurt so much?'

'A good hurt,' Deborah said.

'The symptoms and the sickness and the secrets have many reasons for being. The parts and facets sustain one another, locking in and strengthening one another. If it were not so, we could give you a nice shot of this or that drug or a quick hypnosis and say "Craziness, begone!" and it would be an easy job. But these symptoms are built of many needs and serve many purposes, and that is why getting them away makes so much suffering.'

'Now that I have the . . . realness . . . will I have to give up Yr . . . all of it . . . right away?'

'Never *pretend* to give it up. I think you will want to give it up when you have the real world to replace it, but there is no pact with me. I do not ask you to give up your gods for mine. When you are ready, you will choose.' Then she said gravely, 'Don't let them torture you every time you let some of the world's good light in your windows.'

The 'burn-squad' was waiting for her when she got back on the ward. It was Doctor Venner this time. She had nick-named him 'Lost Horizons' because he never seemed to see anyone, but kept looking out as if to sea, past the people he was supposed to be treating. The name had stuck. Now he was impatient because she had not been ready and waiting for his ministrations in a properly chastened frame of mind, because the burns had resisted for months now, and because cleaning them should have given her the pain she deserved and yet she seemed always above it. Deborah did not like Doctor Venner and she expressed this by joking to Quentin Dobshansky, who held the bandages and winced whenever the doctor's rough swabbing pulled the raw flesh away.

'Hold that arm still,' Venner growled at the limb held motionless before him. In his anger he jerked the swab hard and blood from the healthy tissue underneath welled up and covered the wound. 'Damn it' he breathed.

'Heck, Doctor Venner,' she said softly, 'you don't have to get angry. I've got a fake tumour that more than makes up for what I'm missing here.'

Dobshansky bit his lip to keep from laughing, but the instrument dug sharply again and he drew in his breath. 'Uhh! Easy, Deb!'

'The hurting is only theoretical, Quentin,' she said. 'What

hurts is being kicked by the forces that everyone else lives by and years of being nuts and not being able to tell anyone and have them believe you. Every time you double up with a theoretical tumour pain, some professor is there to tell you why it can't be hurting. As a courtesy, they give you a shot or two of the experience the other way.'

'Keep quiet!' Doctor Venner said. 'I'm concentrating on this.'

Dobshansky winked at the nurse who had come in and Deborah was grateful to them that they had permitted her to be a witness.

The New Doctor came up a few days later to do his stint as call-doctor for the day. 'It's time for another look at those burns,' he said.

'Venner was the last one and if he didn't hit bone, no one else will.'

The comment was disturbing and took New Doctor by surprise. 'I've been worrying about those burns,' he said quickly to cover his unprofessional reaction, and she caught him in another professional blunder as he remembered some page 892 of some tome that preached, 'Never Tell a Patient You Are Worried.' His surprise at what he had said was plain on his face, and he began the wiping away of the look, hastily and piecemeal, so that a part of it was left. 'Well, let's say *concerned*, and I thought of something that might just work.' He took a little tube of medicine out of his pocket. Then he dismissed the massing burn-squad and the two of them smiled a little at each other like conspirators. They both breathed easier.

He looked at her arms. The bandages were rank and the flesh around the burns was beginning to take on the mushi-ness of the burnt area.

'Well, we'll give it a try.' She saw in his face that the burns were worse than he had remembered. When he was through, he said, 'I tried to go easy. I hope it didn't hurt too much.'

'Don't worry,' Deborah said, and rose the tremendous distance from the falling Anterrabae to be capable of a smile. 'Someday, maybe it will.'

When the nurses cut the bandages two days later, the putrefaction was gone.

'What was that stuff he used?' The head nurse shook her head in wonder.

'He left it for her in number six cabinet,' said little Cleary.

Deborah turned to the nurse. 'I'll have my contribution ready.'

'And what is that?' she said with the impatience of the expert.

'Why, the smile.'

23

BECAUSE SHE WAS going to live, because she had begun to live already, the new colours, dimensions, and knowledges became suffused with a kind of passionate urgency. As form and light and law became more constant, Deborah began to look into the faces of people, to talk with them and hear them. Although she was shy and stunted in the subjects on which people spoke to one another, she began to find the D ward with its lost patients and harried staff too thin a reality. Impatient and eager on the hospital's ponderous wheel, she began her slow ascent; she could almost hear a creak as the wheel groaned under her weight. Bit by bit she regained the distance by which the doctors measured responsibility: Alone to Her Doctor's Office (100 ft × 1 hr sane); Alone on Front Grounds (200 ft × 3 hrs sane); Alone on Front and Back Grounds (1 mi. × 5 hrs sane); and at last she applied to go to B ward, where the foot-hour rule would be given the whole inward sweep of books and pencils and sketch pads. Now that she held this tremulous but growing conviction that she was alive, she began to be in love with the new world.

'If I'm alive, then I must be of their substance – the *same substance*, don't you see!' she told Furii in her excitement, gesturing outward to the world. The last time she had been

on B ward there had been only darkness and silence except
for the roaring of the Collect and the building up of the
volcano. She had been no one and nothing, but the way to
the bathroom and the way to the food and sedative line. This
time she took her bedding eagerly, looking into the faces
of the nurses, and asked their names and hoped for a room
up front where it was noisy and alive.

The head nurse cocked her head. 'You know Carla
Stoneham, don't you?'

'Is she back? I . . . I thought she was gone.'

'Well, she was an outpatient for a while,' the nurse said,
trying to keep anything but the dead level from her voice.
'She's back now.'

Carla was sitting on her bed. Looking at her, Deborah felt
a special warmth in the eye.

'Well, you girls know each other.' The nurse put the extra
blanket on the other bed and left.

'Hi, Deb . . .' Carla seemed glad to see her, but Deborah
could see that she was subdued because of shame, and Deborah's mind, warm as her eyes towards Carla, began to
plead: I am your friend – don't be ashamed because of this.
She closed her eyes and pushed the English words of commitment across her Yri tongue.

'I don't care if it is selfish. I'm glad you're here because
it's where I am.' Then she began to make her bed and put
her clothes away while they gossiped about this and that:
Miss Coral, Helene, Mary's latest crack, and the nurses on
B (which one would come if there was trouble and which
would not).

Then Deborah said, 'Grapevine never told me you were
back.' She looked straight at Carla while she said it, and
with that look she meant everything that would have been
an intrusion had it come in words.

'It gets awfully lonely out there, that's all,' Carla answered.
She had given Deborah the privilege of a question; Deborah
tried to make it a simple one.

'Was it hard to come back?'

'Well . . . it's being defeated,' Carla said, and she nodded
the question away with her head and went off, gently, on a

tangent. 'I was all alone in my job ... the long ride in the morning to work gets you kind of hypnotized and there was no one except the technicians and "good morning" and "good night". In the evenings I went to the movie show or stayed in my room and read technical books to catch up. Soon the streets began to remind me of the other streets back in St Louis and the way the days were back there – the feeling of it all seemed the same—'

The look of the familiar pain was stamped on Carla's face as she talked, but suddenly she pulled herself away from her thought. 'I'm not saying that no one succeeds,' she said hurriedly, 'or even that I won't make it again – it's just that I go out sometimes in defiance, when I'm not ready—' The ringing of a bell interrupted her. 'The OT shop is open,' she said. 'Come on – I'll show you around.'

Outside, the winter air was sharp with cold. Deborah found the world incomparably beautiful. Somewhere beyond the hedge of the Preserve there was smoke rising and she caught the smell of it occasionally. Next to her was a friend and in the craft shop a drawing pad waiting to be filled. She tried to stop the gratitude and hunger that were overflowing inside her, but her eyes filled with the colours and dimensions of the world and the laws of the consubstantial human race – motion and gravity, cause and effect, friendship and a sense of a human self. She heard a sound high up and behind her, and turning, saw Miss Coral waving from a window on D ward.

'She must be in seclusion again,' Carla said, counting the windows. They waved back and for a few moments drew signals in the air to talk to one another.

(I was in a fight) Miss Coral said, spreading her gestures in the space of the fenced window.

(I am free!) Deborah answered, breaking chains and doing a caper.

(How far?) Miss Coral asked, making the sign of looking out to sea.

Deborah made a wall with her arm and stopped before it with her hand.

(Nurse is coming!) Miss Coral shouted, hands to head for

the two wings of the white cap and then the flip of a key.

(Good-bye!) A quick wave and gone.

An attendant had come out the back door and seen them gesticulating in the walkway.

'What are you girls doing?' she asked.

'Just practising,' Carla said, 'just practising.' They walked on to the craft shop that was in one of the outbuildings.

The shop had a warm, normal look of work being done until one looked close and saw that it was only imitation. Patients were sewing or modelling in clay, reading or making collages with paste and bits of fabric. Most of their activity was make-work of the most obvious kind, and Deborah felt quietly embarrassed. Outcasts from the laws of the world seemed to be warming their hands before the illusion of satisfying labour. They were vainly seeking its textures, paper, and materials, and ravelling out old woollen scarves to extract reality from them. In a land where usefulness was extolled above all, the 'therapeutic' make-work seemed to Deborah an unconscious slap at the pride which the patients were supposed to be developing. An Occupational Therapy worker in her blue-and-white-striped uniform came towards them.

'Well, hello, Carla,' she said, a little too cheerily; then, looking at Deborah, 'Have you brought us a visitor?'

'Yes,' Carla said. 'We just wanted to look in. This is Deborah.'

'Why, of course!' the worker said enthusiastically. 'I've seen you before – it was up on D ward!'

Heads shot up from work. Deborah saw in her mind a sudden vision of the occupational-therapy worker in the clothes of a hunter shooting over a wind-bent wheatfield and causing the scared and sudden rising of a flock of birds. Carla understood what was happening and turned away for a moment. Then she turned back, and said, 'She's on B ward now, and she's my roommate.'

A few of the faces relaxed and a few of the hands moved to work again.

They stayed for a while and Deborah was introduced to

some of the male patients, wondering as she heard their names what could possibly make *men* sick. When the two girls left, they walked towards A ward, which was open and where there was a coffeepot for both patients and staff.

'It's mostly for them,' Carla said, 'but it shows you what you can hope for, and maybe, if no one wants any coffee, they will let us have what's left.' Deborah did not want to go in. One shot over the wheatfield was enough for the day.

'Carla . . . you've been out – I mean really out. Is that the way it is outside when one of us comes into a room?'

'Sometimes,' Carla said. 'Getting a job, you have papers you have to show, and sometimes there's a social worker checking on you. It can be very, very tough, but people are sometimes better than you think they will be. In lots of jobs you have to show your "sanity papers" and they make a big thing of it, but the best people on the outside make you feel honoured to share the name "person" with them. The part that's hardest is the feeling you get when everyone is polite and says "good morning" and "good night" while the distance between you and them is getting wider and wider. The doctors say that it's the fault of the sick one – my fault. If I were less anxious, they say, it would be easier for friendships to come, but that's easy to say. I don't think any of the doctors ever tried to break into a new group with a heavy stigma on their heads and having their first acceptance in that group hinge on pity or morbid fascination.'

Deborah laughed. 'Doctors! Spend a glorious year in Foreign Travel. Visit your nuthouse as a patient!'

Carla laughed. 'Tour without your prestige, your civil rights, or your self-respect! Thrill to the false fine-fine when you are on the receiving end!'

For a while they indulged themselves in the game of getting even with all the doctors who used their prestige and a certain sense of private ownership of reality to separate themselves from their patients. It occurred to Deborah that Doctor Halle and Furii and New Doctor would not need Foreign Travel because they had never completely shut the gate between themselves and their patients.

'I forgot to tell you,' Deborah said when they were walking back to the ward, 'it's about Helene. You know, we've been laughing at her jokes, but until lately, they were awfully cold. Somehow lately, there's been something like a caring in her.' Deborah told Carla how Helene had been at the door when she was leaving the D ward. Helene had waited until they were alone for a moment and then had said, 'Why couldn't I be the one going?' Deborah had said, 'Well, why not?' and she had answered abstractedly, 'Maybe ... maybe ...' as if she were thinking of it for the first time. Helene had never been so unguarded, even in her sleep. Of course, when the nurse came to take Deborah down, she had covered it up, putting out her fist and calling Deborah 'a stupid bitch' and yelling after her, 'Don't you forget it!' But Deborah had smiled, knowing that Helene had been cursing the Maybe and not her at all.

They went through the keyless south door and met New Doctor coming out. When he saw Deborah, his face brightened. 'Hey!' (with the eye-deep smile) 'I heard about your change of address. Congratulations!' His tone had respect. She had not taken into account that there might be some heady wine in the first tasting of the new world. *But he may not really know enough to judge*, Deborah whispered to the gods of Yr in propitiation.

'Something strange – something I never thought about before—' Deborah said to Doctor Fried, '—that Jews have their own form of intolerance. I never knew anyone well who was not Jewish, and I never gave my last particle of trust to someone who wasn't Jewish. Doctor Hill, the new doctor, and Carla are Protestants, and Helene is Catholic, and Miss Coral has kind of a frantic-Baptist background ...'

'Well?'

'Well, I've been doing something funny in my mind. I've been *making* them Jewish so that they could be close to me.'

'How do you do this?'

'Well, it's one step more than forgetting that they're gentiles – the ones we were always told betray you in the end. I also have to forget that they're not Jewish, too. Yesterday, Carla asked me what I thought of someone. I said, "You know that type – he wants to be an individualist, so he cries through Purim." It took her look, that sudden stop of surprise, and a long, long time to remind me that she didn't know what I was talking about *because she isn't Jewish.*'

'Can you let them be what they are and be what you are, and still love them?'

'The hospital gave me that,' Deborah said slowly. 'When you're nuts, it hardly matters that you're a nutty Jew or a nutty Holy Roller. . . .'

Doctor Fried's thoughts drifted for a moment to an article she had written once discussing the question of how a doctor tells a recovering patient that her own newborn health must grapple with symptoms of madness in the world. The health in this girl might weigh someday towards larger reason and freedom. Then discipline caught her up and she said, 'How glad I am that you have discovered this! But beside the point. You know, I have listened to that memory you told me – the one about your almost having thrown your sister out of the window when she was a baby – and something has been bothering me about it; something is not right about it. Tell me the thing again.'

Deborah told the memory again: how she had reached into the bassinet for the little darling whose ugliness was so apparent to her and so invisible to everyone else; about the window out of which she had held the little creature, the arrival of Mother, and the shame of hating and being caught at it; how later, when love came, she had shivered at thinking that she might have ended Suzy's life that day. Over the whole happening brooded the spirits of the knowing, shamed, and sorrowful parents, silent in their charity.

'Was the window open?' Furii asked.

'Yes, but I remember opening it wider.'

'Did you open it all the way?'

'Enough to lean far out with the baby.'

'I see. Then, after you opened the window and tested it by leaning out, you went and got the baby?'

'No – I picked her up first and then decided to kill her.'

'I see.' Furii leaned back like Mr Pickwick after a good dinner. 'Now I turn detective,' she said, 'and I tell you that your story stinks to heaven! A five-year-old lifts up a heavy baby, carries it to the window, holds it on the sill with her own body while she opens the window and practises leaning out, lifts the baby out over the sill, and holds it at arms' length out the window ready to drop it. Mother comes in and in a flash of speed this five-year-old whips the child inside where it starts to cry so that the mother takes it—'

'No – by that time it was back in the bassinet.'

'Most interesting,' Furii said. 'Now, am I crazy or did you make that story up when you were five years old and walked in and saw that baby lying there and hated it enough to want to kill it?'

'But I remember . . .'

'You may remember hating, but the facts are against you. What did your mother say when she came in? Was it: "Put that baby down!" or "Don't hurt the baby!"?'

'No, I remember clearly. She said, "What are you doing in here?" and I remember that the baby was crying then.'

'What astonishes me about this whole business is that I was so busy listening to the emotional content – the hatred and the pain – that I lost the facts and they had to shout at me again and again before I could hear them. The hatred was real, Deborah, and the pain also, but you were just not big enough to do any of the things you remember doing, and the shame you say your parents felt all these years was only your guilt at wishing your sister dead. With the false idea of your own power (an idea, by the way, that your sickness has kept you from ever growing out of), you translated those thoughts into a memory.'

'It might as well have been real; I lived with it for all those years as if it were real.'

'Yes, that's true,' Furii said smiling, 'but no longer will you be able to flagellate yourself with that particular stick. Our would-be murderess is no more than a jealous five-year-old looking into the cradle of the interloper.'

'Bassinet,' Deborah said.

'Those ones on legs? My God, you couldn't even reach into it then. I turn in my detective badge tomorrow!'

Deborah was back in the room being five again and

standing with her father for a view of the new baby. Her eyes were on the level of the knuckles of his hand, and because of the ruffles on the bassinet she had to stand on her toes to peep over the edge. 'I didn't even touch her . . .' she said 'I didn't even touch her. . . .'

'As long as you are back in those days, we might as well see them together,' Furii said.

Deborah began to talk about the year of brightness before the gloom had settled in for good. She explored the brief and magical time when looking forward had been with expectation. Now it came to her that for that one year, even with the false weight of the murder and her dethronement as princess, she had not yet been under the sentence of destruction. There had been that season – it came again now with a powerful surge of meaning – when she had still been committed to life and had lived with a joyful hunger because of a present and a future.

She came from the sunshine of that fifth year with tears running down her face. Furii saw the tears and nodded. 'I approve.'

Deborah understood now that the very early happiness was proof that she was not damned genetically – damned bone and fibre. There had been a time when she suffered, yet shone with life. She began to cry in full earnest. It was still a novice's cry, harsh, random, and bitter, and when it subsided, Furii had to ask if it had been a 'good one', with healing in it.

'What's the date?' Deborah asked.

'December fifteenth. Why do you ask?'

'I was just thinking out loud. Yri time is internal. You know about the two calendars and how days are measured between meetings for trial by the Collect.'

'Yes.'

'Well, I just remembered that today is *Fourth Englift towards Annot*. It means that we are on a rising calendar.' She was still too frightened to say that, by some miracle, it seemed to have raised her from Hell to Purgatory.

When she left the doctor's office to return to the ward, an icy rain was falling. Cold of the casual world made her shiver, and she was grateful because it was a cold responsible to the laws and seasons of the earth. In the Preserve the tree limbs were wet and black. She saw Idat high above her, walking on a great branch. Her veils were all shimmering like the air above a fire.

Suffer, victim, Idat greeted her.

Oh, Idat! Deborah answered in Yri. *The earth is so good now – why is it walking in ruin to have both Yr and Elsewhere?*

Am I not beautiful in this tree? the goddess asked. Questions had a particularly poignant quality in Yri because they used a familiar form and because they gave hint of the quick and ephemeral quality of asking anything. Idat was the Dissembler and her answers were always difficult. *I think I shall be a woman always,* she said now. *You can have something on which to model yourself.*

Deborah knew that she could never use Idat for a model. They were different in every way, mainly in that Idat was a goddess and impossibly beautiful, not bound to the world at all. When Idat cried, her tears crystallized into diamonds splashed on her face. Her laws were not those of earth.

Stay with me, Deborah begged to Yr, using the word which meant forever. There was no answer.

At dinner Carla seemed particularly nervous. Her hands were shaking and she had a pale, sick look. Deborah tried to warm her by looking at her with 'pure' Earth eyes, but it was no use. When coffee came, Carla tried to pick up her cup, but it leaped from her shock-wired hands and fell, breaking like the brittle crust of reality on which they all walked. While the sound of the breaking crockery still echoed, the others at the table made quick reference to their own places on that crust, while the fright ran all along the familiar pathway traces inside of them.

Then Deborah took Carla's hands and held them. The hands rested. Carla rested. The act was a sudden thing, more sudden than the recollection that Yri time and season were measured by the internal climate and that *fourth Englift towards Annot* was a strong position to venture from;

more sudden than the recollection that a debt to Sylvia still had to be paid and that she still wanted to give a kiss to McPherson, long away. She looked at Carla. The face was still pale and slapped-looking, but it was better than it had been. The hands relaxed. No one said anything and soon the nurse whose particular job it was to signal the end of the meal raised her discreet white arm, just enough to be seen, and everyone, more or less, got up and went. It was then, at the signal, that Deborah realized that she had unhidden herself for Carla. On the way up the stairs it came to her that perhaps – no, perhaps was too strong – that three short of maybe, she might be more than only an ex-almost-murderess. She might be something more nearly – the word hit like a fist, but it was there and she could not cancel it or keep it out of her mind – more nearly *good*.

24

HER DREAM BEGAN with winter darkness. Out of this darkness came a great hand, fisted. It was a man's hand, powerful and hollowed by shadows in the wells between bones and tendons. The fist opened and in the long plain of the palm lay three small pieces of coal. Slowly the hand closed, causing within the fist a tremendous pressure. The pressure began to generate a white heat and still it increased. There was a sense of weighing, crushing time. She seemed to feel the suffering of the coal with her own body, almost beyond the point of being borne. At last she cried out to the hand, 'Stop it! Will you never end it! Even a stone cannot bear to this limit . . . even a stone . . . !'

After what seemed like too long a time for anything molecular to endure, the torments in the fist relaxed. The fist turned slowly and very slowly opened.

Diamonds, three of them.

Three clear and brilliant diamonds, shot with light, lay in the good palm. A deep voice called to her, 'Deborah!' and then, gently, 'Deborah, this will be you.'

25

ON THE FIRST of January, with eagerness outrunning terror, Deborah went home for a five-day visit. Although she knew that she wore a strange look, that besides the scars of scrapings and burnings, a subtler mark was on her – an aura of withdrawal and loneliness – hunger for the new world propelled her into it.

She was received at home as if she had won the world. Suzy had been warned, Jacob had been warned, Grandmother and Grandfather had been warned, and all the old aunts and uncles warned, so that they held their love up, quivering with pity and fear, to show her that it was still whole. All her favourite foods were served and all her favourite people came to bear witness to the fact that 'nevertheless' and 'no matter what . . .'

Deborah tried to eat the holiday food and speak to the people who came to see her, but exhaustion would claim her as she sat. The hospital relationships had been brief and fleeting and never complicated by more than two or three people at a time and conversation ended abruptly when darkness fell on any of the speakers. Now here was chatter and threads of talk that wove in and out like a complicated cat's cradle. It was not possible to tell them how immense she found the distance between herself and the rest of the human race, even if she were of human substance.

Jacob's warmth and pride, pathetic and vulnerable, flowed towards her as he saw her sitting again at his table. 'I'll bet they don't serve a piece of meat like this at That Place.'

Deborah was about to answer that the cutlery alone was sufficient challenge, but she caught herself in time.

'Soon you'll be home for good,' he said.

Deborah paled so markedly that Esther threw herself into the talk like a suicide from a skyscraper. 'Well, we'll see, we'll see – I think the mushrooms are delicious – you see, Debby, all your favourite foods!'

Suzy sat across the table looking at Jacob and Esther and the homely, tired, older sister who was really younger than she, and who was being feasted and catered to as if her homecoming were some kind of miracle. She knew that she had to protect this latest Debby. It was not the sister she had wanted – the prom-going sister, all boy-friends, college football games, and glamour – but in her somewhere, and by some mistaken magic, the family happiness and peace rested.

'Look, Debby,' she said, 'Mother and Daddy told me already about that place not being a school, so if everybody would stop dying over the big secret, it'd be a lot easier.'

It would be easier, she thought, to go into the bedroom and make a telephone call, and tell her friend that she would not go on the outing they had planned for so long. Mother and Daddy needed her now, and Debby needed her, too, in a frightening sort of way. It was really too bad. . . . She felt the tears coming because she had wanted to go on this trip so much. She dared not wipe her eyes where they could see her.

She got up, knowing that they wanted to talk without her. 'Excuse me, I have to call Annette.'

'You're going with them, aren't you?' Esther asked, remembering how long Suzy had been talking about their 'weekend'.

'No . . . I'll go next time.'

'Is is because I'm here?' Deborah said.

'No – no, I just don't *want* to, this time.'

A bad lie. Deborah's mind, already exhausted and dulled by another day in the world, grappled for Suzy's feeling. 'Were they supposed to come up here first or something?' she asked.

Suzy turned, and almost answered, but the open mouth bit it back, and she said, 'You're not here that much. I want to see *you* this week.'

'Don't *mother* me, *tell* me!' Deborah said, sinking under the world.

'No!' Suzy shouted, and she turned and went in to make her call.

'She really loves you very much,' Esther said. 'The whole family is doing everything it can – all the roads have been smoothed over.' All Deborah heard were the sounds of her own gasps of exhaustion as she climbed an Everest that was to everyone else an easy and a level plain. As she reeled and pulled on the endless, vertical cliff, she felt that every favour, every easing, was an unpaid debt heaped upon her by loving tormentors and weighing like lumps of lead. Among equals gratitude is reciprocal; her gratitude to these Titans, who called themselves average and were unaware of their own tremendous strength in being able to live, only made her feel more lost, inept, and lonely than ever.

When Deborah had gone to bed, Esther and Jacob came embarrassedly to her bedside with the ration of sedatives prescribed by the hospital. As Deborah took them, Jacob looked away, but when he kissed her good night he said winningly, 'It's nice here, isn't it? It's where you belong.' The tumour heaved inside her. He continued, 'Debby, you don't need to stay with all those . . . those screaming women.'

'What screaming women?' Deborah asked, wondering if he had ever heard her louder than a whisper, and hoping with all her soul that he had not.

'Well, when we visited . . . we heard it—'

The pain of looking at him escaped in a laugh. 'Oh, I know – that must have been big, dumb old Lucy Martenson. She gets even with everybody by playing Tarzan out the front windows of the D ward and scaring the visitors to death.'

It had never occurred to Jacob that the screamer who still haunted his dreams might just be a person, someone named Lucy, and the realization eased him a little, but he hugged Deborah hard when he said good night.

In the dark her room was luminous with Yri personages. *We never hated you*, Lactamaeon said, shining on his hard-ridden horse. *The cruelty was for protection!* Anterrabae said in antiphon, waving a sheaf of sparks in his hand.

We came in the era of dryness and the death of hope, called Lactamaeon.

We came with gifts, said Anterrabae. *When you were laughing nowhere else, you were laughing with us.*

She knew that it was the truth. Even now, delighting in a world of rich colour and odours that actually referred to what one was smelling; even profoundly in love with cause and effect, optics, sonics, motion, and time all obedient to their laws; she wondered if Yr would be a fair trade for all of it. Of course, the Yr she mant was the once-upon-a-time Yr; not the anarchic Yr of world's end, the latter-day Yr that sent its queen hurtling endless distances into pits of mindlessness, but the ancient kingdom of the early years: with a crag for an eagle, an illimitable sky, a green landfall where wild horses grazed, and falls with Anterrabae that showered light behind them.

The change had begun with the coming of the Censor after a long time of horror that she now knew had been the collision of the two worlds. He had promised protection and had told her that he would keep the worlds separate so that she might go safely between them, paying lip service to the grey and lonely Earth while being free in Yr. In the times of greatest joy, the happiness was so great that her feet could not bear the ground and she went to flight. The time of the pure flight, the joyful and perfect flight, had been pitifully short, and the Censor had begun to rule like a tyrant in both worlds. Yr still gave beauty and great joy, but the beauty and joy were at the tyrant's erratic whim.

Now the choice was to be made again, but this time the scale that weighed the Earth's virtues had a new quantity to add to the rest – hope, the little, little Maybe. Still the Earth was a place full of peril and treachery, especially for an alien. The sedative began to dull her senses, but at the last moment of vision the brightness of Yr prevailed.

Suzy stayed home the next day and the next. Members of the family were still coming for visits, carefully grouped according to the state of their ignorance about Deborah's 'condition'. She had brought a package of her drawings home to show Esther, who had always been her first judge, and Esther displayed them proudly to group after group of aunts and great aunts, who looked with the bemused and tolerant pride of relatives. There were no hospital scenes at all, but there was Helene, a string-haired, vacant-eyed mad-woman looking into a mirror at the lovely college friend of the photograph, and there was Constantia and the two nurses it took to give her a walk seen as tiny figures in a Preserve that went off into infinite distance. These and others she had Deborah explain for the technical aspects. Most of the visitors contented themselves with extravagant praise such as they always gave, leaving with a kiss and a joke for Suzy about her latest conquest. ('No, Aunt Selma, he was *weeks* ago – I just went to the party with him.')

At dinner, Esther praised Deborah's poise and charm, while it seemed to Deborah that Suzy had somehow darkened over these two days. She had been free to go out and leave the prodigal elder sister to all the praises, but she had stayed. Was it perhaps the virulence after all – the slow poison of Deborahness which conscious will told her did not exist, but which still whispered, 'They lie! They lie!' deep in the places beneath logic and will.

She took her sedative early that night and went to sleep. As she drifted away, she heard Suzy's and Esther's voices from the living room. They were voices of argument, and full of anguish. 'God help us!' Deborah said, and slept.

'You don't hear them,' Suzy groaned, 'because when it isn't about Debby, you just don't hear anything, but I'm more than just a careless and brainless dope!'

'You're not being fair,' Esther said. 'It's that she's only home for a few days so we seem to be making a bigger fuss.'

'Every letter,' Suzy cried, 'every visit that you make to her! I draw, too; I dance, and I wrote two of the songs for the camp follies last year. They may not be as "profound" as Debby's pictures, but you never stop Grandma or invite Aunt Natalie and Uncle Matt to hear the new song that *I* wrote or the smart thing that *I* said.'

'Don't you see, you stupid girl,' Esther said almost savagely, 'I don't have to! Praising you is bragging. Praising Deborah is – excusing—'

Their voices were so loud that Jacob came in from the bedroom angrily and growled, 'Enough! You'll wake the dead!'

They all caught the slip, the unconscious but accurate allusion to the drugged and sleeping cause of all these years of heartache and argument. They went to bed guiltily and angrily, loving and despairing.

When the visit was over, Deborah went back to the hospital with a suitcase full of new clothes.

26

SPRING MOVED IN again and winter drew off the Preserve and off the streets that led to the town. Deborah still in the first urgency of hunger and love for the world's forms and colours, had radiated her artistic gift into a dozen media and styles. The materials in the craft shop were scanty, but she worked with whatever there was: silk-screen and block-printing, water colour and *gouache*. She yearned to play with all the toys of the earth, while Yr and the world's darker parts fought it out inside her. To Earth's usages and people she felt she could never come, but to the material things there was new access and freedom and great reward. A new patient asked her what she was, meaning her religion, and she found herself answering, 'A Newtonian'.

The new patient was very like Helene. Deborah felt that, underneath her vagueness and sudden crying out as if she had been shot, there was a trueness and a strength. Her name was Carmen, her father was a multimillionaire, and Deborah knew that she was destined for a long stay on D ward. The three-month 'honeymoon' that most people spent clutching the last rags of sanity to cover an awful nakedness was almost over for her. Sometimes, when Carmen passed, Carla and Deborah looked at each other and said with a look: When she blows, she's going to cover the ceiling.

'Hey, Carmen – let's go over to A ward and play ping-pong.'

'I can't. My father's coming to visit this afternoon.'

'Do you want us around or not?' Carla said, and Deborah knew that she was volunteering their aid. Though they were no beauties, she and Carla would wash up, get combed and rigged, to help their ward-mate by running interference between Carmen's father and the more bizarre-looking of ward B's cuckoos.

'No,' Carmen said in her listless way, 'he wouldn't understand. I just hope I can do it . . . just right.'

'Which is how?' Deborah asked.

'Agreement . . . always. Just absolute . . . agreement.'

It was Sunday and the craft shop was closed. There was a weekend desertedness about everything. Even in the safety of the hospital, Sundays were hard to take. Carla described how agonizing they had been when she was 'outside' working, and Deborah herself remembered how treacherous the world made its Sundays. On regular days the Semblance could be pulled up like a screen over body and mind, but Sunday called itself Rest and Freedom, and threw one off guard. Sunday promised leisure, peace, holiness, and love. It was a restatement of the wish for human perfection. But it was on Sunday that the Semblance never fully covered, and Sunday afternoon was a frantic struggle to hide the other worlds before Monday arrived with its demand that the lies be repeated and the surface be perfect.

Deborah and Carla ambled idly in the half-warm mists of the early spring, looking at the cracks that winter had left in the walkway and playing their dreamers' game, which they had made up to pass the time. In it they would shatter the world a dozen times and rebuild it, half as a punishment, half in a secret, fragile hope.

'In my university, we won't allow any special groups or cliques.'

'In my factory, the bosses will work on the most routine jobs just so they can see how murderous they are.'

But it was hospitals that they knew best and they built and staffed hospitals endlessly, equipping and administering them as the main part of the game. As they talked, they found themselves walking far beyond the doctors' buildings and student nurses' residence.

'I would do away with all the bars on the windows,' Carla said.

Deborah wasn't sure. 'The patients would have to be strong enough to stand it, first,' she said. 'Sometimes you have to fight what won't yield and put yourself where it's safe to be crazy.'

'Let's make our doctors-on-call really on call.'

'All my attendants will spend a week as patients.'

They found themselves in the meadow far beyond the last hospital building.

'Look where we are.'

'I'm not allowed out here,' Deborah said.

'Neither am I.'

They felt good. The afternoon was settling into evening and a light rain was beginning to fall, but neither of them could bear to part with this small and special mutiny against Sunday, supervision, and the world. They sat in the field, stupid with pleasure and let the Sunday God's rain fall on them. The day went to twilight. The rain got cold. They stood up in their sopping clothes and began wistfully to walk back towards the hospital.

As they neared the last building, they were seen by Henson and little Cleary, who had come out of Annexe 3 and were going towards the main building.

'Hey, you girls – do you have night privileges?'

'No,' Carla said. 'We were just going in now.'

'All right then.' The two attendants waited for them, flanking them when they came. It was not the way to go back; they could not go back that way, not after the freedom, the laughing, and the good rain. They looked at each other. Their eyes said, 'No.' When they came close to the door, the attendants closed in automatically; and so, defeated, they went in. On the other side of the door the moment came. Carla and Deborah saw it together, and, as if they had been trained for it all their lives, they took it together. Henson and Cleary had relaxed unconsciously.

Beyond the door was a set of swinging doors, and when they had all passed through them, Carla and Deborah simply turned on the same footfall, back through the doors, which swung back on the surprised attendants, and out the front door without a break in stride. As they ran, they heard the buzzer that signalled to the hospital a patient's escape.

They ran, laughing until they were breathless, for a long, long time, down the dark back roads. The rain beat hard on them and there was a fast rack riding the sky. Anterrabae was singing gloriously out of Yr, songs of the beauties of the world which he had not given for many, many years. Deborah and Carla ran on until the breath sobbed out of them and their sides ached, and then they slowed down, shivering with cold and freedom. From a distance a light came on. It was a car.

'They sent searchers out!' Carla said breathlessly, and they dived together into a side ditch until the car passed. After the light had disappeared in the rain, the fugitives came out of the ditch and walked on, laughing because they were quick and able. After a while they saw another car.

'More searchers?'

'Don't flatter yourself, nut. It's still a public road.'

'Might as well play it safe, though . . .' and they dived again for the ditch.

Huddled cold and alert in their hiding place, Deborah wondered for the first time what they intended to do. They had no dry clothes and no money. They had no plan and no desire to do any more than they were doing. She tried to remember what Furii had taught her about doing what she really wanted, and sat back against the embankment wondering what it was. Beside her, Carla was shaking a stone from her shoe. When the car passed they clambered up, looking like twins for the mud, and went on walking.

'We have to turn back sometime,' Deborah said aloud.

'Sure,' Carla answered. 'I see my doctor tomorrow. I just had to be alone, that's all, not led or taken.'

Deborah smiled in the darkness. 'Of course. That's what I wanted.'

It was a long walk back. They sang through some of it

and laughed at the way they slid in their sopping shoes. They were not 'caught' until they were through the front gate and inside the front door of the B-C-D ward building. In retaliation, it seemed, for having gone and come with such sweet ease, they were phalanxed and separated. Two attendants guarded Deborah while she took a bath. They were Second Night Staff, which meant that it must be after midnight.

'You'll be in for it now,' one of them said self-righteously.

'Do I have to go . . . up?'

'You behave here and take your sedative and go to bed and you'll be here tonight,' the attendant said. 'You girls will have to be in seclusion.'

After the bath Deborah and her guard passed Carla and her guard on the way to the end of the hall, where a small group of rooms were kept for seclusion. Their glances, still free, caught over the heads of the nurses and they winked at each other. Later, when Deborah began drifting towards sleep, she thought: It may be a hell of a price. But she remembered the smell of the rain.

A new doctor, a Dr Ogden, was administrator for B ward. Deborah did not know him yet and couldn't tell what he was like. She hadn't seen Carla since they had exchanged the wink of complicity. All she could do was to try to remember all the grapevine talk about escapes in the past, and think of something that would make their reasons sound good enough. At 11.00 that morning, she was sent down to the administration offices under guard. The attendant knocked at Dr Ogden's door.

'Come in.' Deborah went in and there, sitting at the desk, was Doctor Halle. The surprise and delight she felt must have been spread all over her face, since he smiled slightly and said, 'Doctor Ogden is down with the flu, so I am taking over the B-ward work for a while. Being here for B-ward duties keeps things straight.' Then he leaned back, rubbing his thumbs together. 'What's it all about?'

She told him where they had been. He stopped her twice for details and when she was finished asked, 'Whose idea was this in the first place?'

She groped for an explanation. There was an Yri word that described how they had felt and its presence in her mind made it difficult to concentrate on speaking English. She decided at least to translate the single word and hope that he could understand. After her false start he looked at her and said, 'Just tell me.'

'Okay ...' She hesitated because of the awful need to sound sane. 'Well ... if you're clumsy and bungling the way I am, you venerate people who aren't. Where ... I ... Where I came from we called such people *atumai*. For such people the extra step is not there to trip them, and the string that they tie packages with is never two inches too short. The traffic lights are always with them. Pain comes when they are lying down and ready for it and the joke when it is fitting to them to laugh. Yesterday, I got to have that *atumai*, just for a while. Carla had it, too. We both had it together. You don't decide to sneeze, you just do it. No one had the idea or was the leader; we just did it and were.' She thought of the way they had swung back together through that second door and the smile came back and broke away from her.

'Was it fun?' he asked.

'It sure was!'

'All right,' he said. 'I'm going to talk to Carla for a while and I want you to wait outside.'

She left the office and saw Carla, right outside, waiting her turn likewise guarded and looking very frightened. Her eyes questioned. Deborah shrugged the imperceptible shrug of the experienced patient, prisoner, spy, or nun. Carla's eyes took the gesture like a blow. She went in. After what seemed a long while, she stuck her head out and motioned to Deborah.

'Come in – he wants to see us together.'

This time it was the guards who exchanged glances.

Deborah went in, scenting the air. Doctor Halle looked very grim, but Deborah breathed out with relief when she saw that he was fighting a smile.

'You broke hospital rules – eight of them, I believe,' he said. 'Very reprehensible. Your descriptions of your actions tally with each other's. It was fun, wasn't it? It was shared fun. That's rare here. I'm kind of proud of you. . . .' He rearranged his look towards discipline. 'I see no reason to change the status of your privileges. That's all.'

They left, closing the door behind them. Doctor Halle swivelled around in his chair to look out the window. Outside, the trees were in small leaf, the springtime filling out along the branches. The hedge was raining green. He thought of the two girls in the stormy night, walking and singing, and of a trip he had once taken, running away. 'Kids!' he exclaimed. In his voice there was impatience, admiration, and a little kernel of envy.

'Where's Carmen?' Carla asked Deborah. 'I want to tell her that it's all okay. She saw us go in the afternoon and she must have heard what happened.'

'I don't know, I haven't seen her.'

They asked the nurse.

'Carmen's gone home. She left last night.'

'But didn't her father come just to visit?'

'Yes,' the nurse said, 'but I guess he changed his plans. All I know is that she left with him about seven last night.' The nurse's tone told them to ask no more, so they questioned each other. 'What could it have been?'

'Terry, did you see Carmen yesterday?'

'Yeah – I saw her.'

'What happened?'

'She disagreed.'

Deborah and Carla looked at each other, shivering, with the world's perversity and Doctor Halle's praise circling each other in their ears.

'My parents—' Deborah said. She knew that they had seen more of her hatred than her love, but they had let her stay. They had let her stay without a sign of improvement for a long, long time. They had never demanded of her a recovery to heal their prestige. She looked down and found her hands working in Yri again, passionately, framing words to speak to her own mind. Carla, sealed in her own cell and shut off at the eyes from all else, filled in her special words.

'It was freedom they gave me, after all. Carmen's didn't give her a chance, but mine . . .'

It came to Deborah that it was her parents who had bought this fight for her. They could have cut her off from the minute that she failed to make their progress. They had kept faith with a future which might never sing their praises.

'Carla . . . if I weren't scared to death of it, I would be so grateful!'

27

DEAD PALE, cold-handed, in a lilac-flowered dress that ill suited the lithe tiger wearing it, Helene came to B ward. Her 'normal' smile seemed wired, like a booby trap. When Deborah and Carla told her they were glad to see her, she told them they were hypocrites and liars, and her true smile crept behind the display one, so that they saw she was inhabiting her body and they were happy for her.

They took her over to the craft shop when she was given her privileges. Deborah went, too, because she remembered that it was a wheatfield and that the hunter there had a very sudden gun. With Helene's violent past, legends of which were still current, the gun would be a cannon.

Carla left early for her doctor's hour and they didn't see her again until just before supper. She came quietly out on the hall where Deborah and Helene were sitting with sketch pad and curlers, and walked over to them.

'Deb – it's about Carmen.' She handed her the newspaper clipping. Newspapers were not allowed on B ward, but there was a brisk bootleg trade going on. Deborah looked at it quickly and slipped it in her sketch pad. The headline said, MAGNATE'S DAUGHTER SUICIDE. She held the pad so no one could see the clipping and read it through. Under the headline there was an article with details about the mess that can be made when a human being fires a gun into her ear.

'Do you know her? I mean did you know her?' Helene asked. 'How long was she here?'

'Just long enough to learn to disagree,' Carla said.

'She could have made it,' Deborah said flatly, as she stood up.

'Oh, Deb, how can you be sure?'

'You're not just rubbing it in good to get a little free suffering out of it?' Helene asked in her bitter voice.

'I didn't say that she *would* have made it, but that she *could* have.'

Their voices brought others out of their rooms. Everyone knew what the talk was about and there was a rippling tension on the ward. The nurses stood by, not knowing whether to speak or be silent, and Deborah began to feel the mood was less about Carmen's suicide than an argument between the cynicism that was in each of them and the blind, small longing to fight.

To her surprise, Deborah found herself on the side of the little Maybe. She knew what she was thinking, but wondered if she could speak to these women who were both so much saner and so much more terrified than the D-ward patients were.

'Oh, Deb, you said yourself that Carmen was going to blow sky-high any minute,' Carla said.

Deborah looked at Carla, wondering if Carla was trying to keep her from saying something that would make trouble and need recanting, or spoil something between them that had weathered all the suffering.

'Carmen could have made it, that's all. She had a good healthy sickness.'

'That's a contradiction in terms!'

'That's impossible!'

'No, it isn't – think about it for a minute – a sickness with a good, hard hurt that's direct and doesn't cover with an appealing surface or exercises in normal-faking the doctors.'

There was an embarrassed silence and without meaning to, Deborah found herself looking at Linda, the 'psychological authority', who had read everything and gave jargon

218

like currency, recklessly improvident because she hoped never to be touched by the pain that was wrapped in the words. Linda, frightened of the look and the definition, came back angrily. 'Ridiculous – you're just rationalizing your own defensive system!'

Deborah tried to say it better, and make it more real. 'Look at that bunch from the Men's Admitting – they're all very rational and "sane" and witty. The staff likes them, even as people, but they're here and they've been here for years and they aren't helped by anything or anybody. They don't seem to suffer much because they don't feel anything much. That's sick-sickness. Miss Coral up on D may be sick, but she's feeling and fighting and alive ...' Her voice petered out in the face of their anger and disbelief, but suddenly she felt again the quiet power of the opening of the world which she had felt that evening on the D ward. Only now it came more urgently and passionately. 'Alive *is* fighting,' Deborah said. 'It's the same thing. I still think that Carmen could have made it.'

The nurse stopped them then, and Deborah looked around at the faces suffused with anger against her. She had hit a particularly sensitive nerve. It was B ward's nerve; a desperate hope that the false 'fine-fine' might see them through if only they acted *long* enough and tried to make it be the truth. Was it as frightened a clutching at convention on the outside?

'You sure like to rattle the cages around here,' Carla said later as they got ready for bed.

'You're wondering how I ever made it to this old age, as thorny as I am?'

'I'm going to miss you, Deb.'

In Yr's distances a cannon went off. 'Why should you?'

'Because I'm going out to try again.'

The fear, like a backhand slap, caught her unprepared, but her lessons with Furii had been well learned, and while she shook, she questioned: Fear for me or for Carla? If for me, why? Lose a friend? Lose a friend to the world? Fear because soon *I* will have to go?

Part of it was of the same fear that had made the others

back off from her definition of a 'good, healthy sickness'. She smiled at it ruefully.

'It should be strong enough, this therapy,' Carla said, 'to go a lousy mile into town. I'm going to start looking for jobs where I won't be sealed up in a little room somewhere. Maybe that was the main trouble before.' She sounded frightened and tired.

'I'll miss you,' Deborah said bleakly.

'Maybe soon you can come, too.'

Deborah tried to say 'sure', but she knew that her fear might translate the words into some other language, so she lay on her bed and felt the fear settle over her like fog.

The girl who took Carla's place in her room was a gentle, generous veteran of mechanical psychiatry in a dozen other hospitals. Her memory had been ravaged, but her sickness was still intact. She gave herself dozens of sets of wildly divergent parents. 'It was always a musical family ...' she would say vaguely. 'My father – he's Paderewski, and my mother is Sophie Tucker. It's why I'm high-strung.'

Deborah liked her and after a while they did not speak of families at all, or the marital frictions of her parents, Greta Garbo and Will Rogers.

The hunger for the new world which had awakened in Deborah forced her to seek more and more of it. She would sit near the student nurses on the hall and in the craft shop to hear them talk. She would question them about their lives and families and where they lived and what they wanted to do after they finished their training. She would walk into town and back often, learning all the ways there were to go and come, looking, smelling, watching the seasons change.

The hunger made her go even where she was not wanted, into the social life of the town. She joined two church choirs and talked to the Methodist minister about the young people's group. They both knew that belonging was a hopeless quest; the hospital and its inmates had been feared and ridiculed far too long in the small, insular community. But the tired, quiet ladies of the church choir could not measure or reckon the passionate hunger of a new-born worlding for her birthright. Although they ignored her, she came anyway. They made her invisible, yet she still came.

And finally, in fear and excitement, restlessness and stubborn will, she set into motion the request for her own way out of the hospital. When the machinery had whirred and the response had come, she saw in her room-mate's face the look which she, in turn, must have shown to Carla and before Carla to Doris Rivera – an awe, a fear, an anger, an envy – above all, a reality-shattering loneliness.

'It doesn't matter to me, you're going,' the room-mate said. 'I'm not really a patient here, you know. I'm just doing research for my degree and as soon as I'm finished I'll just pick up and go!'

When Deborah said good-bye, the woman looked at her as if she had never seen her before.

The social worker had a list of rooms in town that could be let to out-patients. Most of them, Deborah knew from the grapevine or from her walks, were poor and dark, and partook of the shame of the lepers who lived in them.

'There are one or two places which are new and have no patients living in them. They are a little far, though – way over on the other side of town.'

Deborah closed her eyes and put her finger on the list of names.

'The law requires us to state—'

'Yes, I know,' Deborah said, and suddenly remembering her sprained ankle and St Agnes ('Are they *violent*?') she winced a little.

'I'll have to come along,' said the social worker. 'It's a requirement—'

They stood together at the door of the old house, and when the landlady opened it, Deborah looked hard at her, waiting for the guarding of the eyes and the closing of the face as the social worker explained what she was. The landlady was elderly and there was little subtlety in her. Deborah began to wonder if she understood what was being said.

When the worker was finished she motioned to them. 'Well, I hope you like the room.'

'It's a *mental* hospital,' the social worker said desperately.

'Oh? . . . Now, this room has more light, but the other is closer to the bathroom, you see.'

When the worker left, the landlady only said, 'Now, please don't clog up this toilet – it's old and a little cantankerous.'

'Not if my life depended on it,' Deborah said.

As it turned out, the landlady, Mrs King, was a stranger in the town and had not been raised on the bogeymen of 'That Place'. Too many incidents and frightening tales had bred fear and contempt in most of the town's people. Deborah had often seen mothers call their children out of the range of 'The Captain', who had been in the Navy and talked to himself as he walked. To Deborah, who looked somewhat more normal, the town showed no such fear. It showed nothing. Although Deborah had gone to the choir practice at the church and sewing classes at the high school, and even a teen-age outing club (Come One Come All), she went and returned, sharing a sewing machine, a hymnbook, a map, and 'good evening' and 'good night' and no more. Everyone was most polite and so was she, but their lives had been walled against her.

'Is it the town or is it my face?'

'Maybe both . . .' said Furii, 'although your face looks all right to me – perhaps there is a certain anxiety in it when you meet people.'

Deborah and Dr Fried worked without inspiration – a kind of mental day labour, finding in the new freedoms new confrontations with the past.

'I wanted to ask you,' Furii said, 'to look back again to the past and tell me if you see any light breaking through that greyness of which we have spoken.'

Deborah sank back into the memories. The reign of ruin and calamity, which had seemed so total, now, magically, admitted of some patches of sunlight all but lost under the conquering powers of Yr. 'Yes . . . yes . . . I do!' She smiled. 'I seem to remember whole days of it sometimes – and there was that year in the house where we were before we moved back to Chicago – and there was my friend – how could I have forgotten!'

'You had a friend?'

'Until I came here – and she was not one of the ruined either, at least not after she got used to the newness of the city. She started like all the others to whom *nganon* cries – she was lonely and a foreigner – but she learned our ways quickly and she was good – I mean she was not ruined!'

'You heard from her in the last years?'

'Oh, yes! She's in college – why didn't I remember?'

'When you were so very ill, remembering a friend or a partial sunlight would have meant changing a view of the world that could not allow change. One relinquishes claim to the world for a reason. You have to have all the reasons to make so big a renunciation. Now, when you have come again to the world, you are able to remember what was *also* there with the darkness. Much of it was darkness only because it was balanced against the light of loving and experiencing truth.'

'But Yr is beautiful and true also, and there is love there, too.'

'It is not the language, and not the gods in themselves,' Furii said, 'but their force of keeping you from the world, which is the sickness.'

'It's nice to walk with Lactamaeon when he is in a good mood. After the sewing class, where I don't belong, or the church choir where I am a stranger, it's good to walk home with someone who can laugh and be silly or turn beautiful and make you cry, looking at the stars while he recites.'

'You know, don't you, now, that you made him up out of yourself – that you created him out of your own humour and your own beauty?' Furii said gently.

'Yes – I know now.' It was an admission that gave much pain.

'When were you at last able to see this?'

'You mean with all my eyes?'

Furii nodded.

'Well, maybe I always saw it, partly, far in the place where it was safe, but I guess it's been getting nearer and nearer to me for a long time. Last week I was laughing secretly with Idat and Anterrabae. They had written a choral setting of a poem by Horace, and when they sang it, I said, *That was one of the few texts I know by heart all the way through.* And Anterrabae said, *Of course.* And then we started the kind of banter – the kind you have when you are kidding and hurting someone at the same time. I said, *Teach me mathematics,* and they laughed, but they admitted at last that they could not go beyond my knowledge. Then we were insulting each other and laughing, but giving pain too. I said to Anterrabae, *Is that my fire you are burning in?* and he said, *Was it not worth the fuel?* I said, *Does it do for light or heat?* and he said, *For years of your life.* I said, *For all the years? Forever? A disputed land, your land.*

'Do you see the Collect now as the criticism of parts of your own mind?' Furii said.

'I'm afraid, still afraid that they are real somehow. It would be wonderful if I could dismiss them when I wanted to.'

Furii reminded her how merciless the Collect had been, and how lacking in real beauty for a long, long time the gods had been. Only now when she fought them did they come with their allurements of wit and poetry, because it is harder to fight an amiable spirit.

While the memory of light was still in Deborah's mind, Furii said, 'What about your new friend, Carla? Do you still see her sometimes?' And Deborah began to tell Furii about the strange thing that had happened.

She had not seen Carla much lately, but when they were together there was a special closeness between them. They might have been friends anywhere, but because they had been sick together and had fought out of it at the same time, their comradeship was tinged with the aura of emergent life and struggle. Carla was busy during the day at a lab technician's job, and at night she had to spend time studying the new techniques which had passed by the barred windows of her five years and three hospitals.

They had shared much of their pasts, most of their fears, and all of their tenuous and fragile hopes, but Deborah had noticed over the years that whenever she mentioned her art, or something on which she was working, a subtle change would come over Carla. Her face would harden almost imperceptibly; her manner would edge towards coolness. Because it was a subtle emotion in a world of erratic oscillations of feeling, of violence, and of lies told by every sense and perception, Deborah had not noticed it in their sick times. But one day the world had cleared enough so that she realized that at any mention of her art, her friend drew back. In their new eagerness for experience and reality, the strange aloofness stood out clearly. She did not remember Carla ever having seen her work, but there must have been scraps of it about during their days of paper-collecting on D ward. It must have been that Carla hadn't liked what she had seen and was guilty, being a friend, and angry because of it. So Deborah had decided to spare Carla the ups and downs of her art. There was so much to share in the new world that they never missed the view from that one window.

The Saturday before, Deborah had gone to sleep looking forward to telling Carla about a new boarder and the landlady's son-in-law. She had a dream.

In the dream it was winter and night. The sky was thick blue-black and the stars were frozen in it, so that they glimmered. Over the clean white and windswept hills the shadows of snowdrifts drew long. She was walking on the crust of snow, watching the star-glimmer and the snow-glimmer and the cold tear-glimmer in her own eyes. A deep voice said to her, 'You know, don't you, that the stars are sound as well as light?'

She listened and heard a lullaby made by the voices of the stars, sounding so beautiful together that she began to cry with it.

The voice said, 'Look out there.'

She looked towards the horizon. 'See, it is a sweep, a curve.' Then the voice said, 'This night is a curve of darkness and the space beyond it is a curve of human history, with every single life an arch from birth to death. The apex of all of these single curves determines the curve of history and, at last, of man.'

'Can I know about my curve?' she said, begging the voice. 'Will I hold part of the sweep of the age?'

'I cannot show you yours,' the voice said, 'but I can show you Carla's. Dig here, deep in the snow. It is buried and frozen – Dig deep.'

Deborah pushed the snow aside with her hands. It was very cold, but she worked with a great intensity as if there were salvation in it. At last her hand struck something and she tore it up from burial. It was a piece of bone, thick and very strong and curved in a long, high, steady curve.

'Is this Carla's life?' she asked. 'Her creativity?'

'It is bone-deep with her, though buried and frozen.' The voice paused a moment and then said, 'It's a fine one – a fine solid one!'

Deborah wanted to plead again for the shape that her art would draw in time, but the dream faded and the voices of the stars became dim and died out entirely at last.

In the morning the vividness was still with her, so that when Carla came and they sat idly and talked, Deborah was distracted and her mind was still hung with heavy stars and her hands were still gripping the smooth curve of bone.

'Please don't be angry,' she said; and then she told Carla the dream. When she got to the part about digging in the snow for the curve, Carla was with her; when she pulled up what was buried, Carla said, 'Do you see it? What is it like!' moving a little whenever Deborah moved as if to brush the snow away from it. When she described it to Carla and told what the voice said, Carla began to cry.

'Do you think it's true – do you really think it's true?'

'I told you as it happened.'

'You didn't make it up – I mean you really dreamed it that way—'

'Yes, I did.'

She wiped her eyes. 'It was only a dream, your dream . . .'

'It's true anyway,' Deborah said.

'The one place I could never go . . .' Carla said musing, '. . . the one hunger I could never admit.'

When Deborah finished, Furii said, 'You always took your art for granted, didn't you? I used to read in the ward reports all the time how you managed to do your drawing in spite of every sort of inconvenience and restriction. You were rich in your gift, even at your sickest, and now you see how it can be with others who are not so lucky to have a creative calling into which they can grow and grow. The healthy friendship you had to bury in forgetfulness, and the times of sunlight you banished from your memory. I think this dream was to remind you of another joy as well; it was the understanding of Carla. There may be many who envy you a little – yes, yes, I know it sounds like the old "lucky girl" business, but it isn't. You have been taking for granted this rich and prolific gift of yours that so many others would give so much to have themselves. By this dream you were perhaps awakening to it a little. It is part of the call of the world.'

As Deborah listened to Furii's description of her, it did not sound like a cursed and ruined life. Together they recalled the old Yri cry: *Immutably, in sleep, in silence, nganon cries from itself.* It had been the secret cry to the damned and had made Deborah an engine and accomplice in their destruction. It would seem now that this horror had been lifted. Was it possible that she could touch things without causing them to become diseased? Was it possible that she could love without poisoning, witness without blighting? Could she give testimony from the elemental bone in a friend's good need?

28

DEBORAH SPENT THE next months simply, working on a series of pen-and-ink drawings and cleaving the past in heavy hours with Dr Fried. As the world began to gain form, dimension, and colour, she started to find the sessions of choir practice and sewing class too fragile a scaffold on which to build hope. No matter how pleasant, sane, or co-operative she was, invisible and inaudible was all she would ever be. She would know the Methodist liturgical year and some of the gossip of the Ladies' Altar Club, but she would never penetrate an inch under the politely closed faces whose motions she duplicated in those places. Over the text of John Stainer's 'Seven-Fold Amen', she looked out into the congregation on Sunday and wondered if they ever thanked God for the light in their minds, for friends, for cold and pain responsive to the laws of nature, for enough depth of sight into these laws to have expectations, for friends, for the days and nights that follow one another in stately rhythm, for the sparks that fly upwards, for friends. ... Did they know how beautiful and enviable their lives were? She realized more and more that her few spare-hour pastimes provided too little in which to test or exercise her fragile 'yes' to a newborn reality.

Although she read Latin and some Greek, she had never graduated from high school and her memory of it was now almost four years old – the memories of an occasional visitor from a foreign place. She looked in the town papers and was surprised at her feeble knowledge of the world and its requirements. No job, even the simplest, was open to her. The town was small and slow; a waitress or 5 & 10 girl would not be under the pressure of hurrying crowds; these jobs required little intellect; but she did not have enough education to qualify for them.

For a while there was no help from the hospital. The psychiatrists were all themselves strangers to the town and had been long years away from considerations of skilled and unskilled labour. Dr Fried implied subtly that it might be Deborah's problem to solve, and the outpatient administrator, after saying somewhat the same thing, mentioned offhandedly that he would look into the problem. When he called her back to his office two weeks later, he seemed a little surprised.

'I've talked to several people,' he said, 'and apparently you'll have to get through high school before you can get any job.' To her terror-stricken look he said, 'Well ... think about it for a while. . . .'

He did not know that Deborah had gone during the day to look at the town high school. It was a great and sudden stand of buildings all the way over on the other side of town.

The stone heaps brooded like a great moa, too big to fly. She might have to be one of the students at that school. She had been broken in a school like that, years ago. Certainly the sickness had been building up inside her for years, but the final terrors of it – the missing days, the sudden falls into dark Yr – were all walked through in halls like the ones inside that building, among faces like the ones that would be there. She remembered the struggle before she had given up the pretence of consubstantiality. She thought again of the secret Japanese, bearing untreated the wounds which had led to his capture, secretly dead and bearing unnoticed the pressure-crazing Semblance, secretly a citizen and captive of Anterrabae, the Censor, the College, and the Pit.

Even as she had compromised her captors, she had lost the wish for Semblance – to be a picture of belonging at all costs. She knew the costs now; in a tightened, frightened small town where her classmates would be three years younger and light-years distant, she knew that at best such a world would be a no-man's land. Even if she no longer belonged to Yr, there would still be the awful alienation from Earth that had once made her run to otherness in pain day after day. Yr or no, it was too late to join students such as these again, too late for the proms, the cliques, the curlers, and the class pins. She had had quite enough of a 'special vocabulary of belonging'.

'I'm nineteen . . .' she said to the heap of buildings. 'It's too late.' She turned shivering in the Yri wind that blew over all the miles of a real and unreal separation.

'I can't go back to my merry high-school days again,' she said to the out-patient administrator, 'volleyball in the gym and teeth-teeth at the school dances.'

'But unless you have that diploma to show . . .'

'*Non omnia possumus omnes* . . .' she said, and reminded him that it was Virgil, but she knew that what he said was true.

'Why don't you make a list of all the things you can do?' he said. She knew that it was make-work, 'doing something useful,' something Deborah felt was nothing more than juggling dead-end signs. The administrator wanted to get

229

off the hook, he wanted not to be bothered with the world of commerce and livelihood, and Deborah, seeing this, was moved out of sympathy to be dutiful and do what he said. Perhaps she would find hiding in a word some preference or talent, or something that could really be used. There it was again, the little Maybe, building its compelling heat from a small and vulnerable spark.

She went back to her little table at the rooming house, sat down, and ruled a piece of paper down the middle. On one side she wrote KNOWLEDGE and on the other, POSSIBLE JOB.

KNOWLEDGE	POSSIBLE JOB
1. Ride a bicycle	Rural delivery girl
2. Know all of Hamlet by heart from beginning to end	Tutor of Hamlet to kids who are taking it in school
3. Can wake up from dead sleep in full possession of faculties	Night watchman
4. Have a tremendous vocabulary of obscene words	Language consultant
5. Some Greek	(Not enough)
6. Some Latin	Tutor of Latin for kids who are taking it in school
7. Have potential for callousness	Professional assassin
8. Artist for 10 years	Not genius—not commercially practical
9. Know the components of most forms of mental illness and could act them realistically from seeing the original	Actress (too dangerous)
10. Don't smoke	Wine taster

She rewrote the list leaving out numbers 4, 5, 7, and 9. She felt a special poignancy at having to leave out 'Professional assassin'. She realized that she was too poorly co-ordinated and clumsy, and professional assassins should be very wiry and graceful. She was so lacking in *atumai* that she knew her victims would always fall the wrong way, and picturing herself trying to crawl out from beneath the body of a three-hundred-pound former wrestler, she knew that 7 was a lost cause.

The next day she took the list to the administrator, but did not stay to see him read it. Even Anterrabae was embarrassed by the poor showing of his queen and victim, and the Collect was jubilantly self-righteous. She was frightened by the choices that the world offered her. The possible futures stretched before her like the hall down which she was now walking from the administrative offices: a long road with carefully labelled doors every ten feet of the way – all closed.

'Oh, Miss Blau—' a voice called behind her. It was one of the social workers. (What now? she wondered. I have a room, so I don't need a room-tracker, unless there's one to rescind the other's trackings.) 'Doctor Oster was talking to me about you going to the high school.' (There it was again, the lock-step-lock of the world; they had reassigned her to her place under the juggernaut.) Redness seethed upwards from the tumour until she was hot to the eyes with its pain.

'I should have thought of it right away,' the social worker was saying. 'There's a place in the city that might be able to prepare you for them.'

'For what?' Deborah said.

'For the examinations.'

'What examinations?'

'Why, the high-school equivalency. As I was saying, it seems the practical way ...' The social worker was looking at her quizzically. Deborah wanted to tell her that it is not possible to hear through a red wash, and that the relief of her news, which had turned her face a chalk white, was also giving her 'the bends' from the change in pressure.

'I wouldn't have to go to the town high school?'

'No, as I was just saying, there is a tutorial school in the city—'

'I could choose, then?'

'You could talk to them about the possibilities—'

'Does one call for an appointment?'

'Well, you are still a ward of . . .'

'Could *you* call them for an appointment?'

'Yes, I could do that.'

'And will you tell me what they say?'

The social worker said that she would, and Deborah sat down and watched her walk away. The pain in the red wash was fading, but the panic was not withdrawing from her. *Listen to your heart,* Anterrabae said, falling beside her. She heard it slamming like a latchless door in the wind.

What is it? What is it? she called to Yr. *I was real, just here, just before!* Her vision was ragged and distorted and the words came in an odd Yri form, as if even Yri had been coded for secrecy. *Why? Why is this happening?*

Her question broke the earth's silence, and she sensed people near, perhaps Doctor Oster coming out of his office. But her hearing was distorted like her vision, and when she stumbled into someone, she cried, 'The senses are not discrete!'

'Is she going to be *violent?*' (or something like that) came in bored annoyance from the blur. Deborah began to answer that violence to a volcano is natural law, but she could no longer communicate at all. Flanked and followed by the handed blurs, she entered the steel patient-elevator and was carried up to D ward – the beginning all over again.

When she cleared – again, all over again, wrapped and restrained yet again – she laughed down at herself looking the length of the case.

'Now I know, you sudden, falling calendars. Now I know, Lactamaeon, you sad god. Now I know why Carla and Doris Rivera were so damned exhausted!' Her throat seemed to be breaking with the hard, hurting laugh.

After a while Quentin Dobshansky came in to take her pulse.

'Hi . . .' he said, trying to figure out if he should be cheerful or grave, '. . . is the pack helping?'

'Well, I can see again,' she said, 'and hear, and talk.' She looked at him. 'Are you still a friend of mine?'

'Well, sure!' he said uncomfortably.

'Then don't do anything to your face, Quentin. Just leave it hanging there.'

He let his face go, and it fell back into disappointment. 'Just ... well, I liked to think on you being outside and starting along, that's all.'

He was beginning to feel an ache of anxiety because this person towards whom he felt kindly was a crazy person (even though the doctors had told him to call them mentally ill) and he could make her crazier if he said the wrong things. The doctors and all the books he had been reading told him not to be too definite, not to argue or show strong feelings, but to be cheerful and helpful. In spite of these instructions, he knew that he could move her, and this made him try, and the trying made him feel something for her, and his success at this feeling made her a human being to him. She was homely and straggle-haired, but he had been laughed at for his looks, too; and he had been defeated once as she seemed to be now. He had been in an accident which had left him lying on a road all broken, his father beside him. The rescuers had taken him to the hospital tied up in a blanket, as she was tied up now, and he remembered that trip. Before the pain there had been something worse: the awful feeling of being crushed to a pulp – body and soul. It had whispered to him over and over with the turning of the wheel rims: stove-in and broke, stove-in and broke. Of the later pain he was curiously proud. His father's death left a raw, clean sorrow; the broken ribs made each breathe-in-breathe-out a kick in the face of death, a hurt of being alive. Now he looked at Deborah and heard his mind go again around the rims of the wheels, stove-in and broke, stove-in and broke. It must be what she was feeling now.

'You want a drink?'

'No, thank you.'

Suffering, shy with each other, waiting for his disappointment and her fear to make their weights known between them, they looked at each other, and Deborah was suddenly struck that Quentin Dobshansky, her friend, was a man – a sexual man – a passionate man who seemed to be sounding a cry of passion into the echo-places of her emptiness. Only at that moment did she become aware of them as empty. And at the instant she discovered emptiness, she discovered hunger. It was a long, hard hunger, years late and never plumbed before. But the measure of hunger was the measure of capacity. Furii had been right; nuts or not, Deborah could feel.

She looked up at Quentin. He was pausing at the door, waiting to give hope, of which he had less than he wanted to show. 'You have another hour,' he said.

'It's okay.' She knew that she was ugly and she didn't want to hurt his eyes or his mind's eyes, so she turned her head and let him close the door.

Now it was not Anterrabae who mocked, but Lactamaeon, the black god with the icy blue eyes. *The fisherman has won, and the fish is in the net, but it does not die and be dead. It keeps flapping against the sides of the boat, turning and seeking for its element and suffering the deprivation of the essence by which it lives. This distresses the fisherman. He does not want to think about the death-throes of the fish, which is his prize and his victory. Thus are you to the world and to us also. Re-die, and let things stand as they were.*

Don't you see! she cried out at him, *I don't know* how *any more!*

Back on the ward that afternoon, an attendant left a smouldering cigarette in an ashtray near the nursing station. Deborah picked it up, hid it, and took it to the dormitory where she was staying, now between an Ann and Dowben's Mary. She sat on the floor, hidden by the other beds, and looked at her scarred arm. The tissues would have no feeling, the burn do no good. She began to start a new place, moving the burning cigarette to put it out against undeadened flesh. As it came closer she felt the warmth of it, the heat, the burn. The first singe of hair brought a red-hot stab with it so that she jerked her arm away, astonished.

'It was a reflex!' she said incredulously to the bedrail. She tried again and again, but at every place, a burning hot pain prevailed upon instinct and she had to pull away from the burn before it had even closed upon the flesh. She put out

234

the cigarette against the bed-leg and said aloud in Yri:

'*To all gods and Collects of all the worlds: No more burn-ings and no more fires, for I seem to begin to be bound—*'
She had begun to cry because of the terror and joy of it. '*I seem to begin to be bound to this world. . . .*'

When it was time to see Furii, she ran to her office, terrify-ing her tracker, and burst in to the beginning of the session. 'Hey! You know what happens when you burn yourself? You get burnt, that's what! And it has a hurt called a burn, that's what!'

'You burned yourself again?' Furii asked, drawing away the smile with which she had answered Deborah's.

'I tried to, but I couldn't.'

'Oh?'

'Because it *hurt*!'

'Oh, I'm glad!' They smiled at each other. Then Furii saw the tracker behind Deborah and asked her why she was with her and was told. When the nurse left to wait outside, Furii gave the quizzical look that Deborah knew and had winced at long in advance of its coming.

'I always had warnings before – an explanation of why it was going to happen—'

'Maybe "it" knew that you needed help. You were in call-ing distance of that help, but you didn't dare ask for it out-right, lest it be refused.'

'But the oncoming was so sudden and severe. How can I be getting any better at all when it is so sudden and com-plete?'

'These defences against getting well and casting with the world are at their last barricades. Of course, there is a des-peration to save everything that can be saved of your sick-ness.'

Deborah told her about the school, how frightened she had been and how despairing at the thought of three years inside the town's vast silence, and how she had thought that it was predecided, the lock-step-lock of being a victim. She came to the part about meeting the social worker and hearing her suggestion, the sudden release of forgiveness and hope, and how she had sat down with 'the bends' and been overwhelmed without warning. As she described the oncoming of the Pit, it struck her that there had been a change in it. 'Something ... funny.'

'What, funny?'

'Well, Yr used to be the logical and understanding place, and the world the anarchic thing. There were sets of formulas to help in the escape. They got more and more elaborate, but always ... they were predictable ...'

'Well?'

'Well, when I began to have the world, it was as if Yr said, "We'll take the other way of it, whatever it is." When the world was without logic or law, Yr was the place with form and caused effects. When the world began to be the rational one, Yr stopped giving reasons at all.'

'Yes,' said Furii gently, as she did when she wanted to remonstrate without an overtone of anger. 'When will you stop straddling these two worlds?'

'I'm not ready yet!' Deborah shouted.

'All right,' Furii said mildly, 'but you will never be able to grasp the world really, with all of its advantages, until you relinquish your double allegiance.'

The wind of panic beat over Deborah and her heart began to rattle with it. She called silently to Anterrabae and he came, fleet and reassuring to her. *Suffer, Victim.* (The familiar Yri greeting.)

Is it true that you bring me beauty lately only when you are threatened? she asked him, waiting for his sardonic half-smile. He did not give it, but winced instead.

Pity me.

She was thrown by the surprise of this action. *Of what do you suffer?*

Of burning.

But you are not consumed.

When you were exalted and beyond the range of human fire, I was also. Since the flames burn you, they burn me also. He breathed in again, sharply, and she saw the upward planes of his face as they were lit by his fire, shining with sweat and tears. *Oh!* she cried out for him, so that he turned his eyes towards her again.

You see — you endure and share with me. We are of a voice, of a look. Could you ever hope or imagine to be so sharing with anyone of earth? And he made the gesture of turmoil and renunciation that was Yri hand-language for the world.

'Where have you gone?' Furii was asking. 'Take me with you.'

'I was with Anterrabae. He's right. The world may have law and logic, even if it is dangerous and twisted sometimes. It has challenge, too, and things I don't know to learn, like mathematics, which the gods can't teach me, but where else' — and here her eyes suddenly filled with tears — 'where else is there the sharing that I have with them?'

'What are those tears?' Furii asked, still very softly. Deborah looked at her and recognized the opening words of their formula, hers and Furii's. She had to smile.

'Of ten units; four self-pity, three what Yr calls "the Hard Rind" and one desperation.'

'That is only eight.' (Still the formula.)

'And two miscellaneous.'

They smiled again. 'You see,' Furii said, 'it can be as clear between the two of us as with your gods. I never hid my nature, but sometimes you forget that I am and have always been a representative of and a fighter with you for this present world.' And she blew her nose as if to show how typical a member of the world she was. 'What is that which you call "the Hard Rind"?'

'Well, when I first came to the hospital I was not unhappy. I didn't care about anything and that had a kind of peace about it. Then you made me care and as soon as I did, Yr punished me and I got desperate with it. When I begged for mercy from Yr, Anterrabae said, "You have eaten down hope from the red to the rind." I thought that I would have to live and watch that old rind shrivel up and get hard and be thrown away at last. He used that allusion now and then, and when I realized that I was alive, really alive and of the same substance as the world's inhabitants, I told him that I would chew that dry rind and keep chewing until it gave me nourishment. This time, when I was back and everybody was so disappointed in me, Anterrabae said, "That hard rind is cracking your teeth – why not spit it out at last"?'

'And what do you feel about doing that?'

'I can't stop chewing now, even if I don't seem to be getting anything much,' Deborah said. 'Since I have the reflexes and instincts of a world one, I guess I'm stuck with it . . .,' and she smiled sheepishly because it was an admission; it counted and someday she might have to hang from it.

If only I could tell her . . ., Furii thought. How do you tell someone born and raised in the desert what rich and fertile lands there are, just out of sight? Instead she said, 'How is it going for you on the ward?'

'Well, of course the patients are mad at me, and the staff is kind of disappointed. I'm down to see Dr Halle today.'

'Oh, something special?'

'No . . . I have to tell him to let the social worker know that it's still on with me, and that if it's okay with the people down at that place she mentioned, I'll be ready whenever they are.'

REQUISITION

Date: Sept. 3	*Ward:* D
Patient: Blau, Deborah	*Ward Administrator:* Dr Halle, H.L.
Items:	*Date:* Sept. 5 *Time:* 8:30 A.M.

1 dress, suitable for city wear
1 pr. hose
1 pr. shoes
27 'clip-type' curlers
1 coat
1 tube lipstick
$.80 suburban bus fare (for social worker and self)
4 city bus tokens (for social worker and self)

The above to be requisitioned from patient's rooming house.

Signed:

H. L. Halle

Miraculously, her need had been seen by Earth ones. Deborah found that her exceptional problem was common enough to be covered by a statute. If she could prove to the Board of Regents her conquest of high-school subjects, she could get a certificate of equivalency without having to undergo three years in the big stone school. If she could ride the two hours to and two hours back between the hospital and the city's Remedial and Tutorial School, there might be a quicker and less perilous bridge between Never and Maybe. She fell into her work dizzily and full of doubt, found her balance, took the books, and dove into them. Buried in pages, she sounded to the bottom like a whale, rose, took breath, and plunged again. Despite the dangerously hypnotic effect of the double two-hour ride each day, pride in the stubborn battle gave her the strength she needed. She struggled to stay up to the demands of the study and travel. In time the teachers were able to open a tiny crack in the wall of her separation. During the month that she went to school from B ward the nurse woke her before full light. Each morning before she was ready to leave for school, she was allowed by doctor's order (medicinal) one cup of coffee, and after a week of fidelity to the early hour, the night nurse added toast and a glass of juice on her own responsibility. Deborah was proud of the respect that the little extras showed. Except for the extraordinary ones, the hospital workers tended to give the flat requirement and no more, but lately, at the moment when she stood at the door with her morning schoolbooks – symbols of responsible sanity – and waited for it to be unlocked with the large 'madhouse' key, the attendant would say, 'Good-bye, now,' or even, 'Have a good day.'

With such extras, Deborah achieved a certain pride and status on the ward. When she moved back to the rooming house, and went to the hospital just for supper and therapy, the shadow that she cast along the walkways was lengthened by more than the coming of evening. She began to understand why Doris Rivera, who had been well enough to work and live with her own keys in her pocket, had spoken so sparingly to the hungry and terror-stricken audience of D ward. She, too, had seen her shadow lengthened by hard-won hairbreadths, and though she was still dwarfed on the flat-faced walls of the world; to the hope-stunted sick from among whom she had gone, she had had an outline larger than life. How it had swayed and faltered with her return.

One day, coming from an exhausting session with Furii, Deborah saw a knot of people in the hall, and coming closer she saw that they were writhing, slow motion, like creatures under water. At the centre of the knot, all but hidden by it, was Miss Coral. Because Deborah's loyalty had not shifted with her commitment to the world, she had to choke back a guffaw. The bed-flinging genius of fulcrum, weight, and thrust was at it again! Deborah wondered how she had gotten off the ward. She was standing almost still in the middle of the mêlée, taking on five attendants by drawing them into battle with each other. Her rant was a low mutter, like an engine, full of long sibilances and obscenity. Deborah passed by and tossed a 'Hello, Miss Coral,' more for the attendants than for the lady herself. Miss Coral removed her concentration from her war and smiled to Deborah.

'Hello, Deborah. You're not back, are you?'

'Oh, no; just a doctor's hour.'

'I heard you were home for the Christmas holidays.'

'Yes . . . It was easier this time – almost like real fun.'

Miss Coral's lightning eyes softened; her rigid stance and the whole five-man writhe about her relaxed into a half-comic, yet strangely moving, truce, while Deborah and Miss Coral faced each other, socializing.

'How is Carla? Do you still see her?'

'Oh, yes, she got that job she wanted. . . . Hey, is it true that Dobshansky got married to a nurse on one of the male wards?'

'Yes, a student. It's a secret marriage, though, because of

240

her training. No one knows about it,' and they smiled at each other for all the cold-water pipes and all the ears on all the wards.

'How is everybody?' Deborah asked.

'Oh, the same, more or less. Lee Miller is leaving for another hospital. Sylvia looks rather better, but she still doesn't talk. Helene's back with us on D, you know.'

'No – I didn't. Say "Hello" for me. Throw something at her and be rude so she'll know it's me.' Deborah looked hard at Miss Coral. It was difficult to confront the pain she saw so nakedly in the face of her modest and gentle teacher, the bed-thrower and bearer of Catullus. 'Are you okay?' she asked, knowing that anything more would be an imposition.

Miss Coral looked apologetically at her retinue as if they were all one great, embarrassing social blunder with which she was not connected.

'Well . . .' she said, 'it comes and goes.'

'Can I bring you anything?'

She knew that Miss Coral could not ask, but she was hoping for something in code. They had shared a thing rare for their sort of illness – a touching of minds, a touching of feelings. Horace, shouted through the two-inch-thick doors of a seclusion room and into the dark wastes of a private world, had been more than Latin, more than beauty.

'Oh, no . . . no.'

Deborah realized that the bus would be leaving. 'I have to go—'

'Well, then, good-bye, Deborah.'

'Good-bye.' She moved past. The hardness came back into Miss Coral's eyes; the muscles tensed. The writhing began again; the machine hum started. The truce was ended.

When Deborah sat in the bus, she thought of Miss Coral and trembled a little. How many of the dead could be raised? Of all the D-ward women, how many would be free someday? In her three years there many faces had come and gone, and many had stayed. Of those who had gone, maybe three-quarters had left for other hospitals. Some had improved enough to live a kind of half-life as outpatients.

How many were really iut, alive, and free? You could count them on your fingers! She shivered. She would have to force herself to her books tonight.

The months went on and the high-school subjects began to fill in the notebooks. If sanity was measured in feet and hours, learning was weighed in pounds of books carried to school and back again. The heavy textbooks gave her a kind of pride, as if she might someday weigh in the world what her schoolbooks weighed in her arms. The city remedial school was mainly for young children with reading problems or speech impediments, but apart from sitting at tiny deal tables, Deborah liked it. She liked not having to be uncomfortable with her teachers, working alone and hard and with no precocity, and not unbelonging in the middle of the Varsity Drag. After a while her teachers began to praise her for her tenacity. Steady and steadfast, they said, and she was greatly pleased. It was only when she was returning to her room in the afternoon that the world hurt. Young and rustling, loud with charm-bracelets and giggling, the high-school and young college girls would overwhelm the buses, and she would once again find herself peering into the world of the elaborately vain, mirror-mad, fearing and predatory young girls – a world where she had failed, a world that she knew looked much better than it really was, but to the eyes of its outcasts, a world that glowed with mysterious brilliance. She looked down at her own school skirt and sweater. She looked the way they did, but she was still a stranger, the imitation of a young schoolgirl.

And am I not as that world is? Idat asked from Yr. *I am veiled and mysterious; I am rewarding and full of splendour. If you leave me and Lactamaeon, who loves you, and Anterrabae, who is your friend, with whom you laugh and are easy, will you ever have such light?*

Then, strangely, the images of her tutors at the remedial school appeared in Yr to speak to Idat.

Are you joining the Collect? You too? Deborah called to them.

Certainly not! the English tutor said. *We are against those creatures of yours!*

Listen, you, the math tutor said to Idat, *that girl works hard. She is here every day with sharp pencils and conventional dress. She is prompt and obedient and never insane in the classroom. She's not overbright in math, but she works hard for what she gets and that's the good, solid truth!*

Hardly a shower of stars, Idat said drily. *Hardly a silver raven.* (It was an Yri metaphor for flattery – because of the high polish.)

Suddenly, one by one, members of the Collect began to appear in the Midworld. One carried a trumpet, one a fiddle, one a drum, and one a tambourine. *We are going to the Dance,* they said to Deborah.

What dance?

The Grand Dance.

Who will be there?

You also.

Where will it be?

The Five Continents.

Sick or well, the English tutor said, *sick or well you are one of the dancers, don't you see that?* Teachers and Collect began to trace the Yri words of separation on a piece of paper. In Yri and English they copied the old, old words, 'You Are Not Of Them'. *There it stands,* the math teacher said. *All your old reality.*

Then they tore the paper into shreds and gave it away to the wind.

That evening at the church, Deborah invited her hymnbook mate out for a soda. The girl blanched and stammered so badly that Deborah became frightened that those who had seen might think she had said something indecent. She saw a momentary picture of the ancient fear, as Onward Christian Soldiers marched onwards against the little girl of the past. Slipping back to invisibility she sang on through choir practice about Compassion.

'Adolescence again?' Furii said. 'That at least you can grow out of, but do you really think you are poisoned still?'

'No, it's just hard to get rid of the old things all at once. I was always so careful of my *nganon*, and so jealous of the

243

clean things that other people had. It's hard to think differently about everything all at once.'

'But you have friends—' Furii said, more as a question.

'In this town, though I sing beside them and take classes at night – they don't see me. They will never see me.'

'Are you sure it isn't your attitude?'

'Trust me,' Deborah said quietly. 'It's true. There are brightnesses, but they are small except for one or two friends from the hospital.'

'And the small brightness?'

'Well, my landlady was babysitting for her daughter. The little granddaughter is just two months old and the landlady had to go out. She came to my room and just said, "Deborah, will you mind the baby 'til I get back?" Then she went out and that was all. I sat with that little baby for an hour and a half, hoping against hope that it would keep imitating itself – breathe in, breathe out, and not die while I was there.'

'Why should the baby die?'

'If I really was just a Semblance after all – only alive one eighth inch inward; alive to fire perhaps, but no deeper—'

'Tell me, do you love your parents?'

'Of course I love them.'

'And your sister, whom you never murdered?'

'I love her – I always did.'

'And your friend Carla?'

'I love her, too.' She started to cry. 'I love you, too, but I haven't forgotten your power, you old mental garbage-collector!'

'How does it feel to go about without all that old, stinking garbage?'

Deborah felt Anterrabae begin to rumble. Was he, Lactamaeon, Idat, and all the beauties of her many places in Yr to be lumped together with the Pit, the Punishment, the Collect, the Censor, and all the plagues of past reality?

'Does it all have to go? Do we pile it up and throw it *all* out?'

'It cannot be a decent bargain now – don't you see?' Furii

said. 'You have to take the world first, to take it on faith as a complete commitment ... on my word, if no one else's. Then, on what you yourself build of this commitment you can decide whether it's a decent bargain or not.'

'How about the shining things? Must I never think about Lactamaeon, so black on his black horse, or Anterrabae, or Idat, now that she keeps her form and is so beautiful? Am I never to think of them again or of the words in Yr that are better than English for certain things?'

'The world is big and has much room for wisdom. Why have you never drawn pictures of Anterrabae or the other ones?'

'Well, they were secret – you know the laws against mingling the worlds.'

'Perhaps the time has come to share the good parts, the lovely and wise parts of Yr, with the world. Contributing is building the commitment.'

Deborah saw Anterrabae falling faster in his own spark-lightened darkness, and while Idat's tears had been diamonds, his were flame-bits; Lactamaeon was weeping blood like Oedipus. The blood made her remember something and she spoke absently.

'I once went to a lady's house and saw blood coming out of her kitchen faucets. There used to be blood clotted in the streets and people were bug-swarms. At least I don't have that any more.'

'Oh, Deborah! Health is not simply the absence of sickness. We never worked this hard just so that you might be unsick!'

Again Dr Fried yearned silently as if before a blind patient to whom she was trying to prove the colour of light. If only Deborah could know what a life of reality and experience *means!*

'If I gave you a picture of Lactamaeon in his hawk aspect or as a rider, would you look at it as my old nuttiness, or as a "contribution"?'

'I would have to see it first,' Furii said.

'All right then,' Deborah said, 'perhaps I might begin to open Yr.'

The high-school equivalency examinations will be given on May 10th at the County Courthouse.

As a registrant for these examinations you will be required to fill out and send in the appended forms and be present at the County Courthouse on Tuesday, May 10th at 9.00 a.m. Failure to comply with both of these requirements will disqualify you for certification.

Deborah put the notice on one side of the table and on the other, the sketches for a picture of Anterrabae. She had taken the notice from its envelope quickly, surprised that the time for it had come so soon. She had filled out the enclosure immediately, had looked twice to see that the address was right, and had gone out to mail it right away, lest it be forgotten or misplaced. When the letter was in the gullet of the mailbox, she had felt the first fear.

Now she sat before the table and tried to laugh it back, knowing with what eagerness and excitement part of her mind was functioning. The real feeling was hope, not fear. It was too late to pretend that she might not cast with the world this time.

Expectation bore her along for the two weeks until the test, and then she went forth in the clothes of reason on the specified day, to the musty, wainscoted room in the old courthouse building. There she found others taking their high-school educations at one gulp – a group of hard-handed day labourers who sweated and grunted over their papers as if they were blocks of granite. She was surprised and then humbled that they, too, though not prisoners or insane, had somehow missed beats in the rhythm of the world, and now were sharers with her in this necessary thing. McPherson's wisdom was at her elbow: you have no corner on suffering. When the time was up and the papers had to be given in, Deborah put hers with the others and left, unable to measure what she had done.

An arrangement had been made at the school for her to go on with the tutoring until the results came in, as much to keep her from worry and idleness as out of fear that she might fail and have to apply again. It was a time of innocence before decision. She pursued her studies, but not breathlessly; followed the season of budding fruit trees in front of the Methodist Church; looked at the changes of the sky; fell in love with poplar trees; went to the movies every time the picture changed, which meant that she knew Tarzan at least as well as Hamlet; and had a month of singular, idle happiness. She called it 'childhood'.

At the end of the month the Regents of the State called her out of the springtime to open their letter. She had passed well – well enough to be certified by the state as having an education equivalent to that of students who had attended high school – and there were enough points over to make her an acceptable applicant to any college. She phoned home, especially proud to give her parents that second bit of news, and glad that their time of pride, while hedged-about and deferred, was still possible.

'Wonderful! It's wonderful! Oh, wait until I call all the family! They are all going to be so proud!' Esther said.

Jacob, by comparison, was almost still. '. . . very proud,' he said. 'It's fine, just fine.' His voice seemed on the verge of breaking.

The high-school graduate hung up the phone, ashamed of her father's pitiful pride. The sunlight still pulsed through the room, the air still bore the odours of spring – sap and greenness, flowering bushes, and moist, warmed earth. She walked slowly outside and down the road and around the old Catholic graveyard and past the auto wreckers', intending to go to the high school and stare its windows down. It was a ritual she had promised herself if she passed the exam. There was no joy in going now; she was going simply to keep an old promise. She walked into the school grounds and skirted the huge ball field, on which four boys were still practising. Suddenly she felt very tired, and sat down against the fence that bounded the back of the field.

Why had he been so pitifully proud? She had given all her strength, all her struggle, all her will to succeed at her study. Now it was over and what had it been, after all, but what everyone else did without half trying, and it was two years late. She was nineteen and a high-school graduate, with parents who were calling the good news all over Chicago by now. *But I wanted it!* she whispered to herself in Yri, turning towards the fence in sudden helplessness.

On the field the boys were running with the late-afternoon magic of their ten-foot shadows. They seemed so young and strong and golden in the late sun. It had taken all of her capacities, every drop of her will, to come as far as they had come laughing and easy. The wall between them was still there and it would always be there. She could see through it now, to where the world offered its immense beauty, but she would burn away all her strength just staying alive.

Across the field, gleaming in the sun, two other figures walked. A slender young girl, all grace and innocence, held the hand of the boy who walked with her. His jacket hung loosely on her slim shoulders. Slowly they walked around the field past her. A few times they stopped, playing or saying something that ended in laughter; he would lean over, nuzzling her gathered-up hair or her cheek.

Deborah talked to herself out loud, the way crazy people do. 'I will never have that,' she said. 'Not by fighting or study or work or withstanding will I be able to walk with one of them or be warmed by their hands.'

Carla told you that long ago, Lactamaeon said from the fence. *Your studies, your job – it's all the same: 'good morning' and 'good night.'*

Quentin will give you water, Anterrabae said, *from the feeding tube. He will never move over your face with his hand. No one . . . no one . . .*

It was almost dark. She got up slowly and walked back towards town. The faces of the church choir seemed to challenge her from the yard of the auto wreckers. *Good evening. Good night.* They never spoke her name.

I spent my hope singing and sewing with you, and when I stand next to you, you don't remember who I am. They were at the graveyard, Anterrabae scattering his flames in the darkness, Lactamaeon moaning in a dog-howl, the Collect building again – *Work hard, lazy girl; fight hard, clumsy girl . . . never . . . never . . . never . . .*

248

I won it hard! she cried to them, *I showed up even when I was sick. I showed up neat and on time and sane every day. I have some certain pride—* But they had drowned her out in a great wave of laughter. She called Anterrabae, watching into Yr for his fiery passing, but there was only his laughter, a savage hollow laughter of terrible scorn. He flashed by, shrieking with laughter, joined suddenly by another figure, a figure which she recognized from a distant book, one of the forgotten books in grandfather's study, a book with engravings, a book out of fashion now, but which had once been *de rigueur* in cultured homes. It was Milton's *Paradise Lost*; her original brilliant vision of a god falling perpetually in fire was none other than Milton's Satan. She had gone over the pictures a thousand times in visits to Grandfather's house. The nine-year-old had caught some of the ponderous thunder of the lines she did not know she had read, and while the artist in her had studied the etched angels and fine engraved lines that had blessed them with dimension, the secret-kingdom-seeker had subtly stolen the proud archangel for the first inhabitant of her world. Even Anterrabae was not hers!

In back of the vision the tumult mounted. *You will create ... the Collect roared. Nothing! You will lie down in the fields ... nothing! Study and work ... nothing!*

They screamed her down the road into town and through the streets; she went vacant-eyed, listening into Yr. Past the church, where she sang on Wednesdays and Sundays, the gods mocked her father's breaking voice. Past all the familiar streets the Collect hooted over Quentin's smile and the golden people on the ball field. Male and female created He them. She was nearly at the hospital now – she could make out the two lights where the cars turned in. She went as if by habit, blindly. The Pit was waiting. Soon. She was terrified. Sight go soon. Voice ... nothing. Up the steps to the door. Now, open it. Someone there, please! Inside: 'Hello, Miss Blau.' And then, 'Are you all right, Miss Blau?' One thing left: make a sign. Though a god screamed she could still hear the other sound–three buzzes: emergency. The Pit.

She emerged again back at the eternal beginning, with her

heart just slowing from the terror. Because she was still alive, still bearing the insolent pumping muscle in her chest, she began to fight and struggle in her bonds, hoping to become exhausted and die. Exhaustion came, but death was adamant against her. After a while Dobshansky came again. This time his face had been carefully strained to remove all but the bland hospital expression. The books had won.

'You feel okay now?'

She was very tired. 'I guess so.'

'We had to call your landlady and tell her you weren't coming back there tonight and that you were here. She got worried about your school and came over with your books and some clothes. She was concerned about you.'

'She's a good person,' Deborah said, meaning it, yet wishing that she did not have to wear everyone's virtues as a weight that somehow counted against her own. She congratulated Quentin on his 'secret' marriage and watched his face struggle with astonishment.

When he and little Cleary had gotten her free, she put on the ratty hospital robe and went slowly out on the ward. The faces there were empty or hostile, the same as ever; the first shock of a return was always brutal. It was early evening; she had lost all of the previous afternoon and most of the morning. The trays were just being given out. In the corner, Dowben's Mary was muttering rites over her dinner. Miss Coral was in seclusion again, probably; Helene was hiding from her in bitterness and envy . . . and friendship. Deborah sat down, heartsick, and looked at the meal.

She heaved a sigh over the lukewarm substance on the plate, and suddenly Dowben's Mary stood up and flung her coffee cup and saucer, and it hit Deborah a sharp, glancing blow on the head. She turned to face Mary and saw her unchanged, as if she were unaware of what she had done. The attendant came, slightly menacing them both because he didn't know what had happened even though he had been sitting there and he felt guilty at having missed it all. Deborah felt in her hair for the wetness and remembered, as if it were medieval history, another gesture like that – her gesture years ago after Helene's attack with the tray.

She looked again at the faces on the ward. Her presence was making them struggle with Maybes. Suddenly she realized that she was a Doris Rivera, a living symbol of hope and failure and the terror they all felt of their own resiliency and hers, reeling punch-drunk from beating after beating, yet, at the secret bell, up again for more. She saw why she could never explain the nature of her failures to these people who so needed to understand it, and why she could never justify scraping together her face and strength to go out again . . . and again. In some ways reality was as private a kingdom as Yr. The dimension of meaning could never be made plain to people whose survival depended on its abridgement or eradication. Mary's cup and saucer glancing hard off Deborah's head, and the unshielded fear and anger that Mary turned at her, made Deborah understand why the anguish had begun to come as her hand had hung up the telephone after delivering a triumphant piece of news. Yr was forcing her to choose at last. With her acceptance as a member in the world, a person with a present and a possible future, a Newtonian, a believer in cause and effect, the final lines of choice were drawn. It had come in agony and violence, in the familiar terror of the Pit, only because she was still very inexperienced in her knowledge of the difference between problems and symptoms, and so the sickness, which was also a source of her only defence and strength, had placed her where it was safe to make a choice. It was time for true allegiance.

When the trays were cleared away, she asked for her schoolbooks. The attendant brought them out and handed them to her with something of a respect for what they symbolized. She opened the first one.

'AN EQUILATERAL TRIANGLE IS ONE IN WHICH THE ANGLE OPPOSITE AC IS EQUAL TO THE ANGLE OPPOSITE AB AND IS ALSO EQUAL TO THE ANGLE OPPOSITE BC.'

'You rotten whore! Let me go!' sounded from the dormitory.

You are not of them, Anterrabae said quietly.

I am of them. Furii says that you will be a contribution,

but I don't yet know how, Deborah said to him. *I will have to learn how. Then, maybe . . .*

'A line bisecting an 80-degree angle forms two angles whose sum is 80 degrees.'

Mary: 'I wonder if insanity is catching. Maybe the hospital could sell us for antibodies.'

Will you not save us as a shield against your hard rind, Bird-one?

I can't do that any more. I am going to hang with the world.

But the world is lawless and wild . . .

Nevertheless.

Remember your own childhood – remember Hitler and the Bomb.

In spite of it.

Remember the blank-wall faces and the 'sanity papers—' and hungering after ones that go hand in hand.

No matter. No matter what.

We could wait until you called us . . .

I will not call. I am going to hang with the world. Full weight.

Good-bye, Bird-one.

Good-bye then, Anterrabae. Good-bye Yr.

'Technological advances affected Western Expansion in many specific ways.'

Constantia: 'Can't you see that I'm suffering, you goddam pigs!'

'The invention of t.n.t. made possible the joining of the coasts by railroad.'

'I am the secret first wife of Edward VIII, Abdicated King of England!'

'Jenna's going again. Call Ellis; we'd better get a pack ready.'

'And both railroad and the morse telegraph maintained the contact indispensable to modern industrial society.'

'Full weight,' Deborah said.

Arthur Hailey

The book that remained for over six
months on the American bestseller list,
now filmed with a star-studded cast —

HOTEL 5/-

Against the background of a great
New Orleans hotel move the characters —
tycoons of the hotel industry, guests,
and staff; men and women, young and old,
dedicated and amoral — sealing their
own destinies in five days of
dramatic change.

'Compulsively readable' DAILY EXPRESS

THE FINAL DIAGNOSIS 5/-

The engrossing story of a young
pathologist and his efforts to restore
the standards of a hospital controlled
by an ageing, once brilliant doctor.
'Probably the best and most
potentially popular medical novel
since *Not as a Stranger*'.
NEW YORK TIMES BOOK REVIEW

Arthur Hailey
and John Castle

FLIGHT INTO DANGER 3/6

High over Canada a crippling emergency
strikes an airliner — on the ground,
helpless observers wait and pray . . .
A brilliant novel of suspense in the air
that enthralled millions as a TV play.

David Beaty

an author noted for his subtle
blending of flying expertise and
razor-sharp observation of men and
women under emotional stress.

THE WIND OFF THE SEA 3/6

Book Society Choice. The commanding
officer of the world's most powerful
nuclear rocket station disappears.
Has he defected? Or is it another
woman — or suicide?

'A dynamic novel of absorbing interest'
THE BOOKMAN

THE HEART OF THE STORM 3/6

A gripping story of a major air
disaster and of two love affairs in
part responsible for the tragedy.

'First-class story . . . dramatic'
MANCHESTER EVENING NEWS

THE SIREN SONG 3/6

A story of passion and subtle hate
played out against the background of the
air age and its advancing technology.

'Enough suspense to grip you to the end'
OBSERVER

John Braine

Author of ROOM AT THE TOP

THE JEALOUS GOD 5/-

Vincent — thirty, a schoolmaster,
Catholic, and still a virgin.
Laura — erotically attractive,
intelligent, sincere, everything that
Vincent needs — but divorced.
An emotional and domineering mother,
a seductive sister-in-law, the
disciplines of his Church — all
contributing to a conflict in which
one man's world is shaken and
another man's life destroyed.

'In this novel more than any
other, he shows that he knows what men —
and women — are like' DAILY TELEGRAPH

'Written with tremendous compassion . . .
white-hot emotional violence . . . tempered
with gentle understanding' DAILY SKETCH

'By far his best yet' DAILY MAIL

The author of ONE PAIR OF HANDS

Monica Dickens

has now written her most important
and powerful novel:

KATE AND EMMA 5/-

Set in today's London, the story of two
young women whose friendship is doomed
to tragedy by social forces beyond
their control.

An extremely moving novel, lit by a warmth
of humanity that would have delighted the
author's eminent great-grandfather.

For information about current and
forthcoming PAN titles write to:

PAN LIST
PAN BOOKS LTD 8 HEADFORT PLACE
LONDON SW1